THE STRIP

IAIN RYAN

ultimo
press

Published in 2024 by Ultimo Press,
an imprint of Hardie Grant Publishing

Ultimo Press
Gadigal Country
7, 45 Jones Street
Ultimo, NSW 2007
ultimopress.com.au

  ultimopress

 A catalogue record for this
book is available from the
National Library of Australia

The Strip
ISBN 978 1 76115 230 6 (paperback)

Cover design Andy Warren Design
Cover image Courtesy of Pexels
Author photograph Courtesy of Shannyn Higgins
Typesetting Bookhouse, Sydney | 11.5/17pt Minion Pro
Copyeditor Deonie Fiford
Proofreader Camha Pham

10 9 8 7 6 5 4 3 2 1

Printed in Australia by Opus Group Pty Ltd, an Accredited ISO AS/NZS 14001
Environmental Management System printer.

 The paper this book is printed on is certified against the
Forest Stewardship Council® Standards.
Griffin Press – a member of the Opus Group – holds
chain of custody certification SCS-COC-001185. FSC®
promotes environmentally responsible, socially beneficial
and economically viable management of the world's forests.

Ultimo Press acknowledges the Traditional Owners of the Country on which we work,
the Gadigal People of the Eora Nation and the Wurundjeri People of the Kulin Nation,
and recognises their continuing connection to the land, waters and culture. We pay our
respects to their Elders past and present.

For the Diablo victims and their families

Ruben James Davis
(1952–1978)

Theodore 'Teddy' Adams
(1926–1978)

Edward 'Eddie' Phillip Edgar
(1946–1979)

Barton Westerby
(1911–1979)

Violet Rosemary Burke
(1956–1979)

Leonard 'Lenny' Gibbs
(1921–1979)

Joel Howard Delaney
(1942–1980)

and

Brian Arthur Amstell
(1938–1980)

The natural tension which exists between the community and any powerful group or institution is exacerbated by the nature of police work.

—TONY FITZGERALD

For where God built a church, there the Devil would also build a chapel.

—MARTIN LUTHER

IN THE BEGINNING

WEDNESDAY, 20 FEBRUARY 1980

JOURNAL OF EMMETT HADES

(SELECTED EXCERPTS)

No future. No past. Just an endless present rolling on like some locked groove of a broken record, locked on to summer and the new decade on the Gold Coast. I used to be a policeman. Twenty years, I gave it. Fifteen as a detective. Haunted by it now. Haunted and broken. Untethered. Living in my back shed, tormented by daydreams and sweating through the night, seeing the names in my sleep, clawing and moaning in the sheets, trying to draw them back in.

Ruben, Teddy, Eddie, Barton.

Henry.

I see the devil now. Whisper to him . . .

I see the killer.

I see the name of the nameless one. He who binds us all together, hidden away, occulted and rotten and vile and—

The names:

Violet.

Lenny.

Joel.

Brian.

The names are like curses.

Like lightning and promises.

Like the broken record, turning.

CHAPTER 1

DETECTIVE CONSTABLE LANA COHEN doesn't recognise a soul. All eyes are on her, but it's not her district, not even her end of the state. Thankfully, the ancient street cop posted to the scene perimeter knows the look, can spot the particulars of her get-up. Her hair pinned back. The neat press of plainclothes worn like a uniform. The cop barely glances at her badge.

'You on your own, luv?'

'Looks like it,' Lana says. 'SIB yet?'

'On their way. You've got the place to yourself.'

Seeing the empty street ahead, it feels like she has the whole world to herself.

'Who called it in?'

The old cop whistles at two uniformed blokes idling nearby. 'These two.'

'Okay. Thanks.'

Lana leads the two uniforms down the street. They're both young. One is fresh out of cadets, and neither is chatty this morning. To loosen them up, she asks after the local beat. It sounds like a snooze: routine break-ins and stolen cars, angry tourists and upset neighbours. 'Either of you two done something like this before?' she says, pointing to the crime scene.

'Nah.'

It doesn't matter. They've taped it off correctly, played it by the regs.

'We could see the blood from back here,' says the younger one.

His partner: 'A woman spotted him from her car. Just driving past, apparently. She's back there, waiting.'

Lana writes it down. 'Good. You guys did good.'

Both nod. Chuffed, but containing it.

'What do we do now?' says one of them.

Lana tells them to stick around, then ducks under the tape. She takes a deep breath and processes the morning's torrent: the early pre-dawn call from dispatch, the siren-ride here, the surge of petrol station coffee. She lets herself feel it—the excitement and dread of a new case—before putting it aside.

She looks around.

Terranora Creek. Border country. Queensland, just across the water.

Today, there's a bright blue sky overhead.

A wash of wind through the eucalypts.

Salt in the air.

Paradise.

And in the middle of it, a dead body.

CHAPTER 2

LANA CREEPS CLOSER. THE body is a white male, in his late thirties or early forties, and in good shape. He's dressed for running. A grey marl singlet, black nylon shorts, and a pair of black sneakers. Lana kneels by the man's head. He has brown hair. Brown eyes, open. Clean-shaven. A small black crater on the forehead and another under the left eye. Best guess, someone stepped out of the trees by the shoreline and shot him at close range. A small amount of blood spatter on his shirt front, suggesting he probably fell exactly as he now lay.

Lana rolls on a pair of latex gloves and pats him down.

No ID.

No cash or watch or jewellery.

No tattoos that she can see.

A working guy rather than a crim.

Lana strips the gloves off and steps out a cursory grid search, praying for a discarded wallet, a shell casing or a boot print. She finds none of these. She broadens the radius. The roadside gravel is clear. The sand on the bank of the creek is clear. She can find no scuffed tree bark or discarded cigarettes. By the look of it, the killer played it smart, kept to the grass and used a revolver or collected his casings on the way out.

It wouldn't have been much.

Some rustling footfall behind the victim.

A flash of panic.

A loud crack.

Here, under the trees by the water.

Not a bad way to go, all things considered.

•

The morning unfolds quickly. The Scientific Investigation Bureau comes through. A coroner follows. A time of death is estimated between 4 and 6 am. One of the scientists confirms Lana's assessment of *two shots fired*—'Certainly looking that way'—but remains tight-lipped about the rest. An hour later, two local detectives walk through, shaking their heads at the body, deciding on the spot that they're *not strictly involved*. Lana plays along.

She interviews the woman who discovered the body. She's a seventy-year-old who lives two streets back and spotted the victim from her car. Figuring it for a heart attack or a stroke, she pulled over. 'I've seen him before,' she says, suggesting she's been close to the body. 'I don't know his name, but he lives around here.' She has little else to add, and nothing about her feels off. She works in the local newsagency—quickly confirmed—and she has not fired a gun recently. Her hands smell of old lady and potting mix. At worst, she touched the body just to know, or out of sheer panic. Lana sends her to the station to get printed and give a statement.

As the morning turns, the sun beams down, bringing on a chorus of cicadas. Everyone on scene starts sweating. Brows are mopped. Sunglasses appear. The local blokes don't seem bothered by it, nor the onlookers gathering, but Lana struggles. It's like working in a sauna. A humid, hazy dream.

•

Just on ten thirty, a group of Gold Coast detectives from across the border swan in. Moving like a pack of rangy dogs, they bustle through the scene, shit-talking all and sundry. The medical team is about to move the body when one of the Gold Coast men—a paunchy white-haired bloke in Crimplene trousers, shirt stretched across his gut—pulls them up. 'You witchdoctors need to take five. Have a bloody smoke or something.'

The local crew listen to him. They stop and disperse.

Lana has no idea what's happening.

The same paunchy detective points at her and yells, 'Who the bloody hell let a reporter in here? What the fuck is this? You need to get the hell out of—'

CHAPTER 3

DETECTIVE HENRY LOCH STUDIES the body, squatting down beside it in the grass, staring at it with silent intensity. The world seems to quieten around him. The sneering and jostling of his colleagues, all their cursing and disappointment.

Two shots to the back of the head, like the last one.

Out jogging, early morning.

Well planned.

Simple.

The chatter fades back in.

Henry's partner, Lowell Sennett, leans over Henry's shoulder and quietly says, 'Same MO.'

'Shooting people ain't an MO,' says Ron Bingham, but it comes out exasperated. Ron's the boss—or thinks he is—but it doesn't matter. They all know it's their case already. It's in the air.

Another of the lead detectives arrives. Mark Evans, with his notepad and his steel-frame eyeglasses, looking for all the world like a lost bookkeeper. He nods at Henry and Lowell, then gently looks under the victim's skull, prising it up with the end of a plastic ruler.

'Did they go through?' says Henry.

Evans shrugs. 'Doesn't look like it.'

Same guy.

Evans looks over at the female detective and says, 'Any shell casings?' Her name's Lana apparently, up from Sydney CIB, something Bingham just learned the hard way, copping a serve after calling her a journalist.

Lana shakes her head. *No.*

'Did you look?' says Bingham, still shitty.

Lana doesn't take the bait. She stays silent, the best way to deal with him.

'What was that, dickhead?' It's one of the local guys, trying to front for the home team.

Bingham barely registers it. 'Calm down, son.' To the Gold Coast men, he says, 'Okay, we better bloody decide what we're doing here. You wanna do this or not, fellas?'

Evans looks out at the creek. 'Can't see how we can let it go. I mean . . .' He looks sad, Henry thinks. *Sad.*

'It's him,' says another of them, Pete Reynolds. To punctuate his point, Pete spits on the ground. Pete isn't much for SIB and their *forensics bullshit.*

Bingham doesn't wait for more bad news. He turns to the New South Wales crew and starts rattling off commands.

An air of confusion ripples through.

Henry walks.

As he passes Lana, she whispers, 'What is this?'

'A nightmare,' he says and keeps moving.

•

Henry drives and broods. Lowell rides shotgun and smokes. They're very different men. Henry is broad and menacing: a twenty-six-year-old standover cop with a military buzz cut. He's neatly dressed today, but his frame is not built for subtlety or grace. Lowell, meanwhile, is tall and louche. He's fit-looking and popular with the ladies. All for show, though. Lowell is rotten on the inside. Midday beers and carton cigarettes, all the way, their branch car like a rolling buffet.

Henry stays quiet from Terranora Creek to Tweed Heads to Currumbin. And Lowell does too, until he tires of it and yawns, saying, 'Go on, then.'

'It doesn't make sense.'

'Yeah, yeah.'

'We've got a long way to go and we're just getting further away,' says Henry.

'I'll say,' says Lowell. 'I'm starting to forget I'm not actually in Homicide. This fucking thing.'

The two of them are seconded to Strike Force Diablo from the Gold Coast Consorting Squad. Consorting is agreeable work for Lowell, concerning as it does his three favourite pastimes: prostitutes, illegal casinos and SP bookmaking. Strike Force Diablo, on the other hand, is a sinking ship for everyone involved, a real CV killer. Six murders in two years. All unsolved.

Seven now.

The first Diablo victim was Teddy Adams. Teddy managed a massage parlour on the Glitter Strip in Surfers Paradise. When their second victim dropped—brothel bartender Eddie Edgar—Henry and Lowell landed in Diablo to assist, due to the sex industry angle. Then the bodies piled up and there was no escaping it. But unlike Lowell, Henry doesn't want to escape it. Homicide is Homicide. He's been chasing it his whole career.

'Emmett still reckons we're looking for two different blokes,' Henry says, as they come into Burleigh.

'Emmett? Jesus, don't start with that shit again,' says Lowell. 'I'm begging you.'

'You know he's right. If you saw that body today, and Teddy Adams back in '78, would you really think they were linked?'

Lowell sighs. He lights a fresh smoke off the last. 'Who gives a shit? We're not catching this bloke, not you and me. I know that much.' He rests his hand out the window, feels the air.

Henry changes lanes. 'I used to look up to Bingham and Reynolds when I first got here.'

'Some detective you are.'

'And did you see the look on Mark's face back there? He normally seems okay, but—'

'Evans can't decide what to eat for lunch these days,' says Lowell. 'I mean that literally. Never eat with him. Look, at least that foul weather has pissed off.'

Henry doesn't respond.

Lowell slaps his bicep. 'Mate, look around. It's another sunny day in Strike Force Dildo. Come on!'

Henry grips the wheel.

'With honour we serve,' says Lowell. 'With honour we serve.'

•

Henry's main worry is sprawl. The first two Diablo victims make sense. Teddy Adams and Eddie Edgar. There are connections: Teddy and Eddie were business partners. They both owned a piece of a suburban knock-shop out in Ashmore. Independent witnesses put them together a fortnight before Teddy's passing. Reynolds and Evans even interviewed Eddie about Teddy. More importantly, both men were killed the same way. Both snatched off the street at night. Both choked with a rope or sash. And then both dumped on two different residential streets in rolled-up carpeting. 'Put out like hard rubbish' is how Bingham described it. An unmissable MO. An outright provocation.

The third victim, Barton Westerby, was choked and dumped the same way, except his body was banged up beforehand. There was a different tone to it, but it was the same killer. Barton was a fifty-five-year-old alcoholic, flush with cash from a public service severance. He was recently divorced, living alone. He may not have worked with Teddy and Eddie but every atom of Barton's sad little life screamed *regular john*, and Henry had booked enough of them to know.

No, it wasn't until Lenny Gibbs that the wheels came off. Lenny was a socialite, and his death wasn't quite like the others. There was no roll of carpeting involved. He was shot in the head on the street and left there. The details were slightly off, which irked Henry, because their guy didn't do *slightly off*. He's precise. A planner. Not that it mattered, not with what came next.

When the death of Lenny Gibbs hit the press, the higher-ups went berserk. By that stage, the public had cottoned on. The word *serial killer* started appearing. The *Gold Coast Bulletin* ran a piece telling people to keep their kids inside. Politicians entered the fray, and the buzz mounted. The overtime flowed. Strike Force Diablo worked round the clock, going nowhere but looking busy.

An unknown killer.

No leads.

No fingerprints.

No motive, no actual suspects.

The tip-line introduced pure chaos:

The killer's car was red.

The killer's van was green.

The killer's truck was black.

Witness accounts gave them tall men and short men; Black men, Asian men and white men.

They had nothing.

That's why the Diablo lead detectives folded the death of Violet Burke into the investigation, despite a string of inconsistencies. She was shot out in the bush behind Tugun a few months before Lenny. That officially made her victim number four and Lenny number five. Overnight, it seemed, the serial killer had changed his MO, forsaking his usual strangulation for handgun assassination. Violet Burke worked as a prostitute—there was that—but the rest of it looked like a stitch-up to anyone paying close attention.

Then, two days into the new year, Joel Delaney wound up dead the same way. He was some accountant in Surfers Paradise. Shot in the head at close range while out fishing. That gave everyone pause. *Maybe the killer really did switch things up?* That's how the politically expedient lie became the official reality.

Two MOs, one killer.

Fresh energy pumped into a dying case.

Back to work.

They turned the overtime up. Sent the Diablo men out to interview further, canvass harder.

Then again: re-interviewing, re-canvassing, re-interrogating.

They all went at it.

They all prayed.

Then, as the summer of 1980 hit—the second summer of Diablo—the floor came out from under the whole thing. Rumours circulated. Despite everything, Diablo was going down. Management were going to fire people—Bingham, Reynolds, Evans probably—and the rest of them were headed back to their real jobs, or to early retirement in disgrace.

Henry couldn't stand the thought of it.

He wanted out of Consorting, permanently. There were too many ghosts in Consorting.

His ticket? Solve the original murders.

Teddy Adams.

Eddie Edgar.

Barton Westerby.

Stick to the plan.

Emmett's plan. His mentor.

If Henry landed the original cases, he could have any position he wanted. He'd save the day and it would remake him on the Force. *Resuscitate* him. Because, before all this, Henry was on the shit-heap for life. Diablo was his last gasp.

CHAPTER 4

DISPATCH READ OUT THE name of the Terranora Creek victim as Henry parked the car. Victim number seven was Brian Arthur Amstell. Forty-two years old. A doctor with a practice across the border.

'There you go,' says Lowell, working on a sausage roll.

'I want to stay away from that one.'

'Fine by me, mate.'

'It's the gun.'

'Bloody hell.'

'Switching up the weapons makes no sense.'

'Maybe he just got sick of choking people?' says Lowell. 'I'm sure it's hard work. Or maybe our bloke got bored? A bit of strange goes a long way.' Lowell crushes the sausage roll bag in his hand. 'Speaking of . . .'

'What? Oh yeah, we're on for tonight. Trina has us booked in for ten thirty.'

'It's going to be a long day. I don't mind telling you, Henry, I'm as toey as a Roman sandal.'

'Good to know.'

'Okay, let's get this over with,' says Lowell. 'Hand it over.'

He means the list. The two of them are following up registration checks on green vans across the Gold Coast. It's needle-in-a-haystack stuff. Going over old details. *Eating cold vomit* as Lowell likes to call it.

Henry shuffles his murder book.

'Is it in there?' says Lowell.

'I think so.'

It takes another minute.

The file is as thick as a telephone directory.

CHAPTER 5

THE GOLD COAST DETECTIVES identified the body of Brian Amstell from a photo in his wife's purse. It was him, all right. The local doctor. A man with three teenaged daughters and a house not far from the crime scene.

At the Amstell residence, a uniformed cop makes tea and mills about, while Lana waits for the first waves of grief to wash through the house. It's bad, as always. The daughters are loud, sobbing openly and squabbling with each other because they're not sure where to put the grief. The wife, Erin, keeps to a back room. After an hour, Lana slips inside and helps her to the en suite for a tab of Valium. With the widow sedated, Lana brings everyone together in the living room for a chat. 'I'm sorry to have to do this now,' she says, meaning every word. 'But the sooner we do it, the better.'

Erin Amstell can hardly hear it. In the pause that follows, Lana notices how beautiful she is. A delicate nose and mouth. Long, cared-for hair. Her daughters are clones, all of them symmetrical and perfect.

'Mum?' says the oldest one, ushering her to speak.

'Yes?' says Erin.

Lana clicks her pen, trying to draw the woman's attention. 'Can I start with your full name and date of birth?'

Nothing.

'Mum?'

Erin rattles it off. Maiden name is Donaldson. Thirty-eight years old. Lana pushes through the rest.

Erin is a stay-at-home mum. Her marriage is solid. 'We had our ups and downs.' Both are practising Catholics. In terms of money, Brian's business is thriving. No financial issues.

Lana turns a page in her notebook. 'Can you tell me what happened this morning?'

Erin and her daughters put it together piece by piece. Brian got up early, as he tended to on weekdays, and went for a run. He was not a lifelong jogger, but was in training for a charity half-marathon. He was late this morning, but that wasn't out of the ordinary.

'You were stopped at the roadblock in your car,' says Lana. 'Were you out looking for him?'

Erin shakes her head. 'No. I ducked out for milk.'

'Do you own a gun?'

'What? No.'

'Can you think of anyone who might want to hurt him?'

'No.' To the best of Erin's knowledge, her husband had no problems with anyone. No vices. He didn't drink or smoke or do anything particularly hazardous to his health, except work too much. By the sound of it, he was a regular dad, with a nice wife and a nice family. Lana can see that they all loved him. The dawning horror in all their faces is self-evident, the youngest one especially.

'Can I have a proper look around?' says Lana, getting up.

Erin gives a silent nod.

Lana wanders through the house. It feels empty already. She's done this dozens of times now as a detective, but she notices some slippage today. Her professional veneer isn't holding tight because she lived in a place like this once, lived through a terrible fork like the one branching off in front of the Amstell family. She remembers the murky days of a traumatic upset, the missing father. She opens Brian Amstell's closet and his bedside table and looks in the study. They are all painfully neat. Brian isn't big on objects or clutter. He has two expensive-looking cameras on a shelf. An industry award gathering dust. On his desk, Lana finds a Rolodex full of doctors' names, and three photos of his kids, all perfectly aligned. She sorts through the bin beside the desk, finding used tissues, a magazine subscription card and a note that reads, *Back soon, Maddy called.*

The oldest daughter appears in the doorway. 'Find anything?'

Lana holds up the note. 'Who's Maddy?'

'She works with Dad.'

'Let's go back out and wait,' says Lana. There isn't much point getting too carried away with the search. The science team will be through soon.

'Are you a good detective?' says the girl.

'I am, yeah.'

'Have you found many killers?'

'We're going to do everything we can to find the person who hurt your dad. I promise.'

'Good.'

Is it?

The Amstells are standing on the cliff's edge, about to plunge over, and there's nothing Lana can do except her job. She puts her hand on the girl's back and gently steers her up the hallway, into the living room to the rest of the family as they wait by the phone. To stave off the silence, Lana organises another round of tea, doing it herself this time. But, as the tea bags steep, she notices something: there's plenty of milk in the fridge. A half-opened carton in the door.

CHAPTER 6

LANA'S DAY PASSES WITH rising irritation. The detectives who commandeered the Amstell crime scene leave her stranded at the Amstell house all afternoon, and Queensland SIB doesn't arrive until dusk. By that point, Lana only has a few hours left to join the neighbourhood canvass, and out there, the detectives treat her with suspicion, even the local blokes. Still, she goes door to door, learning nothing new. By eight o'clock, the whole neighbourhood has turned in, and the strike force with it. There's no official debrief. No request for Lana's details or notes. In the end, she drives back to the motel in Murwillumbah, from whence she came. Her dinner is an unwashed apple and a packet of salt and vinegar chips.

Later that night, Lana wakes to find her room lights burning bright. She's in her robe, on top of the bedcovers, field notes spread out around her. Across the room, someone's pounding on the motel room door.

A rasping voice says, 'Cohen? *Cohen?*'

She opens up on a tall, ghoulish figure. It's New South Wales Superintendent Dwain Gorst, but it takes her a second to recognise him in the here and now.

'Can I come in?'

Lana steps aside, tying her robe as he passes.

Gorst looks around her room with mute distaste, like it's a crime scene, which it is, in a fashion. Between her court appearances in Murwillumbah, Lana has been reviewing her father's missing person's file. The walls are plastered with photos of vacant spaces and anonymous buildings. There are maps and checklists, grim paperwork and diagrams. A bad energy seeps out of the display, and it's keeping housekeeping away. This on top of the dusty surfaces and severe lighting.

'You want a drink, sir?'

'No. I won't be staying long. How's the trial?'

'I'm done. Just seeing it through. He's going away. There's nothing to it.'

'Good, good.' Gorst clears a pile of paperwork from a chair and sits. 'I want you to brief me on the Amstell matter.'

He looks tired. It occurs to Lana that he's probably spent the afternoon in the car just to have this conversation. She straightens her spine, cautious now. 'Did you put me onto this, sir? I was wondering how the local guys dodged it.'

'We needed someone solid.'

'Right. Well, Amstell was the neighbourhood doctor. Shot in the head while taking his morning jog. It's not looking great. Evidence is going to be hard to come by. No suspects.'

'What's your gut telling you?'

'Nothing substantial. The guy seems squeaky clean. The wife might be slightly off. Part of her account doesn't add up. That's the extent of it, though.'

Gorst nods. He's ex-Homicide and knows that hunches are everything and nothing. 'I heard the Gold Coast CIB blokes barrelled in and took over. Is that correct?'

'Yes. Look, I—'

'I'm not upset.'

She tells him the story. At the end, Gorst says, 'They're yahoos, all right. The coast is where the Queensland police send their deadwood. It's a forced retirement spot, or was, until recently. Are you familiar with the ins and outs of Strike Force Diablo?'

'Not really.' Lana has only heard the gossip.

Gorst lays it out and the story marries up. Loose cops in trouble. *Big* trouble. Six bodies and no arrests.

Seven bodies now.

Lana takes a moment. 'I thought Emmett Hades landed on the coast after Brisbane?'

'Emmett's crook in the head, they say. Diablo got to him, apparently. And now, without his guiding hand, the whole thing is falling apart. They haven't had a serious suspect in months, and until this morning, the brass was getting ready to pull the plug on the whole thing.'

'What, and write off six murders?'

'Pretty much. Heads were going to roll, of course, but they're looking to cut their losses. They're out of options, Cohen. The press is too riled up, and now the premier's spooked.'

'So why are we handing our case off to them if we know Diablo's a loser?'

'That's why I'm here. We're not handing it off. I've spoken to Ron Bingham up in the Surfers Paradise station and he's given it the okay. I want you to go across the border and work up there as our man on the ground.' Gorst stops. 'Our woman on the ground.'

'Okay.'

'It'll be a collaborative affair. They want the extra resources, and we'll be seen to be helping out.'

'And?'

'And what?' Gorst twists his face into what Lana assumes is a smirk.

'What am I *actually* doing?'

'Diablo is a strange beast. It should have turned something up by now. The talk is, there's a dirty element. We want you to go over there and work our case and have a look around, up close.'

'Have a *look around*?'

'Up close,' he says. 'We need to do the right thing by the deceased's family, of course, but we also want to know about any problem areas. There could be lessons there.'

'Respectfully, sir, I—'

'No one's asking you to step out of line, Cohen. This is purely internal, from God's lips to my ear. There will be no charges laid, no blame assigned. This is a fact-finding expedition. You go up there, work the case, and report back whatever you turn up along the way. It might be nothing.'

'And you and the State Commissioners use the information to play office politics?'

'Something like that. Just know there will be no blowback for the troops. None.'

'And what do I get?'

Gorst nods at this, liking the clarity of it. 'There's a restructure coming. Management is angling for an inquiry, and if I were a betting man, I'd say a new day is on the horizon. If this thing up in Queensland goes well, someone like you could end up with her own team, Cohen. Things are opening up for your lot. The Force needs efficient women, pragmatic women, people like you.'

Lana lets it sit for a few seconds. 'I work the case. I tell you what I notice.'

'An easy assignment.'

Lana gets up, puts her hand out. 'No paper reports. I talk to you and you only. If what I'm doing circulates further and causes trouble, I'm out. I don't care if they *are* all dickheads over there. They're still cops.'

'I can live with that.'

They shake hands.

'You know, I've always liked you, Cohen.'

'I should hope so, sir.'

CHAPTER 7

ACROSS THE BORDER, ON the outskirts of Surfers Paradise, there's a brothel called Tropical Touch. Housed above a gaudy tiki bar, the place is even less tasteful than it sounds. Through a haze of iridescent pink lighting and artificial fog, Tropical Touch comes off as sparse and surreal. To Henry, it's the loneliest of all the Glitter Strip knock-shops. A real eyesore. Of course, his idiot partner Lowell loves every inch of the place.

The moment Lowell gets there tonight, he orders drinks and disappears to a back room with two girls. Henry lingers at the bar, feigning indecision, then calls over the bartender. 'Tell Trina I'm here.'

'No date?' says the bartender.

'Nah, I'm good.'

Overhearing this, one of the workers leans over on her stool. 'Do you ever party, Constable? We're all starting to wonder.'

'Wonder what?'

'Maybe you like boys?'

The rest of the girls crane their necks.

'He's too big to be a poof,' says one of them.

Another chimes in with, 'I can be a boy.'

That gets a laugh.

'I think you lot have missed your calling,' Henry says, and pushes off. He walks across the pink foyer to the centre hallway, opening a broom closet. There, he reaches for a latch behind a steel cabinet. A soft click and the entire cabinet comes away from the wall, swinging open on a secret hinge, revealing a doorway. Henry steps into a dark room, lit only by a large window. In the room, there's a leather couch and a marble coffee table, and on the table, a film camera.

Henry grabs the camera and stands by the window, a two-way mirror. On the other side, Lowell—still half dressed, pants around his ankles—kisses one of the girls, while the other squats down in front. Henry focuses the camera lens, testing it. Lowell's hung like a racehorse, another instance of his impeccable luck.

Luck that's running out, Henry figures.

He snaps a photo.

A side door slides open.

'Evening, detective.' It's Trina Chalmers, the madam. 'Everything all right in here?'

Henry keeps his eye to the camera, keeps clicking. 'Yep.'

Trina looks through the window and winces. 'I've heard the girls talking, but bloody hell.'

They both watch the action. Lowell's eyes bulge as he ejaculates on the carpet.

'I just had that steam cleaned,' says Trina.

Henry pops out the first roll of film and hands it over, then reloads. 'Who develops these?'

'Some schoolteacher. Uses the school's art department darkroom.'

'I want to pick these up myself. This teacher have a name?'

'Wesley Bowman. He's a weird guy.' Trina moves closer to the glass, studying the scene. Lowell positions both girls spread-eagled on the bed. He kneels down and gets to work with his mouth.

Henry's camera clicks and buzzes.

Trina says, 'This session is free, by the way.'

'Nothing's free in here.'

'I've got a favour to ask.'

'There it is.'

'You remember Sarah? She was the girl you pretended to fuck last year when you came in with the alderman's son.'

Henry shrugs.

Trina pulls out a photograph. 'This is her. Sarah Utton. She's missing.'

Henry looks. Utton is five foot nothing with bleach-blonde hair and dark eyeliner. He remembers her. They talked that night. She was thinking of buying an apartment in Southport, off the plan. 'How long has she been missing?'

'About six months.'

'Six months? Sounds like she quit.'

'Oh, she definitely quit,' says Trina. 'She emptied the till on the way out of here. Three grand, I'm down. I covered it, thinking she'd pop up again one day, but she hasn't. If you can get my money back, you can take three hundred as a finder's fee.'

'Six hundred.'

'Really? Okay, fine.'

'Does Colleen know about this?'

Colleen Vinton is the owner of Tropical Touch. She runs a bunch of brothels on the Strip, all with an iron fist.

'Christ no,' says Trina. 'Are you kidding me?'

'What happens to the girl if I find her?'

'Nothing, if I get my money back. That's why I'm asking you instead of Colleen.'

'I never took you for the motherly type, Trina.'

'Piss off. But you're right, I'm getting soft.'

'I'll give it a go,' Henry says. 'Any ideas where to start?'

'Not really. The other girls won't say a bad word about her. I know she was dating their weed dealer for a minute, Brad Glynn.'

'Here, keep this going.' Henry passes her the camera.

Through the glass, Lowell is thrusting away, sweat pouring off him.

Henry takes out his notebook, writes *Sarah Utton*. 'Who's she friends with?'

Trina rattles them off, zooming in and tsk-tsking. 'I've got to hook these two up with my wax lady. You hanging around for a drink after this?'

'Nah. Early start in the morning.'

'Thanks for helping me.'

'It's fine. I could use the money.'

'You're a strange bloke, Henry. I dig it, but I can't say I know what makes you tick. I reckon you've got a bit more going on up there than people think.'

'I don't know about that.'

Trina pokes a finger into Henry's chest, over his heart. 'Maybe it's in there?'

'Look . . . don't.'

'You'll tell me your secrets one day, I reckon.'

Henry forces himself to laugh it off, but when Trina gets like this, it scares the shit out of him. She senses things in him. The hidden stuff. Luckily, Lowell picks this exact moment to bring the visit to an end. Through the mirror-glass, he rips the condom off and ejaculates on the floor a second time.

Trina rests her head against the cool glass. 'Please tell me they're going to fire this dickhead.'

CHAPTER 8

HENRY WATCHES LATE-NIGHT Surfers Paradise pan past from the passenger seat of a cab. It's another Wednesday on the Strip, vacant and dead. He leans into the hot air blowing in through the window. Still twenty-five degrees out.

'There's rain coming,' says the driver.

'No one knows what's coming,' says Henry.

'That's true. Maybe God? The Pope?'

'In this mess?'

The driver laughs at that. On the car radio, the eleven o'clock news carries Diablo as the lead story: *The Tweed Heads community tonight mourns the passing of a local doctor, the seventh in a string of recent local homicides. Gold Coast police are actively searching for the perpetrator, claiming an arrest is—*

'Pig's arse,' spits the cabbie, switching the dial.

'You don't reckon they'll get him?'

'It'll be a cold day in hell.'

Henry puts his head on the headrest and closes his eyes. He's tired, but the fatigue just makes it worse. Nights like tonight—with Lowell and Tropical Touch—don't rinse off like they used to. They take a toll now. Build up.

Henry Loch remembers everything.

•

He came up hard. A wrecked childhood. Alcoholic mum. Violent, alcoholic dad. They lived out in the back streets of Logan, down in the suburbs they call Nappy Valley. He was the oldest of three, or was, until Mum cleared out with the other two.

But not Henry.

Henry stayed back with the old man.

All things considered, it's a miracle he ever made it onto the Force. He had every opportunity to mess it up, and came close once or twice, but he managed to hold on. When he told his dad about the police academy, his dad said, 'No son of mine is a fucking dog.' Henry snapped and started in on the old man right there on the kitchen lino. Caught by surprise, the old man went to water, like all broken bullies. It was Henry's house from then on, but the elation was short-lived, accompanied as it was by the sensation of *too little, too late*.

After graduation, the Queensland Police put him on general duties in Toowoomba, where Henry's innate aggression and wildness found a willing cohort. Up on the mountain, they quickly recognised the mongrel in him. The higher-ups started calling on him for special work.

A reputation formed.

His dad's reputation.

Like father, like . . .

As a reward for his exemplary regional service, they transferred him to Fortitude Valley, down into the bowels of Brisbane City, where policemen like Henry reigned free. But Henry couldn't settle in the city. The routine street fighting and everyday mayhem started nagging at him. Three months into Brisbane, he was sizing up options. He wanted more.

A year later, Henry's youngest brother called, wanted to reach out. Henry met him at the Mount Gravatt Tavern in uniform and the youngest filled him in on lost time. They were all doing better these days. 'Mum worked as a pro to get the money to leave him,' his brother told him. 'That's how she got us out.' She had to leave Henry behind because he was too old for the women's shelter. The church wouldn't have it.

Henry tried not to react.

'She wants to see you.'

'It'll never happen.'

And it never did. She died of a heart attack three years later. His father died the following winter. Henry passed on both funerals. Didn't grieve. Didn't see the bodies.

He *was* the body, by that stage.

A chaotic, violent reproduction.

Full of rage.

And in those early years, the Queensland Police Force fed on it, like a tick on the arse of a bull.

•

Back in the cab, Henry points out the windscreen. 'Over here, mate. This is me.'

The cabbie looks the place over. 'Nice,' he says.

'It's a rental.'

Henry pays the fare and stands out on the bitumen tarmac to watch the cab round the corner at the end of the street. He loosens his tie and looks up at the sky. Clouds are brewing.

He takes the photo of the missing girl from his shirt pocket and stares at it.

Sarah Utton.

Six hundred in cash.

Why not?

He could do it. Diablo is probably a bust. A mirage. Years of hustle to get into CIB—years of blood—and then years more to get from Consorting to Homicide, only to land belly-up in this wreck.

No end to it.

'Shut up, you're just tired,' he says to himself.

But the self-talk does nothing as a light breeze stirs, lifting his hair and rustling the trees above.

DAY ONE

THURSDAY, 21 FEBRUARY 1980

JOURNAL OF EMMETT HADES

(SELECTED EXCERPTS)

Names, names like curses, droning on.

Ghosts echoing around.

Time in reverse.

Speeding backwards . . .

Back to 1960 and back to Brisbane and Rick Graham, my first partner. Rick, the dead man walking, the soon-to-be lonely suicide. But not yet, not in 1960. No, in 1960, Rick is still salty and I'm still new. Fresh meat. We were in the Mobile Patrols together, on the move. Our own jurisdiction.

'This city is an encyclopedia,' says Rick, and he isn't wrong. It's all there, especially at night. A crash course in human behaviour and animal biology. Brisbane, the city that seems only two steps ahead of a country town, sleepy and moralistic, but dark and secretive, also. I wanted it that way. As the city opened itself up to me, I gorged on the darkness inside.

I saw it all.

I scraped the bodies from the freeway.

Wrote reports on corpses of every age, race and gender.

I stepped into a thousand domestic disputes.

Drew my gun in anger. Punched people, harassed and suppressed. I met drug dealers, gangsters, thieves, rapists, murderers, paedophiles, pimps, junkies, gamblers, con men, crooks, and every other type of chancer, and all of them took me to the fount of knowledge.

It was glorious, and it went on for years.

I was the perfect understudy, lapping at the flow.

But also . . .

I was making debt, accruing damage, just like Rick.

Rick saw the edges of it before I did.

And that was my big mistake: never expecting a response, always thinking I was riding for free in the city. Never knowing that things can reach back out of that void. I never braced for my mistakes coming back to me, reverberating up. Like a wave . . .

●

I read about the death of Brian Amstell in the newspaper. They ran it alongside a picture of Ron Bingham, on page five. Ron looked terrified in the pic: his stubby body dissected in two by a line of crime scene tape. In better hands, Diablo would have seen Amstell as an opportunity. Unfortunately, the heart of Diablo is clearly rotten now. The corruption complete. The lack of faith all pervasive. It's keeping the good men from solving the thing.

I have my own ideas about what's really happening, and where it stems from, but they sidelined me before I could act. Put me out to pasture. And yet, and yet . . . the Diablo tree keeps shaking and nothing falls out.

Bingham at the helm.

Murkiness everywhere.

When you've got idiots in charge, the laws of physics don't apply.

●

I do my chores.

Take my tablets.

Go for a run.

I eat a breakfast of grapefruit juice and toast and re-read the paper, crossing out the eyes of Brian Amstell before hitting the garage to do my work. By two o'clock, I'm thinking of visiting the grocery store, but ditch it in favour of a drive across the border to my church, to see my priest. Shouldn't have bothered. He's in a foul mood and knows my complaints just by looking at me.

'Look, I know it's hard watching those men of yours suffer,' he says, no kindness in it.

'It is.'

'You have to stay away. Doctor's orders. Do I have to say it too?'

'What sort of hell is this? This day after day, without progress? It feels like a broken promise.'

'What does?'

'Everything.'

The priest sucks on a smoke the whole time. He always smokes in the confessional. 'That's God for you, Emmett. That's the big man to a tee. His MO if you will.'

He's always like this.

CHAPTER 9

LANA DRIVES ACROSS THE border and visits the beach before work. She takes her shoes off, dips her feet into the lukewarm ocean. It's seven thirty in the morning, but the Gold Coast is already bomb-blast bright. There's glimmering glare in the water. White sand ranging up to the esplanade bitumen. Even the encroaching city—cream concrete high-rises and walk-up flats—looks good in the glow of a new day, sun-tinged and bleached clean.

An hour later, she knocks on the open door of Inspector Ron Bingham's office at the Surfers Paradise police station. Ron's the man in charge, the head of Gold Coast CIB, and the mouthy dickhead from the crime scene yesterday. 'Come in,' he says. 'Ah, I see.' He waves a hand at the visitor's chair. 'Figured it would be you.'

For a few seconds they eye each other off, peering between the piles of paperwork on Bingham's desk. The place is murky, lit only by a desk lamp, and the room has no windows looking out onto the outside world. Just a single panel of glass showing the empty squad room.

'Welcome aboard, I guess,' says Bingham. 'But I have to say, I'm not exactly sure why you're here.'

'Me neither, sir.'

'Dwain Gorst tells me you're not as green as you look.'

'I'm five years in.'

Bingham pushes out a breath through his nose. 'You sure you're any good at this?'

'I believe so, sir.'

'You'll need a bit of that moxie to make it work up here. These men are . . . they can be difficult, at the best of times.'

'Yes, sir.'

'You married, Cohen? I suppose not.'

'No.'

'Where do you come from?'

'Sydney. I grew up in Wollongong.'

'I went to Sydney once. It's a real shithole.'

'Yes, it is, sir.'

It breaks the ice. He follows up with questions about her supervisor in Sydney and about the men she works with. Her answers are pure appeasement and, after a few minutes, Bingham seems to lose interest. He cleans his reading glasses and puts them on. 'What do I need to provide you with, Cohen? I have it written down somewhere but . . .' He waves at the clutter.

'Just somewhere to work.'

'And you're available to act in any capacity?'

'My orders are to assist however I can.'

'That'll work. Anything to report so far?'

'My senior sergeant has local men assigned to assist on the canvass over the border this morning. We're fast-tracking the post-mortem, and the prelim print work is in the mail. They'll report any matches as they come in. Also, Sydney CIB is sending another team of scientists up, just to have a look. You're getting the full English, sir.'

'Good, *good*. Now the only rule I have with all this is I want you to keep your enquiries strictly to the Amstell case. Let everyone else deal with the rest of it.'

'Understood.'

'There's a briefing with the superintendent this afternoon. You're expected to attend those. The superintendent can get quite . . . he can be abrupt, Cohen. Please keep our internal goings-on to yourself. This is a difficult situation. There's a lot riding on us.'

She nods. 'My lips are sealed.'

The first outright lie.

'Good. That'll be all for the moment. When Anne-Marie gets in, get her to take you round to Bruno Karras.'

Ron Bingham unfolds a newspaper and starts reading it.

Meeting's over.

•

Ron's secretary, Anne-Marie, proves a prickly soul. The woman looks Lana up and down and says, 'Inspector Bingham sent you to me for this?'

'An hour ago.'

'I see.'

Anne-Marie takes her through the squad room and around a corner, down a small ramp to a bay of carpet-lined cubicles. She raps her hand on the desk of a thin man with slicked black hair and says, 'Bruno, you've got a visitor.'

Bruno swivels in his chair. 'Lana Cohen?'

'Yep.' She shakes his hand. It's soft and Bruno is neat as a pin. He has the regulation look—business shirt, patterned tie and dark pants—but his cream-white shirt actually fits him. 'Bingham told me to introduce myself. Who are you in all this, Bruno?'

'Didn't he say? I'm your new partner.'

CHAPTER 10

BRUNO'S FIRST ORDER OF business is to take her round the building and introduce her to people. Even with Bruno's gladhanding, the reception isn't warm. The two lead detectives stand bleary-eyed by the kitchen urn and don't make it any easier than they did yesterday at the crime scene.

Pete Reynolds isn't having it. 'Sure, okay.'

'I'll take whoever I can get,' Mark Evans says.

'We all know that,' adds Pete.

Between them, they ask Lana the same questions as Bingham, and she gives the same answers, although the practice has softened her patter even further. As the conversation drifts, she can feel them studying her. Evans glances at her hair and neck. Reynolds is pure disdain, unabashed. He's getting more annoyed by her as the minutes pass.

'I'm just here to help,' she says.

'Bruno needs it,' quips Reynolds.

Bruno takes it without comment. 'Let's keep moving.' From the kitchen, they move around to the admin room through the typing pool, and into the Strike Force Diablo bullpen. There, Lana meets a dozen near-identical police detectives—all broad and tall, and all white, except for two Māori blokes. To a man, they are clean-shaven, low-talking, and dead on their feet. Polite, but nothing more.

The grand finale of the tour is a look inside the murder room attached to Diablo. Comprising two adjoining boardrooms, it's big. A panorama of scene photos, wall-to-wall blood, blank stares and ghostly white skin. On the floor are rows of demountable tables, each containing more paperwork than Lana has seen collated outside of a records archive.

'Holy shit,' she whispers to herself.

Bruno swallows deep. 'It's a lot. Isn't it?'

It's more than a lot. *There's madness here*, thinks Lana. No order. No map or structure. Diablo has descended into chaos.

'Can I have a key to this room?' she says.

'It's unlocked most of the time. I don't use a key.'

'You work in here?'

Bruno shakes his head. 'Try to stay away as much as possible. It gets to me. Gets to everyone, I think.'

'Where's the Amstell stuff?'

Bruno points to a corner where someone has cleared a two-metre patch of wall space and affixed a handwritten sign, *Brian Amstell, Terranora Creek, 20 FEB 1980*. A single photo of Amstell's face is pinned underneath.

'Jesus,' says Lana. 'That's grim.'

'It's what the seventh victim of an unsolved murder case looks like.'

'You know, I could use a smoke. Do you smoke?'

'I'm Italian. I can always use a smoke.'

On the way out, they pass a corner office at the rear of the squad room. It's all closed up, blinds and door, but the nameplate remains.

Detective Sergeant Emmett Hades.

Bruno nods. 'Yep, the one and only.'

'I heard he's on leave.'

Bruno whispers, 'Let's talk outside.'

·

They go to the street-side footpath and smoke in the bracing heat. Lana is wilting, but Bruno's yet to break a sweat.

'Hades is out of action,' he says. 'This thing fucked him up. He lost the plot a few months back. They're keeping it on the down low.'

'Really? He's a genius. People down south talk about him like he's Sherlock Holmes.'

'He is. Or was. They reckon Diablo got to him. But I've asked around, and no one wants to tell me the whole story. I mean, I got transferred down here to work with him, and from what I hear, it was this *place* that got to him, as much as Diablo.'

Lana tilts her head towards the station house. 'This lot?'

'No, the coast. The whole thing. They reckon from the moment he landed down here, he's been on the downward slide. The Gold Coast did him in.'

CHAPTER 11

HENRY WALKS JUSTINS PARK to the foreshore with the tall pines of Burleigh Heads towering overhead. He finds a group of surfers hanging out in his regular spot, a worn timber picnic table adjoining the seawall. The surfers eye him off, all of them lean teenagers with wet hair. On his approach, one pipes up with, 'Bit warm for a suit, isn't it, mister?'

Henry flips open his police ID. 'Piss off.'

With the table to himself, he takes a seat and waits. Despite the morning sun, he feels unsettled and haunted, his mind flashing.

This light, like the dawn sun, ripping through the flat country.

A car and a field and—

A seagull squawks overhead.

Burleigh comes back into focus.

And Jack the Bagman strolls down the boardwalk towards him. 'Sorry, mate,' he says, sitting down. 'Got held up in roadwork.' Jack comes off as a nice bloke, some friendly neighbour caught up in something. But behind the scenes, Jack is the *something*. He runs the racket they call the Joke. His only saving grace is his consistency. You can always rely on Jack to be a greedy, self-serving little shit.

'You keeping well, Jack?'

'Can't complain,' he says. 'No bugger would listen. How 'bout you, son? That business down on the Tweed yesterday doesn't sound too good? Sounds like a right mess.'

'It is what it is,' Henry says.

'Ron Bingham must be shitting himself.'

'Haven't been in yet. He wasn't happy yesterday, I can tell you that much.'

'You still working the first three bodies?'

'Till further notice.' Henry yawns.

'How'd it go with Lowell?'

'You'll have the photos next week.'

Jack smiles. 'Very good, Henry.'

'What did Lowell do to deserve all this?'

'Nothing too terrible. He's got a bit of undeclared work on the side, and he's not paying his dues. I'm surprised you haven't noticed, as his partner.'

'Fuck off. I told you, Lowell keeps to himself.'

This is how the Joke works. The system of graft and corruption is centrally orchestrated, and few can see the whole. Everyone caught in it is siloed off from one another. It's silos within silos within silos, all the way up and down the Queensland Police Force. No one ever really knows what the other guy is up to.

'Just seems odd, is all,' says Jack.

'Are you going to turn up with dirty photos of me next week? Is that where this is headed?'

Jack wheezes out a laugh. 'You'd like that, I reckon. No, we both know where the bodies are buried, mate. Look, I'm sorry you have to dog your partner, but it's for his own good. Think of it this way, if what I hear is true, we're all getting robbed blind by him, and far be it from me to deny a man his payday, especially one he's put together himself, but rules are rules, mate. There are worse things in this world than a few dirty pictures.'

'Okay, well, do me a favour? Hit him up without mentioning the photos. Use that charm of yours. Lowell will roll over. He's a team player at heart. He wants people to like him. Use that before dumping the photos in his lap because he's not as dumb as he looks. He'll work out where they came from sooner or later, and then I'll be in the shit.'

Jack slaps the table. 'That's a good idea, Constable. I've always said you have a real knack for the details.'

'You should tell your mates up in Brisbane.'

'What and lose my best man in the Gold Coast Consorting Squad? No thanks.' To sweeten it, Jack takes an envelope from his jacket and passes it across the table. This is the money. Always the good with the bad with Jack.

'How much?'

'The usual,' Jack says. 'Why? You looking for extra?'

'Not really, but what have you got?'

Jack rolls his tongue around inside his mouth. 'Oh, you'll like this. We're looking for a working girl called Sarah. She's missing. There's a drink in it for anyone who can track her down. A big drink, in fact.' Jack pats his pockets and produces a faded photograph creased down the middle. 'This is her.'

It's Sarah Utton. The same girl Trina Chalmers is chasing, the one who ripped off Tropical Touch. In the picture, Utton sits on Ray Blintiff's knee. *Rotten Ray.* Ray's a big wheel in the Brisbane Licensing Branch. A terrifying bloke.

Henry hands back the photo. 'I don't recognise her, but I can keep an eye out.'

'Good man. There's plenty of people looking for her, so you might notice a bit of movement down here. She's been missing for a while.'

'What's she supposed to have done?'

'Christ knows,' says Jack. 'Laughed at Ray's dick, probably.' He knows more than he's letting on. It's all over him.

Henry taps the envelope on the table before picking it up. 'I better be off.'

He's a good couple of metres away when Jack calls after him.

'Yeah, what?'

'Look at this beautiful day,' Jack says, holding his upturned hands out like a TV evangelist. 'Look at it, Henry.'

Henry gives him the nod and keeps moving.

Fucking Jack.

Every day is his day.

CHAPTER 12

AS EXPECTED, LOWELL SENNETT calls in sick. 'Food poisoning *again*,' says Anne-Marie, loud enough to carry across the Diablo squad room.

'What does that bastard eat?' says one of the detectives.

'What *doesn't* he eat?'

'Vegetables,' is Henry's answer, getting up from his desk.

On the way out, he hears someone whisper, 'Carol from typing reckons he eats all sorts of stuff.'

Muted laughter circulates.

Henry shuts it out.

A day without Lowell is an opportunity, and he's looking forward to the solitude. First order of business is a visit to the archives, to pull the arrest sheets for women working at Tropical Touch over the last two years. In the paperwork, Henry finds six of Sarah Utton's friends, their names matching those provided by Trina Chalmers last night. There are phone numbers and residential addresses. A good start.

Henry takes his list to the murder room and scans the duty book for yesterday's rego checks. Eyeballing it, Henry figures they are about a third of the way through their follow-up interviews with green and blue van owners. He makes a duplicate of the outstanding checks, itemises them by postcode, and matches rego checks to locations near Sarah Utton's friends. The idea is to hit both at the same time. Low-key double-duty.

On the way out to the car, he stops by the Drug Squad to drop in their share of Jack's money. As per usual, the point man for the pickup is an old senior sergeant called Gnomes, and as per usual, he makes Henry do the deal in the squad's putrid bathroom. The tubby prick stands at the urinal and bangs on, 'And Henry, you should have seen the place, it was—'

'Gnomes, do you really need to take a piss every time we come in here?'

'I can't risk taking money off you out there.'

'But can't you piss after?'

'When you're my age, son, you piss every chance you get, and for whatever reason, my bladder likes you.' Gnomes turns and waves his flaccid dick at Henry. 'Take it as a compliment. You're very calming.'

'Steady on. What do you know about a weed dealer called Brad Glynn?' Brad is Sarah Utton's boyfriend. Trina Chalmers mentioned him last night.

Gnomes thinks about it. 'Brad, huh? I know him. What's he done?'

'Nothing. I need to have a chat with him, is all. Is that okay?'

'Yeah, he's on the books. Chat away.'

'You know where I can find him?'

Gnomes starts violently shaking his dick. 'I thought you were a detective.'

'Don't be a cockhead.'

'All right, all right. He has a bunch of spots, but his main gig is outside of Sea World. You can find him there most nights this time of year. If you have to give him a clip round the ear, tell him I said hello.'

'Will do.'

Gnomes zips up.

He counts the money with wet hands.

CHAPTER 13

WHILE HENRY PAYS OFF Gnomes in the toilet, Lana Cohen sits across the station house at her new desk alongside Bruno. Bruno has no agenda for the day. 'All I've been told is to look after you,' he says.

'What do you normally do?'

'Assist, mostly. Paper trail stuff.'

'Fancy a drive?'

Lana takes them south, across the border to the Amstell scene for a look. Bruno wasn't in the cohort yesterday, so it's all new to him. Lana watches him move through the space. The man is careful. He plays it cool but knows what he's doing: takes a lot of notes, chats with everyone. Circling back, he says, 'Yep, it's a crime scene.'

'Any idea who did it?'

'Give me a minute.'

They check in with the Northern Head of Forensics. She's a matronly woman called Pat, up from Ballina. Pat looks and talks like she belongs in the army, but she knows her lab work. She greets them with the usual bluster, 'Lana Cohen, why'd you let them dump this shit in your lap?'

'Somebody hates me.'

'I'll say. This is a real whodunnit.'

'Last I checked, they pay you to tell me things I don't know.'

Pat turns to Bruno. 'You hear how she talks to me, handsome? Disgraceful, isn't it? Okay, I can show you one thing, I suppose.' She leads the detectives to an uncleared residential block across the road. It's a stretch of bone-dry scrub. Inside the tree line, two men kneel in the soil as one pours white plaster into a small ditch.

'Tell me those are boot prints?' says Lana.

'I can do you one better. Those over there are boot prints. Multiple indentations from a single man. The real clincher is that, over there.' Pat points at a metre-long strip of drying plaster lying in the mud. 'Those are tyre prints.'

'Motorbike?' says Lana.

'A single man on a motorbike,' says Pat. 'He parks here, shoots your bloke over there, and comes back to hightail it out.'

'Could the footprints be from another night?' says Bruno.

'Rack off,' says Pat.

Lana adds, 'It rained the night before the shooting. This is good work, Pat.'

'Don't I know it,' she says. The science men stop what they're doing and look over, both stony-faced. One of them clears his throat, causing Pat to cough up a loud cackling laugh. 'Okay, so technically, *these* two found the prints. Thank you ever so much, gentlemen, for doing your bloody jobs. Now if you could please get back to work because it's fucking hot out here, and I'm not built for it.'

On the way back to the car, Bruno asks, 'Is she always like that?'

•

From the crime scene, they venture out into the surrounding suburbs and meet up with the men working the second day of the neighbourhood canvass. Bruno takes the lead and Lana notices he has little sway with the Diablo detectives when they come across them. They grumble at his requests and all their answers are accompanied by a barrage of lurid invitations. That said, they tell him what he wants to know, mainly because they don't know anything yet.

There's a nurse, they say, one who lives two streets away from the Amstell family. She saw a *tall man* lurking on the foreshore on the morning in question. No other details.

A fellow jogger saw Amstell out and reported hearing a loud crack *like a car exhaust* about ten minutes later.

Three motorists who live in the area saw various cars and trucks of various makes and models, none of it solid, except for an emergency plumber who spotted a dark blue van in the vicinity.

This last piece sparks Bruno's interest. He writes it down, mentioning that, 'Maybe Henry and Lowell should be on this?' which means nothing to Lana.

Finally, there's a fisherman who lives at the end of Brian Amstell's street. The fisherman saw a motorbike *hoon up the road* around the time of the murder. The detectives who relay this breeze past it, meaning the morning's scene work hasn't circulated.

'That last one could be our guy,' says Lana.

'Could be,' says Bruno. He checks his watch. 'We've got two hours before the briefing. I know a place for lunch, if you're interested?'

'I want to do something first. I got a hunch I need to follow up.'

'What is it?'

Lana tells him.

He doesn't like it any.

CHAPTER 14

THE AMSTELL HOUSE DOESN'T look like a house of bereavement. It looks like the rest of the houses on the street: a white timber cottage with a neat garden and a neat lawn, enclosed in a square wire fence.

'I hate dealing with the families,' says Bruno.

Lana knocks at the front. 'Everyone hates dealing with the families.'

A man opens up.

'Afternoon, sir, I'm Detective Constable Cohen. This is Constable Karras. We're from the Gold Coast Police. We're investigating the incident from yesterday. Can we come in?'

'They're not home,' says the man, looking at Bruno rather than Lana.

Lana takes out her notepad. 'Can I ask your name?'

'Steve, Steve Jenkins.'

'And how do you know the family, Steve?'

'I'm their house cleaner. My wife and I do it, but she didn't want to come in today.'

'You mind if we ask you a few questions about the Amstells?'

'Nah. Go for it.'

Lana peppers him with the usual: how long he's known them, how he found them as people, did they treat him well? Jenkins gives stunted answers. He isn't dumb exactly, but Lana doesn't peg him for bright, either.

Bruno says, 'You ever see *anything* unusual happen with the family?'

'What, here? No, never. This lot is as normal as you like.'

Lana folds up her notes. 'Okay, that might do for now.'

Jenkins scratches at his beard. 'Actually, what about their other place?'

Bruno says, 'Do they have other houses around here?'

'Nah, I mean the clinic. The missus and I clean Brian's clinic, too. It's not far.'

'What happened there?' Lana asks.

'Nothing recent, but last year somebody smashed the place up pretty good. Broke all the windows at the front with a crowbar or a cricket bat or something. The place was in a right state. Took forever to clean. Had to hire on extra people to help. Wasn't good. Wasn't good at all.'

'Can you remember when this was, exactly?'

He can't. It was *still cold*, he says, and figures it for July or August.

'We'll look into it,' says Lana. 'Thanks, Steve.'

Back in the car, Lana radios the station and requests permission from the widow to enter the clinic. Ten minutes later, it comes through. 'Take the next left,' she says to Bruno. She turns back to the radio. 'One last thing. Can I have someone organise for Erin Amstell to visit the station as soon as she's available? Preferably tomorrow morning. I'd like to go over her statement.'

•

Brian Amstell's clinic is a modern concrete box on the edge of the Wharf Street shopping district. To Lana, the place looks more like a day spa than a doctor's office. The interior fit-out is glass brick on soft furnishings. Bigger than expected, three other GPs work in the building and they're all in today, tending to patients.

'Good morning. Who are you two here for?' chirps the girl at the front desk. She's blonde and looks like something off a postcard. Meter-maid material.

Lana does the introductions. 'We'd like to take a look at Brian's office.'

The girl glances around nervously.

Every eye in the waiting room on them.

Bruno leans close. 'No one's in any trouble.'

The girl nods, relieved. 'I'll show you through.'

In the hall, Lana asks the girl if she's Maddy, the name gleaned from Brian Amstell's wastepaper basket yesterday.

'No, I'm Tanya. Don't know a Maddy. Miriam does Mondays and Tuesdays. She might know her. Here it is.' Tanya opens the door. 'Brian has the nicest one.'

The room is clean. White space punctuated by a wall-sized window overlooking a rear garden. They look the place over while the receptionist waits. There isn't much to find. Brian's desk drawers contain the usual (branded stationery, a street directory, batteries, empty tupperware) and it's orderly up top as well. An empty mug, a desk planner, and a steel rack containing three patient files. Bruno flicks through the files, checking the names.

Lana says, 'Recognise anyone?'

'No.'

'You can't read those,' says Tanya.

Bruno puts them back.

A set of custom-fitted cabinets line the adjacent wall. Lana points to them and says, 'What are these, Tanya?'

'More files.'

'And that?' Lana shifts her attention to a small, freestanding steel cabinet tucked in the corner beside a large potted plant.

'Files. Miriam looks after Brian's paperwork. I handle the other doctors.'

'Do you remember a break-in last year?'

'I was on leave.'

'Surely someone mentioned it.'

'Oh yeah, I knew it happened, but no one really talked about it. It was kids, I think. They had trouble with vandals at the mall around the same time. That's what Doctor Martin said. He's one of the other GPs.'

Lana gives the office a final scan and says, 'I think we're done.'

'I'm done,' says Bruno. 'You know, Tanya, I need a new GP. My regular guy's office looks like a janitor's closet compared to this.'

'I'm happy to book you in for a consult, detective. I'll go fetch the forms.'

Bruno watches her leave.

Lana says, 'You know she doesn't do the consulting, right?'

'I know.'

Bruno lingers around and chats with the receptionist while Lana waits outside and smokes. When he's done, they both jump in the car and head back to the highway.

'You get yourself a new GP?'

'I was working the case.'

'You were working something.'

'Tanya back there told me they've got a day surgery out the back of that place. A little theatre across the hallway from Brian's office. I didn't notice it. Apparently, he does minor surgical stuff in there and makes a killing. That's why he owns the place. The other three doctors handle the day-to-day GP bullshit. Amstell sticks to the boutique stuff.'

'He does surgeries in that little place? Bloody hell. Anything else?'

'Tanya takes her holidays when the other GPs are on leave. They wind back the appointments every August and Brian holds the fort for a fortnight on his own.'

'Good boss.'

'Good boss, but—'

'The vandalism is aimed at Amstell,' says Lana.

'He was the only one on duty. So, could be.'

'Jeez, Bruno. Nice.'

'You're welcome.'

They motor along for a minute.

Lana says, 'Did you get her number?'

'Nope.'

'Can't win 'em all.'

'Winning isn't everything,' he says.

CHAPTER 15

HENRY LOGS TIME ON both cases, Diablo and Sarah Utton, starting with a green van owner in Robina. Name of Simon Tanner. Tanner works in an auto-shop, and the van is right there with him. It's a no-go. Tanner and his van were in Melbourne for the relevant dates. On top of which, the van has a dirty great big logo stencilled on the side, making it an unlikely accessory to murder.

•

The second port of call is a Sarah Utton job, a visit to a shared apartment in Broadbeach occupied by two women from Tropical Touch. This is the home of Nelly Johnson—whom Henry has rousted a few times for street work—and Dianne 'Diamond' Wresting, a high-end girl who pulls the occasional night manager shift in the brothel. He wakes them today, holds up a picture of Utton on their doorstep.

'Sarah, right?' says Nelly.

Nothing from Di.

'I know you both worked with her at Tropical Touch. That's why I'm here. Either of you seen her in the last couple of months?'

'Not me,' says Nelly.

Di goes with, 'We didn't get along.'

'When was the last time either of you saw her?'

Di steps forward. 'Mate, we don't have to tell you jack shit. Time to go, I reckon.'

'You know I work in Consorting, right? Di, there's a file on you back at the station that's an inch thick.'

Di stands her ground. 'Maybe you should go back and read it, then,' she says, and shuts the door in his face.

•

Stop three is an office building two blocks from Diamond Di's apartment. It's a public service place, the Lands Office. Two green van owners on Henry's list work there. The first is Daryl Millman, a short, pudgy property valuer dressed up to the nines. Crisp shirt, gold jewellery (neck and wrist), woollen brown trousers hiked up to the navel. Millman wears a strong cologne, but is a stern bugger, answering Henry's questions with gruff distaste. 'I'm busy here,' he says.

When Henry presses him on times and dates, the man spits back, 'I told the other one. I was at the movies.'

Henry scans his notes. It's true. A previous visit with Millman, from another CIB detective, includes details of a call to Millman's wife for an alibi. That was months back. Henry tries on the dates for the recent murders. 'How about these nights?'

Millman checks his diary. 'Movies as well,' he says.

'All three nights?'

'I like the movies.'

It doesn't look like Daryl Millman likes anything, but the man opens the bottom drawer of his desk and takes out a scrapbook, like something a kid might have. The man has pasted the movie ticket stubs for all the films he's seen in there, alongside brief handwritten descriptions.

The bloke has seen everything.

Henry hands back the scrapbook. 'What's your favourite movie, Daryl?'

'Really?'

'I can get a warrant.'

'Star Wars.'

'Never seen it. Any good?'

'Are we done here?'

Henry is.

•

The second van owner in the Lands Office proves much more interesting. He's a young bloke who works in the surveying department. Ted Freedman. Ted's six two with hands the size of dinner plates. He doesn't have an alibi for the nights in question. 'I live on my own, mate.' He's *heard* about the murders, though. 'All over the news, innit?' And Ted is absolutely dumb enough to be caught out by a routine check like this one. 'Yeah, I've got a van. What of it?'

'You out much at night, Ted?'

'I don't mind a night drive, yeah. Get out amongst it. Beats sitting at home on my arse. No one to look at in there 'cept myself.'

Henry chuckles, keeps it casual. 'Hey, Ted, how would you feel about coming down to the station tonight and giving us some prints? We're doing it with everyone.'

Ted goes wide-eyed. 'Do you have the killer's fingerprints? Bloody hell. They didn't mention that in the paper. I'm getting the inside stuff now, aren't I?'

'We don't have the killer's prints yet,' says Henry. 'This is a routine thing,' which is one lie after another. Diablo has two clear prints from the Eddie Edgar murder and a matching set of partials from the other two on Henry's docket. 'It's just a formality, Ted. But if you could come in, it'll help me out, and I could have someone show you round the station. It'll be fun. Better than a night in front of the box.'

'You know, I reckon I might,' says Ted.

Henry leaves it at that.

In the lift, he thinks, *Be funny if I just solved it.*

CHAPTER 16

HENRY STAYS AT IT. He follows the Sarah Utton leads. A bunch of the Tropical Touch girls live in Surfers Paradise, holed up in rentals around the new high-rises on Cavill Avenue. He spends an hour going door to door, querying and cajoling, getting scraps of info in return.

Sarah lived up the street off and on.

I heard she was moving on to high rollers.

She was a wild one, even by my standards. Light-fingered, too.

Yeah, she was cash-strapped. She was taking on work.

She owes me money.

None of it helps much, but collectively it paints a picture. Sarah Utton needed cash in a hurry. That's a red flag, all the way. Utton had a professional gig with Colleen Vinton. That sort of work is brokered on trust and discretion. When trust and discretion wavers, that's when the shit hits the fan: stealing money or jewellery or drugs, blackmailing clients, selling dirt, you name it. All of it can get you killed when you work for people like Vinton.

One name keeps cropping up in the chatter: Brad Glynn, the pot-dealing boyfriend. Henry flicks back through his notebook and finds his details. Brad works the carpark of Sea World. Henry moves Brad up the list.

Running out of moves, Henry rounds out the morning with three more Diablo rego checks. He talks to a hairdresser on Main Beach. An unemployed bloke in Ashmore. And a painter in Labrador. Three busts. The painter's van doesn't even match the description. It's more of a dark red than a dark blue or green, and the painter himself is a right smartarse to boot. 'Maybe your witness is colourblind?' he says.

'You never know,' says Henry.

'You even sure it's a van?'

'Nothing's for sure,' he says, realising that's the second time he's said something like that in the space of a day.

What's happening?

He checks his watch.

It's 12.14 pm.

The twenty-first of February 1980.

A barren, hot summer day on Strike Force Diablo.

A quiet lunch at the pub might be as good as it gets.

•

Unfortunately for Henry, the Paradise Hotel is experiencing a pronounced police presence. Diablo detectives pack out the front bar. The mood is dour and they're already half-cut for the day. The men are steeling themselves for a three o'clock briefing with Superintendent Albert Beggs. The *Big Boss*. A right bollocking predicted. Henry plain forgot.

He does the rounds. Can't not do it, and it goes about the same as usual. Mark Evans asks after Lowell, with a sneer. Pete Reynolds—the bastard—blows smoke in his face. Ron Bingham, sweating like a heart attack, drunkenly mutters something about the New South Wales police turning up *sweet fuck all* on the Brian Amstell scene.

Henry takes a pour from one of the beer jugs going around and slips out back to the bistro, where he orders bangers and mash and waits for it at an empty table. He spreads his field notes out in front of him and tries to map it all out in his head. After a time, he notices movement in the corner of his eye and a familiar voice.

'How long have you been with the Force?'

It's Bruno Karras. He was mates with Emmett Hades, pre-Diablo and pre-breakdown. They worked a homicide together back when, but Bruno's keeping a low profile of late. Now he's sitting across the way with the New South Wales woman, the one from the Amstell scene.

'I've got to take a slash,' Bruno says.

He gets up.

Henry turns back to his notes.

A minute later, he looks back over and the New South Wales woman is staring at him.

CHAPTER 17

LANA FORCES HERSELF TO smile at Henry Loch. 'Hello again.'

The man stares back with empty eyes.

'I saw you yesterday,' she says.

'I know.'

'My name's Lana.'

'Henry.'

'You want to join us?'

'I've got . . .' He puts a hand on his paperwork.

'Are you working the Amstell case? I didn't see you out there this morning?'

'I'm on the earlier ones.' He looks back down at his work, but then stops. 'Why are you up here?'

'Secondment,' says Lana. 'The district brass didn't want to completely hand over the Amstell thing. It's been a quiet month over there.'

'How long you on this?'

'Don't know. How long's a nightmare?'

'What?'

'That's what you called it yesterday,' she says.

'Oh, right. Yeah.'

'You sure you don't want to join us?'

'Another time.'

She leaves him be. Prodding Henry is pure intuition. He's a knuckle-head cop, by the look of it, but he also seems strangely morose. That's the word that comes to mind. It's all over him, from the thousand-yard stare to the quiet demeanour, to the food he's barely touched. At a guess, Constable Henry is in trouble. Lana files it away.

Bruno returns. 'I just ran into one of the admin girls in the bar. She reckons Erin Amstell's confirmed for nine o'clock tomorrow. Her lawyer's coming with her.'

'That's interesting.'

'You think?'

'I do.'

After a bite of his club sandwich, Bruno says, 'What do you do when you're not up to your neck in this stuff?'

'I don't know. Bit of this, bit of that. You?'

'I'm still working it out. I actually grew up down here, but I never learned to surf as a kid. Been giving it a go lately.'

Lana stops eating. It's hard to imagine buttoned-down Bruno on a surfboard, out with the long-hairs and muscle men.

'Don't worry,' he adds. 'Everyone seems to find it funny.'

'Look, you just don't seem—'

'Hang on.' Bruno gets up and points at the television set mounted to the wall of the dining room. 'Howie, turn that up, please. Howie!'

On the screen, a grizzled mid-fifties man in a blue dress uniform pushes through a crowd of journalists. The scene cuts to the same man shouting—an impromptu press briefing, not going well. The man's thinning black hair is plastered awkwardly across his brow.

'Oh Christ,' says Bruno. 'That's Beggs.'

'The superintendent?'

'Yep, the big guy.'

The sound snaps on.

Beggs, mid-sentence: '—and as you know, the exact status of a homicide investigation isn't anything I can discuss at this time. What I can say is that the Tweed Heads case interests us and is currently under review. Further to which, I have every faith in the Strike Force Diablo men and their ability to determine the case's relevance to our broader investigation. Despite the challenging circumstances, I'd like to confirm, once more, that the apprehension of an offender is not far off.'

Journalists volley for position. The winner shouts, 'What do you make of the recent government memo about Diablo?'

Beggs answers with, 'Total rumour and speculation. I have no knowledge of this memo, whatsoever, and I refuse to play office politics at such an important juncture in the investigation. If such a memo exists, it's a leaked government document, and it has no place in the public domain. Again, I have every faith in the abilities of our—'

The reporters cut him off.

'Oh shit,' says Bruno.

Beggs walks. 'Look, at present I have no further comment.'

The rabble won't stop.

Questions fly.

'What do you make of the appendix of the memo?'

'Do you agree with the assessment of your lead detectives?'

'Is Diablo a waste of taxpayer money?'

Beggs moves faster. 'I have nothing further to add. We'll be holding an official press briefing early next week. Until then, if you could all just excuse me, if you could just—'

The crowd of reporters surge harder.

The audio scrambles.

Hands fumble around the superintendent, over him. One reporter grabs at his uniform, prompting Beggs to put his hands on the man. Then, clear as a bell, he tells the guy to fuck off.

The audio cuts to a stunned news anchor.

A woman in the bistro gasps.

Lana leans forward. 'Did he just say . . .'

Bruno gapes at the screen. 'We better go. We better get back.'

CHAPTER 18

CHIEF SUPERINTENDENT ALBERT BEGGS stands in the Diablo squad room flanked by a cohort of underlings. In person, he's much more intimidating than on TV. Lana can see the street cop in him. The short, broad body, the drinker's bulbous nose and mottled skin. He starts his afternoon briefing like a back-alley interrogation. 'Do you know what they're saying about you fucking idiots up in the city?'

The temperature in the room drops immediately.

'That bloody memo is real,' he says. 'We've had it for a week. And guess what? I agree with every last word of it. Where is the damned thing?'

An underling holds it out.

'Bingham, where are you?' Beggs says.

The inspector steps forward from his hiding place: the doorway of that murky office of his.

Beggs gives him the memo. 'Read it. No, go to the appendix. Read *that*.'

Bingham turns to the page. 'No, I don't think I will.'

'*Read it*. It's not a fucking suggestion.'

Bingham clears his throat, eyes on the document.

'*Can* you read, Inspector?'

Bingham, in monotone, says, 'Despite its idyllic location, the Gold Coast station is widely known amongst high-ranking police officials and relevant government ministers as a punishment posting. It is where the Force sends its weakest officers, those ill-suited for duty in Brisbane and those too unreliable for the unsupervised nature of regional work.' Bingham stops. 'And then there's an itemised list underneath. And . . . we're all on it, pretty much.'

'Give it here,' says Beggs. 'You're too slow, you dumb fuck.'

Beggs goes through the list, reading it loud and clear, naming and shaming. First off the rank is Bingham himself. He's described as *a suspected alcoholic,* and *a once-hardworking detective gone to seed.*

'Suspected?' says someone up the back.

That gets a laugh, but it's the last one.

Next, Mark Evans is said to be *meek. A proven incompetent, incapable of leadership, but driven by unqualified ambition. Not a team player. Not Brisbane CIB material.* Meanwhile, the other Diablo lead, Pete Reynolds, is said to be *insubordinate. Prone to deceit. A poor communicator with questionable judgement, and completely unreliable.*

It keeps going from there.

All the men are shamed.

All are blamed.

Bruno Karras *struggles to conform to the expected norms of policing,* whatever that means. Others are *widely disliked,* or *employed above rank* or *prone to violence.* The worst of it is reserved for Henry Loch. According to the memo, Henry *should have been dismissed years ago. Loch is an irredeemable thug with a slim list of achievements and no track record at all for detective work. He remains in service due to occulted political goodwill, and his placement within Diablo is indicative of the entire operation's complete systemic failure and an obvious scramble for manpower.*

By the end, Lana is scared to look at any of them. Their faces are too much. There's obviously a lot of truth in the room—an informant's truth—and it's all the worse coming from the boss.

To finish, Beggs crumples the memo and throws it on the carpet. 'That, gentlemen, is what the higher-ups think of you. And now, thanks to you lot, this is what my colleagues think of *me.* For the love of god, you better have something to show me today. What *is* the progress? Which one of you would like to go first?'

Total silence.

'No one? Really?'

The men stay quiet.

'Oh, I see. Did I hurt your feelings? Christ. Where's the skirt? The one from down south. Where is she?'

Lana opens her notebook, buying herself a moment.

'Where is she?' Beggs says a second time.

CHAPTER 19

HERE, I'M OVER HERE. Yes, I'm . . .

Henry fumes. Sensing himself spinning out of control, he forces focus, sucks in deep breaths and unclenches his hands, knuckles cracking audibly. Through the haze of embarrassment and shame, he hears the new detective talking, her voice fading in and out.

Victim is a . . .

Lana Cohen runs down the basics of the Brian Amstell case. 'Our forensics team identified several promising leads. We believe the assailant may have travelled to and from the scene by motorcycle. We're following that up. There is also the fact that Amstell's medical clinic was vandalised last year. We're looking into that as well. His wife is coming in tomorrow for an interview. I think mostly—'

'Next,' barks Beggs. 'Who did the background checks?'

Another of the detectives pipes up. 'Amstell has no priors and, at this stage, no links to organised crime or anything like that. His finances are in order. He owns his house, a big boat, and a rental property. He's got plenty of money in the bank. I mean, he did better than expected for a doctor but, apparently, he was a bloody good one. This bloke made the local news every now and then.'

Beggs says, 'Run down the other cases. Go on.'

One by one, the detectives give brief progress reports. It's pure churn. Lots of lists and detail. Lots of re-interviewing and doubling back. No solid leads.

Beggs glares through it, then without warning he pushes his way through to a nearby desk, grabs a pen and takes it to Bingham's office door. He draws three thick strokes on the paintwork, the pen tip screeching in the quiet room. 'See this? See this, gentlemen? One, two, three.

You have three days to make an arrest. Three days from now, if there isn't an arrest, Diablo is done and you're all finished. Anyone I can demote or transfer or retire, I will. Anyone I can bust back to uniform will be back in uniform. So, you have three days. I suggest you use them wisely. And lest you fail to realise the gravity of all this, let me show you how serious I am. Detective Loch?' Beggs scans around, finding Henry. He points a fat finger in his direction. 'You. You're already done. When you come to work next week, you're back on the Consorting Squad until I can find a worse fate for you. You hear me? *Out.*'

Everyone turns to Henry.

Henry stays quiet.

'Good. That's the first fucking smart thing you've said all year,' says Beggs. 'Tell that partner of yours too, because he's going back with you. As for the rest of you, this is your future if you do not provide results.'

Beggs walks. The underlings rush after him.

When it's over, the detectives stand around watching Bingham up front. The man seems stunned. He gently wipes at his neck with a handkerchief. 'Evans, Reynolds, my office,' he says, eventually. 'The rest of you, back to work. Anne-Marie, go get some kero and wipe this nonsense off my door.'

No one moves.

'*Now*, gentlemen,' says Bingham.

The detectives breathe out. They slump into their chairs, scratch their faces and arses, check their coffee cups. One burps loudly.

Henry stays frozen until one of the men slaps him on the shoulder and says, 'Lowell picked a bloody good day for a sickie.'

Henry ignores it. The voice of the chief reverberates inside him:

An irredeemable thug with a slim list of achievements.

An irredeemable thug.

Irredeemable.

It wasn't how this was supposed to work out.

It wasn't the deal.

Deep within Henry's psyche, a shot rings out.

•

He drives north, a blistering afternoon sun burning up one side of the car. The rego checklist flaps around on the passenger seat, but Henry isn't running leads. He's headed nowhere. Just driving.

The question is, Diablo or Sarah Utton?

'No,' Henry says, loud in the car.

The question *isn't* that.

Diablo is a bust.

Everyone knows it. It's the Titanic.

Utton.

He spots a phone box on the boardwalk and pulls the car over, makes a call. Jack the Bagman picks up, first ring. 'It's me,' says Henry. 'I might have a lead on that girl you're after.'

'That was quick. Were you holding out on me, son?'

'I looked into it. You said people were asking after her. How much clout do they have?'

'Plenty, mate.'

'Enough to protect me from Beggs?'

'Sure. Would you like me to make some calls for you, detective?'

'Yes.'

'Is there anything else?'

'What would you do in my situation?'

Jack laughs his jolly fucking laugh. 'As I've told you before, son, the politics aren't that difficult. Just do whatever you have to do to keep your head above water. Survival is the name of this game. It's *everything*.'

'So, find the girl, then?'

'Or solve the impossible case. One of the two.'

Henry hangs up.

Overhead, more fucking seagulls circling.

CHAPTER 20

THE POST-MORTEM RESULTS FOR Brian Amstell come in at dusk. As suspected, Amstell died of two gunshot wounds to the head, fired at close range. 'Shot in fast succession,' says the lab assistant over the phone. 'He would have felt nothing. Pretty clean.' The rest of Amstell's body is in better shape. All his major organs are disease-free. The blood work shows no trace of illness or narcotics. 'His stomach was a little torn up,' says the assistant, 'but it's nothing out of the ordinary. Stress, I'd say. I mean, you cut either of us open and you'd probably find something similar. He didn't smoke or overdo the booze. He was fit.'

'Anything else?' says Lana.

'Nope. A couple of scars. Two on his back from what appear to be mole removals. A couple of nicks on his legs. A small vasectomy incision on the scrotum. In childhood, I'd say he broke his arm.'

'Thanks.'

Lana takes her notes to Bruno. He's head down in the neighbourhood canvass leads.

'Getting anywhere?' she says.

Bruno shakes his head. He makes a show of flicking through the pages. 'There's nothing. If anything, this Brian fella sounds like a nice guy. Kept his yard clean. Said hello to the oldies on the street. He literally drove one of them to church every week.'

'What denomination is he?'

Bruno scans a page. 'His local was Saint Andrews Catholic. Why?'

'He had a vasectomy.'

'Sure.'

'Isn't that against the rules?'

'Not really. Are you Catholic?'

'No. You?'

'I was an altar boy. Vasectomies are what confession is for.'

'Sounds like a good system.'

'It's the same all over, as far as I can tell.'

'Where is everyone?' Lana says. She's expecting the place to be bustling after the superintendent's declaration of war.

'At the pub already,' Bruno says. 'Fancy another session?'

'I think it's my round.'

On the way out, Bruno points to Bingham's office. The lights are off, but the three strike marks remain on the door. Underneath, someone has scribbled, *Freedom awaits.*

•

The detectives of Strike Force Diablo have their corner of the Paradise Hotel and, in that corner, a frenzied energy circulates. Case details are shouted across tables and theories are bandied about. The facts of the investigation are dissected with blunt and lurid clarity. The killer is a psychopath. The killer is an ex-con. The killer is a war vet, a tourist, a genius, a cop, and a dickhead. Or the killer is already dead or already interviewed, already lost in the paperwork. The cases are linked. The cases *aren't* linked. The whole thing is a cosmic coincidence. Or not. No one knows because no one can agree on anything. And as the night tears on, the men stop caring.

Lana wonders what Dwain Gorst and the New South Wales brass suspect of this lot, because—to her mind—there is no level of police corruption or political intrigue that can eclipse this nihilism. One photograph of this session would explain everything to them. *This* is how and why seven cases go unsolved. Whatever trouble lurks, it's just another layer, because there's no perverting something like this. It's already at rock bottom.

Lana refills her beer glass and says to Bruno. 'Let's take a break.'

They bring their drinks across the road to the darkened beach and walk down into the sand with their shoes on. Even down there by the black ocean, the night is humid and still.

'You know,' Bruno says, 'my first day wasn't as wild as this.'

Lana lights a smoke, throws the pack to Bruno. She looks at the lights of Surfers Paradise and says, 'Yeah, no shit. You think they've got a chance of solving this? I worry someone's going to get stitched up just to get it done.'

'It's a real possibility.'

'Who do *you* reckon the killer is? Are they even searching for the right bloke?'

Bruno doesn't answer immediately. He takes a long drag and waits on it. Then he says, 'I think he's a do-gooder.'

'Keep going.'

'Brian Amstell might look squeaky clean, but there will be dirt there, too. Always is. The other victims, they're nearly all ratbags and crooks, either on the surface or underneath.'

'So, they had it coming?'

'That's how our guy sees it.'

'Religious then?'

'No doubt.'

'White?'

'Has to be. Someone would have noticed him otherwise.'

'And definitely a man?'

'Definitely. He killed the first victims with his hands. He might have a female accomplice, though. I mean, this bloke is passing, so that's a possibility. He could have a family, kids, the whole works. He doesn't look like what he is.'

'Which is?'

Bruno points the cherry of his smoke at the buildings. 'A bloke that looks at *that* and wants to burst the bubble.'

'Of Surfers Paradise?'

'Yeah. It's a great place for the family holiday, just ignore the details, you know? Stay in at night. That's the part that gets to you after a while. The hypocrisy of it is so obvious. Everyone can see it.'

'So, we should go harder on Amstell, then? Dig right in?'

'You're running the show.'

'I want your advice. That's why I'm asking.'

'You'd be the first. Look, I'd be shocked if Amstell is one hundred per cent on the straight and narrow. You heard it in the briefing. *He did better than expected.* That's code down here. A lot of these dead people *did better than expected.*'

'Then why isn't the team forensically tearing through his financials?'

'Because that's dangerous stuff around here. If we leaned on every bloke earning above his means, we'd be knee-deep in trouble inside of ten minutes.'

'Do you know anything about that?'

'With our lot?' Bruno shrugs. 'I try to know as little as possible. Come on, we should be getting back or they'll start talking.'

Lana sucks the last gasp out of her smoke. 'Hold on.' Trundling after him, her feet drag in the soft sand.

CHAPTER 21

IT TAKES HENRY HALF an hour to find Brad Glynn. Brad, the drug-dealing ex of Sarah Utton. He eventually spots him near the service exit of Sea World, down in the staff carpark, lurking in the shadow of a shipping container. Brad has a good thing going. The summer casuals are all young and cashed-up, and there's plenty of them.

'Hey, man,' says Brad. 'What are you after?'

Up close, Brad doesn't look so good. His face is covered in sweat and acne and he's wearing grey tracksuit bottoms, despite the heat.

Henry says, 'I'm a cop. I need some information.'

'You with Sergeant Gnomes?'

Henry punches him in the side, crumpling the man. 'Yeah. He sends his regards.'

'Jesus, man, wha . . . why did you do that? Ugh. I'm covered off!'

'This is about something else.' Henry produces a photo of Sarah Utton. 'I believe the two of you know each other?'

Brad squints up at the pic. 'Yeah, kinda.'

'Wrong answer. Where is she?'

'Fuck knows. She's not with me, man, that's for sure.'

'You two break up?'

'I guess. Weren't really *together* together.'

Henry rolls his shoulders. 'Look, Brad, I'm not big on small talk. If you don't tell me what I want to know, I'm going to give you a hiding, and then you're probably going to tell me anyway. So, let's speed the whole thing up.'

'Jeez, man, are you always like this?'

Henry comes closer. 'Yes.'

'Okay, okay, fuck,' says Brad. 'There's nothing much to say, anyway. Just chill. Can I get up?'

Henry gives him the nod. 'Where is she?'

'I honestly don't know. I heard she's crashing on people's couches. She's not with me, man, I promise. I wouldn't let her anywhere near my place, anyhow. She ripped me off last time she was around. Took half my roll. The Agriolis threatened to break my arms over it.'

'When was this?'

'Last year.'

'Why did she take your money? She strung out?'

'I don't know. That's a real mystery, man. She's not using. Not that I know of. She's been clean for ages. All of last year, at least.'

'Are *you* looking for her?'

'Nah. Nah, man.'

'Why not?'

'That's not my style. The day after she ripped me off, she rang and said she'd give the money back in a couple of weeks, but it's been months, hey.'

Henry stands back, gives Brad a bit of space. 'What was she like, the last time you saw her?'

'Scared, man. I didn't really put two and two together at the time, but she seemed *off*, you know?'

'When was this?'

'September, maybe. Around then. Ages ago, man. I could see something was up, but I just assumed it was, fuck, I don't know. No one knows anything with Sarah. That's her deal.'

'And you don't know why she robbed you?'

'Last time I checked, she was flush.'

'Really?'

'Oh yeah. She was making moves, man. Edging into the high-end stuff. Have you seen her? It was always on the cards. She might have just robbed me because she could. She can be like that.'

'Was the high-end work through Colleen?'

'Nah. Solo.'

'Who was hooking her up with it?'

'Don't know.'

'Who were the clients?'

'Kinky rich people. Same as always.'

'Brad?'

'Yeah?'

'Some pretty heavy people are going to come looking for her. If I find her first, she'll be better off. A *lot* better off. If she calls you, tell her to come find me. Here.' Henry gives him a card. 'Also, if I find out you're lying to me, I'll come back, and I won't be nice next time.'

Henry's about to leave but stops when he notices Brad's face. Brad's thinking.

'Come on,' says Henry.

'She has a sister in Brisbane. Carla. Lives in Coorparoo. I went there once.'

'Don't tell anyone else that.'

'You think she's going to be okay?'

'She'll be okay.'

'And you're going to fix it?'

'Yeah. I'm going to fix it.'

•

Henry drives out past Sea World and into the dark corridor of the Spit, through the marsh and scrub. It's getting late, and the sky is dark. Henry parks at the terminus of the gravel road and walks along the low dunes towards the water. They're working to pull this land together, to take all the wild parts of it out and pile in some sort of permanent landmass. The council is all over it. Everyone needs more coast to sell off, apparently. There are even rumours of high-rises going up, but Henry can't see it. You can't build on sand like this. It'd be headed for the ocean, no matter what you did.

Minutes later, he finds the seaway and stands by the water, studying the spot where the river meets the waves, froth and foam churning in the night. Henry's thoughts return to Superintendent Beggs and his black sermon. The thought of it pushes Henry back in time, back through Beggs to all the other men like him, through the ranks of bastards and bruisers and down into Henry's history—to a thousand heaving nights, to high school and the beatings and his father—and back to the loneliest spot of all.

Another night like this one.

Another black, unfounded place on the sand.

Gun at the back of a man's head.

Him gasping his last, wheezing breath.

Suddenly lit bright.

CHAPTER 22

BY ELEVEN, MOST OF the Diablo men are headed home, leaving the rest to hunker down at the pub and brood. Lana calls time on it. She's yet to check into her accommodation and needs to double back to the station for her luggage.

In the station carpark as she's about to leave, she spots a group of Gold Coast detectives passing on the footpath heading east. In amongst them is Ron Bingham. Ron, who made a big show of *going home to the missus.* Yet here he is.

Lana eases her car out onto the street and creeps the walking party as they make their way through the quiet back streets of Surfers Paradise. They arrive at a nondescript white building. Five stories high. Rundown. Shuttered windows. Lana parks and watches Bingham and the men finish their cigarettes on the building's stoop. Sensing something, Lana crawls into the back seat and opens the bench panel. She fumbles around in the boot for her camera, withdraws it, then fixes a telephoto lens, all with her eyes trained across the street.

She zooms in and snaps off a few shots.

Six of them standing there.

Haggard Ron in the centre.

The rest Lana recognises, but the names escape her.

Ron splits off from the group and buzzes the intercom by the door.

After a beat, he pulls it open. The interior of the building is unlit, but the policemen file in, laughing and patting each other on the back.

•

Lana's motel is located a few minutes south, on the line between downtown Surfers Paradise and the residential streets of Broadbeach. She has an open booking at the El Dorado, a musty hangover from the 1960s. It's not bad. Solid bed, a desk, a kitchenette. The real boon is the pool. Despite the hour, she slips into the water, thinking about how the day started with the ocean—with chaotic surf—and now it's ending here, in the cool of night.

Back in her room, she works in her gown as she writes up her notes and packages the camera film. When she's finished, she goes to the wardrobe and pulls out her motley collection of Missing Persons paperwork. This is the stuff she takes everywhere, from case to case. *The eternal investigation. The missing father.* But tonight, it's enough just to touch it, to feel the soft, worn finish of the files. She thinks about Brian Amstell's grieving daughters tucked into their beds and fights back a wave of dread, the same dread that waits for all of them tomorrow. Quietly, Lana sits with the papers and considers calling her brother—her only remaining family—but it's too late. *No.* She puts the files away and settles for a few minutes in an armchair by the window, sitting perfectly still, tuned into the highway and the hum of the air-conditioner.

DAY TWO

FRIDAY, 22 FEBRUARY 1980

JOURNAL OF EMMETT HADES

(SELECTED EXCERPTS)

Five years in the Brisbane Mobile Patrol with Rick Graham and it was just the start of my career, the apprenticeship. Rick was my mentor. Older and smarter. The extra time on duty made him sensitive, but not me. I wanted more, more, more. The Criminal Investigation Branch seemed like it might be the place to find it.

I took the exam and aced it. Got some of the highest scores on record. Never saw myself as the intellectual type, but there it was. Word got around. My transfer came March '65, and I went at it white hot, straight into Homicide, Brisbane CIB. 'Let's see what this genius can do,' was the thinking.

But they didn't know my true self or my true desires.

The city laid bare.

The great encyclopedia, open wide.

More, more, more.

The wash of carnage making me hungrier and hungrier.

More, more, more, more—

They could test for intelligence, you see, but what they couldn't examine was all the heart I had for it.

I was in love.

•

My first case was looking into a dead bloke found in a dirt carpark next to a racecourse in Eagle Farm. Turns out his on-again, off-again boyfriend did it, which was a hard pill to swallow for the widow, seeing as the boyfriend/killer was also her brother. She broke down when we

told her. The brother used to give her a hiding as a kid. 'I should've seen
it coming. I should have known,' she said.

The eternal mantra.

As I learned, everyone has something like that to say, but no one
admits the truth.

The truth is:

Everyone sees it coming.

Everyone knows, deep down.

There's no escape from the violence and mayhem of the city. That first
case may as well have been the tenth, or the twentieth, or the thirty-fifth,
or the last, because it was all one big topography.

•

A couple of months ago, I went back to the station house in Surfers
Paradise for a visit. Snuck my way in during the cover of darkness.
I wanted my Diablo files. My personal work.

It was odd being in the station again, but no one said anything. The
desk sergeant didn't give me a second glance and whoever else was rostered
on was out for the night. Anyway, it's not like I'm banned from the place.
I'm not even officially on leave. God forbid. Instead, I'm perennially 'out
in the field', or 'unavailable', which isn't entirely untrue.

But on this quiet November night back in the station, I took a little tour.
I sat in my old office, in my old office chair. I wandered the squad room
and looked at the desks and the paperwork piled up. I tried Bingham's
office door (locked) and Anne-Marie's desk drawers for his keys (also
locked) before settling into the dreaded Diablo murder room, alone.

It was terrible. My fastidious paperwork had been undone. The place
had no order now, no structure. The decline was clear. The soul of a
homicide case is the paperwork. No one ever says that on TV or in the
movies, but it's true. If the paperwork is orderly, the case is on track.
When the paperwork slides, everything follows.

I had a bit of time. I cleaned it up a little. Then I took what I needed—leaving the important stuff—and came back here to the garage behind the house, to my set-up. Look, it's not as secure as it should be, nor as clean (unsealed floor, dust everywhere, a single globe hanging from the rafters), but at least I can go about my work unfettered. More importantly, there's never any need to explain myself out here in the garage. I should have worked here right from the start. If anything, that's the lesson.

CHAPTER 23

HENRY CAN HEAR THE vacuum going inside Emmett's house. He opens the front door and goes in.

'Irene, it's just me,' he says.

Irene is Emmett's cleaner. The vacuum cuts.

'Henry?'

Emmett Hades appears in the doorway to the kitchen. The old copper is still in his pyjamas, but as with everything with Emmett, his get-up is impossibly neat. He could sit for a job interview in it. 'I wasn't expecting you,' he says. 'Have I forgotten something?'

'I was in the neighbourhood.'

'You want a cuppa?'

Irene restarts the vacuum.

Emmett makes the tea, and they sit out on the little patio area beside the house. 'Tell me what's going on,' he says. There's no small talk with him. It's straight into Diablo.

'I've spent the last week running those rego checks again with Lowell.'

'Any luck?'

'There's one bloke I talked into stopping by the station last night. Could be viable. Haven't checked in yet to see whether he did it.'

'What else? What about the Brian Amstell thing? Any action there?'

'A real whodunnit, by the sounds. Same MO as the last couple. No leads at this stage.'

'Are Reynolds or Evans trying anything new?'

'Not by the look of it. The New South Wales lot sent someone up because it's across the border. I guess that's something.'

'Who is he?'

'It's a woman, actually. Lana Cohen.'

'Never heard of her. Any good?'

'No idea.'

'Interesting. You should probably be careful around her, especially if she's easy on the eye. Is she?'

'Yeah, for a copper. You think she's a plant?'

'I'd say so.'

'Fucking Sydney,' Henry says. He finishes his tea. 'I have to tell you, I'm getting tired of this shit, Em.'

'Diablo?'

'No. The office bullshit.'

'It's the tricky part. You have to block it out. Just keep paying attention to your caseload. Keep it straight. I can see big things in your future, Henry. Remember that. Big things.'

Henry visibly tenses up. 'Don't say that.'

'Everyone's life changes. There are seasons. All you need to do is stay the course and ride this out. If you want to win at Homicide, you need to work the details, do the boring stuff. I've said it a hundred times.'

'I know. You're right. I don't suppose you've had any more bright ideas about these earlier cases?'

'Not this week. Keep working the rego checks and keep an eye out for shifting waters. Use your gut. Let your gut tell you things and then study them. It's the only way out of this. That's the balancing act. Primal instinct versus boring detail.'

'Should I poke around the Amstell thing?'

'Do whatever you think is prudent. But the early cases will be where the mistakes are, mark my word. Those mistakes are the best way into his head. And, Henry, when you know how he thinks, you can work out where he's hiding and how he's moving around. That's the whole gig.'

'Will do,' Henry says. 'It's busy at the moment. I've got some other work on. There's a missing girl.'

He shows Emmett the photograph of Sarah Utton.

'Who filed the report? The family?'

Henry pockets the photo. 'No one. This is off-book. Jack's looking for her too.'

'Okay, well, be careful. And don't get too distracted.'

'I need a break from the other thing.'

'It's a long, long game, Henry. With a tricky homicide case, the winner is always the last person to give up. That's why you still see the old-timers coming in for their cold cases.'

'Do I really want to turn out like that?'

'You rarely have a choice,' says Emmett.

They sit there and think about that. It's a nice morning, but the sun has roasted Emmett's lawn, so it isn't much to look at. Henry can see the dirt through the grass. The garden's a dying trash heap. Inside, Irene finishes the vacuuming and Henry hears the throttling zip of the lead retracting. 'I better get to work,' he says, getting up. He puts a hand out for Emmett. The old man takes the help, but his grip is like a steel vice.

CHAPTER 24

HENRY WAITS IN THE street by Emmett's house.

Irene shuffles out.

'He seems good this week,' Henry says, unlocking the passenger side of his car.

'The episodes have tapered off,' Irene says. 'There's been a lot less talking out loud, and less of his ghosts and imaginary friends and all that stuff.'

'Anything set him off?'

They're both looking for the pattern in his mania, the triggers.

'No. He's always better after church, though.'

Henry nods. Never much for religion. He takes an envelope from the glove box and opens it. This is the Joke money provided by Jack the Bagman. The police union is giving Emmett the run-around, so Henry is paying for Irene out of his ill-gotten gains. It's an arrangement that pre-dates Emmett's unofficial suspension. 'You need any extra this week?'

Irene declines. 'More money isn't going to fix him. You know that, right? We're just treading water with this.'

Henry shrugs. 'He's turned it around before.'

'He's not going to this time.'

'If these are his last days at home, I want him comfortable. Just call me if it gets too much.'

'He's no bother. But I've seen it all before, Henry. I don't think he's getting any better.'

Henry folds up his envelope and says, 'Well, I'm not paying you to think about him, Irene. Just keep him out of trouble.'

It's uncharacteristically brisk, and Henry regrets it, even as the words leave his mouth. He knows why, too. Emmett is a mentor of sorts.

Henry's spent a lot of time with the man. There were lots of late nights in the station house. Hours and hours in that cesspit of a murder room during the early days of Diablo, lots of time to talk and get to know each other. Emmett knows Henry's entire history, and he's the only person Henry has ever met who had anything smart to say about it.

'That pain of yours can be a gift, if you let it.'

He's loved him ever since.

•

Henry drives the Pacific Highway up to the Coomera River where he stops at a payphone. He calls in to the station house and gets put through to Anne-Marie in the Diablo squad room. She tells him Ted Freedman came in the night previous, gladly offering up his prints. The suspect from the Lands Office. 'The overnight guys told me the idiot giggled the whole time,' Anne-Marie says. 'Henry, I think this guy might be too stupid to kill seven people. I guess we'll find out in a couple of days.'

Henry hangs up, then slips another coin into the slot. His second call is to a contact in the Main Roads Department, a woman named Jill.

'Oh, here we go,' she says, her usual greeting.

'I'm fishing for an address.' Henry reads it off his notebook. 'It's Carla with a C. Carla Utton.'

'Detective, you know I'm not supposed to help you with your love-life? Not without a warrant, at least.'

'It's a missing girl. This is her sister. Think of it as your good deed for the day.'

Jill laughs. 'My hero. Hold on.'

Henry waits a full five minutes with the receiver resting on the phone as Jill hits the records room. She comes back with an address in Coorparoo. 'Your girl owns a 1975 green Cortina.'

'Thanks. I owe you one.'

'It's more than one, Henry.'

Coorparoo is inner-city Brisbane, a forty-five-minute drive up the highway and out of Henry's jurisdiction. Still in the phone booth, Henry turns to the back of his notebook, to his contact list. He scans down to Barry. Stares at the number. Detective Sergeant Barry Caller is a dangerous animal, a total black hole of a man. And Henry is in his pocket.

Henry dials. He has to. Into the receiver, he says, 'I'm going to be up your way today, Barry. Just wanted to let you know. I don't want to surprise anyone.'

Barry breathes down the line.

'Henry bloody Loch, well, well, well . . .'

CHAPTER 25

ERIN AMSTELL LOOKS A lot prettier with her make-up on and Lana isn't alone in noticing. Word has travelled around the station and, as Lana brings the woman through, she notices the general duties men loitering, trying to sneak a look. Erin has an older man with her. He introduces himself as Duncan Paterson. 'I'm the family's lawyer.'

'Sure. We only have a few questions, aside from the statement,' Lana says. 'Come on back.'

They use the big interrogation room. When Lana has them settled— seats, ashtray, a cup of instant coffee for Erin—she collects Bruno from the viewing room and finds the place is full of Diablo men.

'Really?' Lana says, going eye to eye.

'Just keeping abreast of the details, luv,' says Bingham.

The men snicker.

'Knock 'em dead,' says one of them.

'Fine by me.'

Bruno and Lana start the interview by running down the specifics. Duncan Paterson keeps quiet, letting his client answer without comment.

Erin tells them that Brian went out running. While he was away, she went out for milk. She spotted the prelim scene on the way back and had a bad feeling. She stopped. A patrolman told her a runner had been shot. That's when she knew. The rest is a blur. She doesn't really remember returning home. 'It was like I was teleported back to the kitchen. Everything was the same, except Brian was dead.'

'Any idea what happened to the milk?' says Lana.

'What?'

'The milk you went out for. The reason you left the house.'

'I don't know.'

Bruno says, 'One of our blokes might've put it in the fridge?'

'Maybe,' says Erin. 'Is it important?'

'It's just that I noticed there was plenty of milk in the house when I was there,' Lana says. 'I made a cup of tea that morning. Maybe you stepped out for something else, instead of milk?'

'No, it was definitely milk,' says Erin.

'Did anyone see you that morning?'

'My kids. Maybe someone at the shop?'

Lana jots down, *Alibi?*

The lawyer smooths his tie. 'Can we move on, please?'

Bruno asks a series of prepared questions, easing them into talk of Erin and Brian's marriage. Once he has her talking, Bruno circles around to infidelity, disagreement and trouble.

Lana watches carefully.

'Our marriage wasn't perfect,' Erin says. 'We had our fights, just like everyone else.'

Bruno keeps at it. Erin Amstell is holding out, playing it more and more elusive. The housewife. The widow.

Lana leans in. 'He made a good living, didn't he?'

'He did. Brian worked hard.'

'Has a patient ever sued him?'

Erin turns to Duncan, the lawyer.

Duncan says, 'I don't represent the practice.'

Lana says, 'We interviewed a receptionist at the practice, one Tanya Corley, and Tanya told us that a while back the place was vandalised. What can you tell us about that?'

'I don't think Brian ever mentioned it.'

'Really? He had to close up shop for a few days. You sure you don't remember him being around more?'

'No,' says Erin. 'I don't remember it.'

Lana checks her notes, taking a moment. Without looking up, she says, 'Did your husband use birth control?'

'I don't see the relevance of this,' says Duncan.

'We're Catholics,' says Erin.

'Does that mean yes or no?'

'No.'

'Our report shows that Brian had a vasectomy.'

'I don't think he did,' says Erin.

She's off kilter now. Bruno spots it immediately and pounces. 'Does your husband have life insurance, Mrs Amstell?'

'I don't know,' she yelps. 'I don't know any of this.'

'We might take a break now,' says Duncan.

'I thought you'd know if your husband had life insurance, is all?' says Bruno.

'I . . .'

Duncan says, 'I think that's—'

'I just have a few more questions,' says Lana.

'No,' says the lawyer. 'I think we'll be having a break now.'

Bruno and Lana file into the adjoining room and watch through the two-way glass as Erin Amstell cries and blows her nose.

Ron Bingham breaks the quiet. 'Bloody hell, Lana, I thought you'd be a friendly female face, not give the woman a heart attack.'

'A man is dead,' Lana says. 'She's got three kids at home about to grow up without a father.'

'I don't think *she* did it,' says Bingham.

Duncan puts a consoling arm around Erin Amstell, but as he does this, his eyes don't soften. Instead, he holds Erin and stares into the mirror, right into the gaze of the onlooking detectives.

CHAPTER 26

ERIN AMSTELL WALKS BRISKLY down the front stairs of the station and across the bitumen tarmac. Her lawyer, Duncan, hangs back, finishing his cigarette on the stoop.

Lana comes out behind him. 'Can I bum one of those?'

'Piss off.'

'Fair enough,' she says, lighting one of her own.

'You really think she knocked off her husband for the life insurance?' says Duncan. 'This isn't a movie, you know.'

'We had to have a poke around. Sorry I upset her.'

'She's a wreck. It's a miracle I got her here and then you two carry on with all this. Fucking hell. I should file a complaint.'

'Was it really worse than expected?'

Duncan studies her. 'How long have you been a detective, if you don't mind me asking?'

'Too long. Why?'

'Would you like some professional advice?'

'Is it on the house?'

'A lot of doctors are terrible husbands. Cheating, gambling, drinking, the lot. They work long hours, but it's also how they get away with it. If I were digging around for dirt on a doctor, I'd track down his assistant rather than attack his grieving widow. The assistants know what they're up to, not the wives sitting at home.'

Lana isn't buying. 'We spoke to the receptionist at the clinic.'

'Tanya? She just answers the phone. Look further afield.'

They both smoke their cigarettes, eyes ahead.

'Thanks,' says Lana.

'You're welcome. Now just leave her alone, please.'

Erin Amstell storms back across the carpark.

Duncan spots it first. 'Oh, I see,' he whispers.

The widow hurls a white object at them.

It explodes on the stairs, warm liquid spraying up in a wide arc. The smell is immediate and clear: off milk. This is Erin Amstell's missing carton of skim milk. It was in her car the whole time.

Erin Amstell screams, 'There you go.'

The milk trickles down the concrete as Duncan wipes debris from his shirt. 'It seems unfair that I got hit with it too,' he says.

CHAPTER 27

SARAH UTTON'S SISTER CARLA lives in a low-set brick cottage at the end of a quiet street in Coorparoo. The house is all closed up. Henry knocks once at the front door before circling around back. In the rear yard, a standalone garage sits beside an empty concrete slab and a dry lawn. The back door to Carla Utton's house sits within a small alcove, providing more than enough cover and—even better—the door is loose on its hinges. The whole thing snaps open on the second kick.

'Hello?' Henry says, stepping into the kitchen. 'Police.'

No sound except for a distant lawnmower.

The interior is spotless. Everything crisp and clean and straight.

There's a pile of papers on the kitchen bench and Henry sorts through them.

Bills.

A month-old newspaper.

And bingo: a pile of mail addressed to Sarah Alice Utton.

She's been here.

He searches the rest of the house, moving fast. There's a spare room that screams crash pad. It contains leftover clothes and a suitcase. Jewellery in a purse. A pile of *Rolling Stone* magazines on the floor of the wardrobe and a shoebox under the bed. Inside the shoebox, Henry finds an uncashed cheque for three hundred dollars, payment coming from Paradise Gaming Pty Ltd—he's never heard of them. In the same box, Henry finds a pill case containing two sets of tablets: orange and blue. At the bottom of the shoebox, there's a church flyer for some Catholic outfit across the border. An Order of Service for Sunday, seven months ago.

Henry deposits the bankbook, pills and flyer into a plastic shopping bag and gets to work on the rest of the house, doing a half-decent job ransacking the place. There isn't much to take: six hundred in cash in the main bedroom, prescription meds in the bathroom, a gold watch. He grabs it all, feeling lousy the entire time.

CHAPTER 28

HENRY KNOWS BRISBANE CITY. He did some of his general duties stint here, '73 to '76. It was his second posting, one filled with mistakes, and dotted across the city like a map. Today he travels that map, vector to vector.

He spends two hours in the Valley, dropping in on daytime prostie beats and hitting up the Valley street cops at their smoko haunts. He shows the picture of Sarah Utton to anyone who'll look and gets zip. Cursing it all, he circles back to the CBD and starts working the station house on Makerston Street. The building is new, but the interior is the same old house of horrors. Sour acquaintances, long regrets. A lot of harsh looks and averted eyes. People are wary of him. People are annoyed and surprised. But there's civility, too. 'Firmness With Courtesy'—but no one likes it. When Henry was sent to the Gold Coast, he was supposed to stay there.

Forever.

Against all hope, Henry ends up at the Police Club on the fourth floor. Neil Winters from the Robbery Branch insists on it, and Henry soon learns why. Neil is two hours into a liquid lunch.

'You lose your surfboard, mate?' says Neil, instead of hello.

The cop drinking with Neil laughs out loud.

Henry doesn't know the other bloke. He stares him down.

The laughing cop takes an impromptu bathroom break.

'Ever the diplomat,' says Neil.

'I need a favour.'

'Have a bloody drink first. Christ.'

Neil orders another round. They take it to a quiet corner. 'Now, what's this bullshit you're getting me into this time, Henry? You're supposed to be dead and buried on the Gold Coast.'

'I want you to keep an eye out for a robbery report on Woodrow Drive in Coorparoo. It'll be for Carla or Sarah Utton.'

'Oh yeah? Who's that then?'

'It's for a case down my way.'

'Then why do I give a shit?'

'Come on, Neil, Carla and Sarah Utton. Do you need me to write it down?'

'Do you have rocks in your head? Don't write anything down. Jesus.'

'Will you remember it, though?'

'I might. Who could forget your fucking face?'

'Come on, Neil.'

'What's in it for me?'

Henry slips him half of Carla Utton's cash under the table. 'Will that cover it? I want this on the down low, Neil. Real low. It's sensitive.'

Neil counts the money above the table, not a care in the world. 'As always, the service is terrible, Detective Loch, but the price is right. Now, I believe this next round is on you.'

•

Henry doesn't get out of there till late in the afternoon, leaving barely enough time to sweep the rest of the station house. He hits the CIB squad room—lightly staffed at this time of day—and with the place mostly to himself, he eyeballs the active cases and assignments.

No sign of Sarah Utton.

No sign of a missing girl or a body matching her description.

He circles around to the Licensing Branch and is about to step inside when Ann Masters appears further down the corridor. They were in uniform together.

She freezes. 'Henry?'

'Yeah.'

'What . . . what are you doing here?'

'Just checking in.'

She comes up to him in the doorway and whispers, 'How are you?'

'Hey!' comes a loud voice from across Licensing.

They both turn to find Barry Caller, the head of the branch, standing across the way nursing a cup of tea.

Barry smiles a big smile and says, 'Ann, stop harassing young Henry. He's taken.' Every word has a cold, hollow ring.

'It's okay,' says Henry.

Ann stands her ground.

Barry says, 'I really like your outfit, Ann. Calf-shit brown *really* suits you.'

She shakes her head, fuming.

'You know, Ann. I think you could be really something if you just—'

'Shut your mouth,' she says.

'—longer hair, a shorter skirt, a couple of pounds off the—'

'Fuck you, Barry.'

The start of tears in her eyes.

Barry laughs at that.

CHAPTER 29

BRUNO PULLS THE CAR up against the kerb, so they can sit there and study the house. It's a modern two-storey joint: stone wall facade, lots of glass at the front, a spiral stair on the exterior. Behind it sits the blue horizon of the South Pacific.

'We're in the wrong profession,' he says.

Lana pops the car door. 'We'll see.'

The Amstell family solicitor, Duncan Paterson, led them here. His quiet tip about Brian Amstell's assistant took them back to the doctor's clinic where it turned out that Brian's current assistant—Miriam, late-forties and openly lesbian—wasn't the woman they were looking for. 'Ha, that'll be the day,' Miriam said. 'I think you're looking for Maddy Santos. She's the one before me.'

A call to the Titles Office gave Lana and Bruno the address, and that was all it took. Madison Santos: former doctor's assistant and primary occupant and co-owner of a mansion on Carlisle Avenue, Mermaid Beach. The other signatory on the mortgage: her old boss, Brian Amstell.

Bruno knocks on the front door, and a delicate woman opens up. She has shoulder-length brown hair and brown eyes and wears a peach silk bathrobe like she was born to it.

'Madison Santos?' says Bruno.

The woman doesn't move an inch. 'You two look like cops.'

Lana says, 'We're investigating the death of your former boss, Brian Amstell. Can we come in?'

Madison doesn't answer. Instead, she turns and drifts back into the house.

Bruno shrugs and steps in after her. From behind, Lana watches Bruno casually scan the living room and kitchen as they make their way through. 'This is a nice place you've got yourself, Madison,' he says.

'It's Maddy. No one calls me Madison.'

Lana opens her notebook, more for show than anything. 'I need to get some details from you. Where were you two mornings back? Do you remember?'

'I don't really talk to cops,' Maddy says.

'And why is that?' says Lana.

'Well, having lived here my whole life . . .'

'You can trust us,' says Bruno.

Maddy gathers her robe around her. 'You know what they say about people who say that.'

Lana says, 'Would you like your lawyer present?'

'No. He's expensive.'

'Well, what about a drive down to the station?' offers Bruno. He wanders the room.

Lana doesn't let her answer. 'So, two mornings back?'

'I was here by myself, I think. Probably slept late, then went out for brunch.'

'Where'd you eat?'

'There's a place on the highway I normally go. Bertie's.'

'How would you describe your relationship with Brian Amstell?' says Bruno, squinting at an abstract painting on the wall.

'I wouldn't.'

'No?'

'I'm not one for gossip.'

Bruno says, 'What do you do for a living?'

'That's my business. You know, I'm not feeling well. I think I'd like you both to leave, unless we're taking that ride.'

Lana clears her throat. 'Did you murder Brian, Maddy?'

'No.'

'Do you know someone who might want to hurt him?'

'No. Now, come on, *out*.'

Bruno pats his tie against his shirt. 'It's a personal question, but were you sleeping with him?'

'More personal than whether I killed him? Fuck off. Your mother's sleeping with him.' She puts her hand on Bruno's arm and steers him towards the door. It's gentle, but there's a manic energy to it as well. She's not quite in control of herself.

Out on the verandah, Lana tries one last time. 'How do you afford this place, Maddy?'

'By not being a cop.'

The door slams shut.

Crossing the street, Bruno makes a clicking sound with his mouth. 'Interesting. Very interesting.'

'I kind of like her,' says Lana.

'For this?'

'No. Just, you know. She was funny, don't you think?'

Bruno unlocks the car. 'Not that funny.'

They get in. Bruno checks the rear-view. 'I told you Amstell was dirty.'

'We don't know that.'

'I know GPs do all right, but not *that* all right. I'll grant him his hot wife, but not a hot wife *and* a hot mistress who lives in a joint like that. No way. Not on a doctor's salary.'

Lana tends to agree. 'Only one way to find out. Let's go pull his financials. Bugger the office politics.'

'Oh boy.'

'Come on, you want to do it too. You wouldn't have mentioned it last night if you didn't.'

'You're the boss.'

The sun is setting. Bruno takes them out along the esplanade, past the pine trees separating the road from the dunes. Lana can see the appeal of the place.

The pink sky.

Men in bare feet and short shorts.

'Sure Know Something' on the car radio.

Salt in the wind.

'You know, Bruno,' she says, 'I've gotta hand it to you guys. It must take some doing to make yourselves miserable in a place like this.'

CHAPTER 30

THE DIABLO SQUAD ROOM is busy this afternoon. A band of detectives crowd around Mark Evans and a whiteboard in the murder room. Fresh from the field, Lana and Bruno watch from afar.

'Any idea what that's all about?' she says.

'That's the Lenny Gibbs end of the room,' says Bruno. 'Victim number five. Mr Money Bags. Word around town is he's a Vinton toadie, despite appearances.'

'Who's that?'

'Vinton?'

'Yeah.'

'Colleen the Queen. Vinton runs all the vice down here on the coast. Started out in gaming with her late husband, but these days she has her mitts in everything going. She's a real piece of work, too. Lots of unsolved cases go back to Colleen.'

'Have they ruled her out for this?'

'To a degree.'

'What does that mean?'

'She's a protected species. Lots of clout. Besides, the old boys are convinced it's not her style.'

'What do you think?'

'I don't like how you keep asking me that.'

'Maybe Mark is changing it up in there?'

'I doubt it.'

They're still standing there watching the action unfold when Anne-Marie comes past with a box of cardboard folders in her arms. 'The inspector's looking for you two,' she says without stopping.

•

Inspector Ron Bingham is in his dreary office with the lights down, just a head and neck barricaded behind the paperwork.

Lana knocks on the open door.

'Yes?' he says, running a hand through his thinning hairline, eyes averted.

'You wanted to see us, sir?'

'Yes, that's right.' He doesn't invite them in. Instead, he sits there until the next thought arrives. 'I've assigned Lovegrove and Webber to night watch tonight, but Detective Evans needs them elsewhere. I'd like you two to take over for them. File the OT with Anne-Marie tomorrow.'

'When do we clock on?' says Bruno.

'I don't know. You'll have to check the roster. I'm sure you can work it out.'

Back out in the squad room, Bruno seems quiet, lost in thought. He snaps out of it and says, 'How about you run Maddy Santos and Brian Amstell through the system, and I'll sort out tonight?'

'Sure. You okay?'

'It's nothing.'

Lana makes the calls and pulls records, sweet-talking administrators down south. Brian Amstell is a blank canvas. If someone is cooking his books, they're a pro. The low-down on Maddy Santos isn't particularly illuminating either: Maddy is thirty-five years old, five foot two, and born in Townsville. No criminal record on either side of the border. No court appearances. She banks with the Commonwealth and owns a light blue car. Lana files deeper searches, recalling education transcripts, family histories, business registrations, tax records and press clippings, anything that might turn up an errant fact, a connection for leverage. It's a slow process, requesting information that moves at the speed of days instead of hours.

Bruno returns. 'You're not going to believe this.'

'Try me.'

'Lovegrove and Webber were due to start their shift an hour ago. We're already late. God, I hate this bullshit.'

Lana checks her watch: 5.40 pm.

CHAPTER 31

HENRY SWEATS THROUGH DINNER with Barry Caller and his Licensing boys. They're eating in some new joint in New Farm. It's loud and humid and made all the worse by Caller's motley entourage, the lot of them squeezed shoulder to shoulder around a lazy Susan. They drink warm beer and ash their cigarettes on the carpet. The Licensing boys are all bluster—no discretion—and for the most part, Henry stays out of it, counting down the minutes with his forearms stuck to the plastic tablecloth.

Of course, the boys have all heard about Brian Amstell. The *dead doctor*.

'I wish you blokes would get on with it,' says one of them.

Another slaps Henry on the shoulder. 'I can't believe they let their star pupil off for the night. What if they solve it tonight, mate? Be a shame.'

'Now, now,' says Caller.

'They've got no chance,' says Ray Blintiff, the crew's enforcer. He stares down at Henry. 'Not with Sherlock Holmes off the case.'

'Who?' says the new guy, Max Pymont.

'Homo Hades,' someone chips in.

'An old friend,' says Caller. 'Henry, a little bird tells me you like to visit with old Emmett.'

That little bird would be Jack the Bagman, guaranteed.

The boys all like the sound of this. A spray of wolf-whistles fill the restaurant. They rustle Henry's shoulder again.

'Get your hands off me,' says Henry.

Caller grins. 'Best do as he says.' A quiet order.

The boys suck on their beers.

'And so, Emmett?' says Caller.

'He's okay. Getting there, I suppose.'

'Just okay?' Blintiff says. 'I heard he's having a nice little holiday while you men have your heads down the gurgler.'

Henry shrugs it off as best he can. 'Emmett's still working the case on his own. I think he needs to keep busy. He's not bothering anyone.'

Blintiff smiles. 'Is the old bugger teaching you a few tricks? Better watch out.'

'It's good you're keeping an eye on him,' says Caller. Barry Caller is unfailingly calm, but every sentence out of his wet mouth is a directive.

Henry nods.

Understood.

Then someone rips a loud fart. 'Bloody hell,' the man says, feigning surprise. 'Sorry, gents. This fucking grub doesn't agree with me.'

The boys cuss him out.

They cover their food.

They choke and cough with exaggerated gusto.

They're dogs, each and all.

•

The Licensing boys tear a blue streak through the Valley, travelling from the restaurant to the pub to the back room of another pub, to an illegal casino, and then up into a brothel off Wickham Terrace. Blintiff doesn't like any of the girls in there, so they stay in the reception and finish a round.

It suits Henry. He shows Sarah Utton's picture to people. Gets a fat zero in response. The Licensing boys have a look. They're all unaware the girl is missing—which is interesting in and of itself. None of them have slept with her either, apparently, but one of them studies the photo like it's pornography. 'I bloody hope she's not dead,' he says. 'Hook me up if you find her, Henry. Hook me up!'

In the second brothel—Bubbles, also on Wickham—some of the men peel off. Henry goes back and sticks his head in the workroom where the girls take their break. He asks after Utton and shows the photo.

No dice.

Back in the bar, he takes his badge out and questions a few punters as they come through. These new johns don't even flinch. In fact, two of them reach immediately for their wallets, like Henry is the fucking valet.

Things have changed in the Valley since his time.

•

Halfway sick with it all, Henry yawns and swishes the dregs of his pot around. It's ten thirty. The new guy in Licensing, Max Pymont, spots the fatigue creeping in and takes Henry to the bathroom, where he taps out two lines of powder on the sink before knocking back the first.

Henry does his share. Light surges. The low throb of an adjoining sound system vibrates under his feet. 'Fuck a duck,' he says, wide awake all of a sudden.

'It's good, isn't it?' says Max.

'I thought it was coke.'

Max snickers. 'That shit makes me run my mouth, and that doesn't go down too well with these blokes.'

Henry knows the feeling well. 'They'll get used to you.'

'I fucking hope so.'

They go back out and Caller immediately starts in, no doubt alert to Henry's altered state. 'Henry, son, when are you going to wet your dick? We didn't take you out tonight to spend the whole time looking at your sad-sack face. You ain't getting any prettier.'

'I don't know, Barry, I'm . . .'

'Let's take him to the new place,' someone says.

'Yeah,' says Blintiff, adjusting his crotch. 'Let's get the fuck out of here.'

They stumble out into the summer night, down the street into a police divvy van. In the back, Henry rides along like a crook on the rickety bench seat beside the boys. They pass a bottle of rum between them, talk about football and old cases. Henry sits there in the dark, white-knuckling it with the road lights flashing and flickering, fantasising about escape.

CHAPTER 32

LANA AND BRUNO SIT in an unmarked police car in a patch of scrub beside Terranora Creek. They're about fifty metres up the road from the Amstell scene, backed into a clump of scrub on an uncleared residential lot. It's the dead of night, but still hot enough to keep the windows down. The car smells of mosquito repellent and cigarettes.

In Lana's view, a night watch like this is good policing. For serial offenders, the crime scene can be an alluring place. The site of immense release and elation. Like any addict, they want more—more detail, more sensation—and sometimes revisiting the scene of the crime is the only mainline.

Bruno is less enthused. 'Pity I never drink on the job,' he says, producing a hip flask from the glove box. For once, he rode shotgun, probably for this purpose.

Lana takes a sip from the flask. Cheap bourbon. 'Yowza. It's gonna be a long night.'

'You'll be happy to know this comes courtesy of Detective Evans. He keeps a bottle of this in his filing cabinet, the cheap bastard.'

'Is Evans any good? He seems like the only one of the old guard who's still switched on.'

'Hard to say. He's one of those people who seems diligent, and smart enough, you know, but he never really gets anywhere. I don't know what his story is.'

They pass the flask back and forth, a sip every half hour. Bruno obviously has a lot of time clocked on surveillance. He hates it, but he's good at it. The art of a job like this is surviving the lull in conversation.

'Why'd you sign up for this?' he says.

'For the Force?'

'No, for *this*. Team Dildo.'

'No, you first. How long were you on the coast before this thing?'

'Five years. My first postings were up on the Sunny Coast, worked robberies out of general duties up there.' That explained the surveillance chops. 'Made a few big cases, but it wasn't enough to get me into Homicide in the big smoke. I came here when my rotation was up.'

'You said you came down for Emmett Hades.'

'That was the plan. If I couldn't get into the big time, I figured a veteran of it might be a good guy to learn from. Didn't work out so well, mind you. Emmett was four-fifths batty by the time I got down here. I did three months of a whodunnit murder with him before Diablo. Ruben Davis. It was just pushing paperwork around, but it wasn't a total waste of time. The paperwork is a whole different thing with Emmett. You've never seen anything like it. He's a good street cop, apparently, but he never left the office when I was working with him. He just reads and collates, reads and collates, like a fucking scholar of paperwork. He worships it. Keeps incredible records.'

'You pick anything up?'

'Bits and pieces. The main thing I got is that I didn't want to end up like him. When I say he lived in the office, I mean it. There came a point where he couldn't really deal with anything else.'

Lana lights a smoke. 'Tell me more about this Ruben Davis thing?'

He sighs. 'It was a household invasion and murder up in Broadbeach. A pretty big deal at the time. They never found the body, but there was lots of blood. The case went nowhere fast. You know, you can go to Emmett's house and meet him if you want. He's around. Is he really that famous down south?'

'Famous enough,' she says. 'I mean, we all read his cases in detective training. The Northside Stalker. The Mount Gravatt bomber.'

'The Johnsons. The Breakfast Creek bookie stuff.'

'Yep, I've read all that. Fuck, it's pretty grim to land up here and not get a Hades story out of it. I'm going to track him down before I go.'

'Well, be careful. You probably don't want the story he's currently telling. You know he was sleeping in the murder room?'

'We've all done that.'

'No, I don't mean falling asleep in there. He was camped out there, for nights on end. It got weird.'

•

An hour later, they each eat another slice of cold pizza from the back seat.

'Your turn,' says Bruno. 'What's the deal? Why are you here? This side of the river doesn't give a fuck about Queensland, so don't bullshit me.'

'There's some politics behind it, but technically, it's my case. I took the call. It's my turn on the roster. I've got more right to be working this thing than you do.'

'Do you really need extra work down here?'

'I don't like putting in time on stuff and not seeing a result.'

'Anyone ever told you that you picked the wrong job?'

'No, you're the first.'

A car passes on the road.

Lana says, 'What's the deal with that Henry guy?'

'Loch?'

'Yeah. He was sitting near us at lunch yesterday. I had a chat to him while you were in the toilet. He seems . . .'

'You should steer clear of him. His partner, too. Lowell Sennett. They're both on loan from Consorting. Henry's got a bit of a rep. Neither of them are on the level. I've seen that much.'

'In on the Joke?'

'That and more, I reckon. Years back, when Henry was fresh out of cadets, he got himself in the shit with Arthur Sorensen, he's the deputy commissioner now. No one knows what he did, but it's something that cuts both ways. You know how that goes.'

Lana knows. A compromised cop can weather any storm. They're like cockroaches. Her own shop has its share. Dangerous men who know too much. The guys who bury the bodies.

'Henry seems to be working on something,' she says, without really thinking about it.

'Yeah, someone's giving him leads.'

'That's weird.' Lana pops the car door open. 'I need to stretch my legs. Can you hold the fort?'

'Go for it.'

She pushes her way out into the scrub, through the broken branches and paper-dry leaves, moving far enough away from the car to squat and pee. In the darkness, she thinks about her own mistakes on the job: the ineptitude of her early patrol work, the bungled witness statements, failed court proceedings, a terrible family homicide out on the Sydney North Shore. When she's done, she straightens herself up and takes a stroll. Out on the shoulder of the road, she notices the creek glistening through the mangrove. Everything is still. No cars. No sudden movement. The trees as silhouettes and shadows.

She decides to visit the crime scene.

May as well.

CHAPTER 33

HENRY'S NIGHT OUT WITH the Licensing boys goes from bad to sinister. Time evaporates. He experiences events in hazy vignettes. All the faces are ghoulish now. Every utterance distorted, fragmented, loaded with double meaning.

It stops making sense.

He finds himself standing in what looks like a suburban backyard, in the sick-inducing humidity, snorting white powder off the back of his own hand.

He hears a car backfire a few blocks over.

Dogs stir.

Memories push their way up his spine.

The thump in the boot, muffled as he drives.

A voice.

His father beating on him, wheezing with exertion.

A strange guttural sound comes out of Henry's throat. 'Fuck you,' he says. 'Fuck you.'

There's a house adjoining the yard, a timber Queenslander. He goes inside and remembers, *This is a brothel. This is a brothel on the edge of New Farm.* The place is lit up like a discotheque. In a corner, by a pile of old car magazines, there's a record spinning and it sounds like it's happening at the end of a tunnel.

Blintiff appears. 'Hello friend,' he murmurs as he comes past. Then he turns and mutters some lurid detail into Henry's ear, some obscenity.

The room tilts.

Henry watches lopsided visions of women in sad worn lingerie and some punter laughing and spitting beer and one of the Licensing boys grabbing on some teenage runaway and Caller, *Barry fucking Caller*, he just watches it all, drinking it in. Barry just watching and waiting, dead drunk or stone sober, like some cop-zombie lording over the carnage.

And then, without warning, there is a woman. Her name is Birdy. Red hair, black eyes, bright and happy despite the horror show. 'Come with me,' she says, and her hand is so soft Henry lets her take him back.

A bedroom.

A folded towel on the bed.

The bed like a grave.

The voice, the muffled voice.

'Your mother, your brothers, you ain't nothing.'

Flashes of gunfire in the night.

A night like this, just like this.

'Nothing!'

Feels the same.

As soon as the door closes, Henry rushes to the en suite and is sick on the threshold, trailing vomit across the tiles around the toilet. When he's done, he slumps into the corner of the bathroom, unable to move as Birdy cleans up, mopping around him, nudging him with the mop like he's furniture.

'That was easy,' she says, sitting on the closed toilet.

'I have to keep moving.' Henry pads around his pockets and finds Max Pymont's bag of leftover speed. He bangs back another toot.

'Can I have some of that?' says Birdy.

'Have the rest.'

Her line is a sharp breath and . . .

Echoes.

You don't have to do this.

You don't have to—

Henry shakes it off. He gets up, washes his face.

Birdy hands him his photo of Sarah Utton. 'Here. You dropped this.'

'Thanks.'

'Do you know her?' says Birdy.

'I'm looking for her.'
'Don't. She's no good to you blokes.'
'Yeah, why's that?'
'She's pregnant.'

CHAPTER 34

THE AMSTELL CRIME SCENE is a reset. A blank stretch of black grass at this time of night. The only sign of trouble is a string of police tape flapping in the branches of a nearby tree. Lana stalks around. She's never seen it in the dark like this. She kneels down and touches the ground where Brian Amstell's head lay. No blood or heat or energy now. Just dirt.

This disappearing trick is an aspect of crime Lana understands all too well. It's what crime *is* in the long run. Painful uncertainty. Lana's father vanished when she was eight years old. He was a school cleaner. There one day, gone the next. No foul play suspected.

Her family ruined in the wake of it. A hundred everyday problems metastasising in the grief. It happens slow, so slow it's hard to notice as the years pile on. But it's there, radiating out from the source: *him*, *his* disappearance, *his* choices or lack thereof. Wave after wave. Her mother losing her mind. Her brother acting out, addicted, suicidal. Lana's own life, as experienced in her quieter moments. All of it contaminated and hard to pin down—to remember vividly—because the source of all this trouble is a void.

A shadow.

Gone.

Her own memories going with it.

Her last day with him.

Their last conversation.

The last time the family ate together: brother, sister, mother, father.

Going, going, gone.

She pushes the thoughts from her mind and stands up and looks around again.

If the killer's smart, like they say, he would have cased the place on a night like this. He wouldn't risk being seen here in daylight ahead of the murder.

Did he stand here and decide?

Or there?

There's a tall red gum by the creek's edge, a small pad of sand beyond. Lana sits behind the tree and lights a smoke in the breeze. The cover is good. The sight lines work. She could see Brian coming. 'Neat as a pin,' she whispers. Overhead, the police tape flaps away, making a brittle rippling sound.

A thought edges its way forward in Lana.

It was how—

She senses movement. Spooked, she turns and looks.

Nothing.

The crime scene empty.

She turns back. Lights appear out on the water. A small tin boat, trailing a muffled drone. The creek shimmering in the wake. Lana takes another drag of her smoke. She remembers the thought: the Amstell murder was professional. It's how she would have done it. The killer has the right gun—a revolver to avoid expelled casings—and he tracked the victim long enough to keep the attack simple, obscured and secluded.

Lana gets up, dusts the sand from her hands. Stepping back out from behind the tree, she finds a lone figure standing in the darkness, metres away from her. *A man.* Something in the shape of him.

'Bruno?' she says, not believing it.

The figure jolts.

'Bruno?' she says a second time.

The man stands there for a long moment, then he runs.

'Bruno!' she screams, going after him. 'Bruno!' Sprinting, hard footfall on the gravel. Ahead of her, the man is partially hidden in the darkness. Lana forces herself to remember him, record the details.

Balaclava.

White hands, white neck.

Five nine, five eight.

Green pullover, dark pants, running sneakers.

She can hear him heaving as she closes in.

'Stop,' she says.

The path takes them out of the trees and along an open part of the creek where the track bows, rounding into a residential area. Unlit houses appear. A canopy of trees rolls back over. Lana pushes herself, pushing her legs to move—

She falls, rolls, realises she's been hit.

A body collapses on top of her.

A fist connects. Lana feels the back of her head bounce off the ground. She brings her hands up, catches the remaining blows, sweeping them away. Then another punch lands. Harder. More direct. Her vision clouds.

There's warm liquid on her face.

'No,' she says.

She slams an elbow around, lashing out with the other fist, punching into him.

The man gasps.

She lashes out again, her fist smashing into his mouth, the sharp grind of his teeth ripping her skin open.

Light blasts through the fight.

Car beams.

And she sees him.

Rabid eyes under the mask.

Upper lip covered with sweat and spit.

Ugly and mean and ordinary and terrified.

In the distance, a voice shouts out.

The man springs up and takes off again.

Lana tries to follow, but as soon as she's halfway to her feet, her head spins and she slumps back down. She reaches for her gun, confused as to why she hasn't grabbed it earlier, then there are hands on her, grabbing at her shirt. She brushes them off.

'I'm trying to help,' says a woman.

Lana looks up. It's a stranger. The woman gets her upright and Lana hobbles off in pursuit again. Cursing herself and concussed, but possessed as well.

Seconds later, she spots him.

He's way up ahead, still running.

He darts across the road to a vacant lot.

To a van.

The interior lights of the van come on.

The headlights flash.

The van fishtails out onto the road and Lana runs onto the street and squints at the licence plate over the barrel of her gun. She can't make it out, and it's not a safe shot, so she collapses down on the bitumen, a rope of drool and blood dripping from her mouth.

DAY THREE

SATURDAY, 23 FEBRUARY 1980

JOURNAL OF EMMETT HADES

(SELECTED EXCERPTS)

Some of the gossip is true. Or true enough. I was once a great policeman. A true detective. But in a city like Brisbane, all the good graces of history and hard work only count for so much. My career thrived under Commissioner Whitrod, but you can't pay down a mortgage with a conviction rate. And in the capital of Queensland, I couldn't sustain my reputation with the law alone. I needed political willpower and I had none at my disposal. Oh yes, I made my resumé and my work went into the training manuals, but it didn't save me in the end.

•

It started with the banks. My first big case. In the mid-sixties, the Johnson brothers went on a tear through the Redlands, knocking over Commonwealth banks. They were brutally effective. Always showed their faces—never wore masks—and they always shot someone. It made people compliant. The tellers and customers fell over themselves to stay alive. Now, I was Joe No One on that investigation, but I worked it to the bone. Went weeks without sleep. Living in my car. Everyone knew who the Johnsons were, you see. It was finding them that proved difficult. But I did it in due course. I followed them from relative to relative, shit-box to shit-box, until the night I caught them in the garage of their second-cousin's husband's holiday house, out on Coochiemudlo Island.

My reward: a photo in the paper and a cold case.

The Northside Stalker.

•

The stalker was a violent rapist of men and women. A phantom.

It took me a year to make him real.

But I did it.

Two from two. I delivered.

•

Then in '68, there was Hanna Schmidt. Hanna killed and maimed bookies. Only bookies. Her husband was a degenerate gambler and ended up selling the family home out from under them. Hanna wanted revenge. It wasn't an overly complicated case, but she was moving fast, shooting and stabbing those blokes every day and night for a week.

We got her.

The coordination effort we installed rewrote the policy.

And yet . . .

•

My big undoing wasn't a failed case or an embarrassing gaffe. I would have worn that. No, they shipped me to the Gold Coast and filed me away for another reason altogether: for doing my job. For doing the right thing in the wrong place. A mortal sin in Brisbane.

•

It was 1973.

A quiet morning in the Brisbane CIB, if I remember. A kid came in. Must've been a new guy on the desk who let him through. The kid said his next-door neighbour was dead, and no one was bothering to look into it. A big accusation. But the kid didn't seem like a rough sort. He wasn't seething with anger. More than anything else, he seemed confused. He was double-checking. I took down the details and put it on my list.

The kid's dead neighbour lived out in Clayfield. The following Monday, I had some errands out that way and stopped in for a look. I spoke to the kid's parents and they confirmed the story. A woman died, and no one seemed to care. The house she lived in was a weird place. Lots of odd comings and goings, they said. I knocked on the door. No answer.

It was winter, so I went back to the car to get out of the wind, and read the case file front to back.

The dead woman was Margaret Brafmann. Ruled a suicide by barbiturate intoxication. Brafmann had an interesting occupation: she was a brothel madam. Recently moved to Queensland from Sydney. She had a family. Three kids. A husband. Aside from that, the file was sparse.

Something was off about it. I was around the office in April '72 and yet this suicide didn't register. I couldn't remember a single mention of it. One of the men I worked with would have caught the case. It should have rung a bell, I thought.

What I did next reveals ineptitude in hindsight. But I was always a straight arrow when it came to corruption. I knew it was around—the dreaded Joke—but I never saw it firsthand. Never knew a single detective on the take, not personally. There wasn't as much of it back then. It wasn't like it is now. When I discovered this cold case, I looked into it without hesitation. Didn't suspect a thing. I did it all out in the open. And for a few days, no one noticed.

•

My downfall was swift. I had summonsed the demons. They first approached me in the lunchroom late one night. 'Would you be interested in some extracurricular work, Emmett? It pays well. It's easy. You wouldn't have to do much.' And so on. As we got further into the conversation, it became clear that I wasn't being asked to do anything at all. I was being asked to stop doing things.

'Refocus your attention,' one of them said.

'The Brafmann thing. It's a done deal, mate. The coroner let it go and you should, too. Don't make work for yourself. It's over. We need smart men like you to focus on the real work.'

I'd never seen these blokes before in my life. To this day, I'm not sure where they sprang from.

I told them I was inclined to work whatever case I wanted.

'Mate, you're not hearing me,' said one of them as I walked away. 'You're putting your nose where it doesn't belong and you're wasting valuable taxpayer money. That's the sort of thing that can bite you on the arse.'

'Or you could just take the drink, make it easy.'

'Do I have a choice?' I said.

I didn't.

But I didn't take the money, either. And I kept looking into the Brafmann suicide. Turns out the place in Clayfield was a police safe house. Brafmann and her family were up in Queensland to give evidence against the New South Wales police. A trip to the state library for the Sydney Morning Herald revealed why: she was blowing the whistle. The New South Wales coppers had a stake in her business and a disagreement turned ugly. She was hiding out up here, awaiting trial, and was going to put a lot of blokes in the shit. Yet, after agreeing to testify and travelling all the way to Brisbane, leaving her businesses behind—with her family in tow—Brafmann topped herself. She only had a few weeks left till the court appearance. It made no sense at all. Every layer was looking more rotten than the next.

So, I continued.

Right up until the axe fell in August.

Got a call, went into the inspector's office. He said, 'You're off-book, Emmett. I run a tight ship here. You know that. I don't let my men work whatever cases they feel like. It's not the done thing.'

I nodded. Didn't respond.

'You've been a big help to me up here, Emmett. A big help. But we need a man like you on the Gold Coast. And to be honest, you could use the salt air.'

'Sir, I'd prefer to stay.'

'It's too late for that,' the inspector said. 'You're not staying. You're going.'

The paperwork was already on my desk.

CHAPTER 35

HENRY WAKES UP IN an empty jail cell in the basement of the Brisbane watch house. Max Pymont is on the other cot, a leg draped over the edge. Max's pissed himself in his sleep and the smell of urine is in the air. No sign of the other Licensing boys.

Henry lets himself out, walks the hallway. A young man in a dirty torn suit looks up from his bunk in the drunk tank and says, 'Hey?'

Henry keeps moving.

'Can you let me out of here?'

Henry's head pounds. 'Fuck off.'

'Hey!' screams the man. 'Hey! Haaaaaaay!'

•

Up in the Criminal Investigation Branch, Neil Winters sits at his desk with his head in his hands and a copy of *Penthouse* magazine spread out on the table in front of him. Neil isn't reading it. He's staring into space.

Henry whispers, 'Neil?'

'What?'

'It's Henry.'

Neil tilts his head. 'Jesus, you look terrible. Big night?'

'Big enough.'

'Did I . . . did we run into each other last night?'

'I hope not.'

'Fuck me. I have no idea what happened,' says Neil. 'What do you want? I have important work to do here.' With bleary bloodshot eyes, Neil pulls the *Penthouse* closer to him. He turns the pages. 'Someone stole this bird's clothes.'

'Did you keep an eye out for the Woodrow Drive break-in?'

Neil looks confused for a moment, then stands up and scans the room. Spotting a man across the way, he yells, 'Jacko, did we have a report on Woodrow Drive?'

'Where's that?' says Jacko.

Henry says, 'It's in Coorparoo.'

'Yeah, that's floating around.'

Jacko fishes out the report and hands it over. Carla Utton embellished the break-in. The removed items list now includes an expensive stereo and a colour TV. Henry hands back the paperwork, prompting Jacko to close in and say, 'I know you're a friend of Neil's, but don't ever pull a job up here again without letting us know. That shit will get you in trouble, buddy.' The kid is out of line and Henry wants to push back, but he doesn't. He's finished. It's time to get out of Brisbane.

CHAPTER 36

CARLA UTTON IS HOME today and she's the spitting image of her sister. Same hair, same eyes, same face. Henry catches her preparing for work. Fresh make-up, in a pressed dress.

'Morning, ma'am.' He flashes his ID. 'Just following up on the robbery. You mind showing me through?'

Carla doesn't like it, but she lets him in. Henry makes a show of studying the entry points: he takes photos of the damage, runs down a list of the stolen goods. Along the way, Carla tells him she works for the Myer department store, which explains the insurance grab for home electrical. Those receipts would be easy to get a hold of.

'What's this?' says Henry at the threshold of the spare room.

'My sister's room. She stays sometimes.'

Henry checks his list. 'Anything missing from in here?'

'I don't know. I doubt it.'

'Your sister lives pretty lean by the look of it?'

Carla says, 'Don't mind her.'

'Oh, I need to write this down. For the report. When was she last in?'

'Let me think.' Carla wanders back to the kitchen. 'It's been a few months.'

'Any reason to believe she might've been the one to break in?'

'What an odd question.'

'It's how this stuff works sometimes.'

'Well, not this time, detective.'

'You have a contact number for her? An address?'

'No.' She takes a thermos down from an overhead cupboard. 'Do you think you'll find the people who robbed me?'

'Maybe. This stuff happens all the time.'

'I don't think it happens much around here.'

Henry asks a few more questions. He firms up the time of day and confirms other aspects of the break-in. Gently, he moves the interview back to Sarah. 'Where does this sister of yours stay when she's not here? Does she travel for work?'

'She has a boyfriend on the coast. Are you putting that in your report?'

'Yeah. You have a name for this boyfriend?'

'For the report?' Carla watches him carefully. She isn't upset. In fact, she seems almost emotionless.

'Maybe we can talk more about the missing stereo and television set?'

'Not much more to say about those.'

'Maybe we could look at where they were in the house, I might—'

'I don't know his name,' she says.

'The boyfriend?'

'She doesn't like me telling people her business.'

'What business is that?'

'I really need to get ready for work now.'

She shows him out. On the doorstep, she says, 'Detective?'

'Yes.'

'If something's happened to my sister, I'm going to remember you. I'm going to remember your face and your name. It was Henry Loch, wasn't it? Detective Henry Loch.'

Henry checks the street. It's empty. He gently puts his hand around Carla's bicep and says, 'Never talk to a policeman like that. Not up here in the city. You don't want to remember anyone up here.' It's partly the hangover talking, but it's also the truth and bad memories and bleak history compacted into a weak moment.

To her credit, Carla doesn't flinch. She peels Henry's hand off and says, 'You don't scare me.'

CHAPTER 37

LANA WAKES IN PAIN. Blinding sun blasts through her motel suite as the telephone rings. Moving to sit up, she finds herself momentarily paralysed, a prisoner in an unwilling body.

The telephone continues.

She forces herself out of the damp bed. Delirious, she staggers to the wall unit across the room and lifts the receiver.

'It's me,' says a gruff voice. 'Report.'

'What? Who is this?'

The man responds angrily, a spray of words coming down the line. As she stands there listening, she catches herself in an adjoining mirror and the image is horrifying. A large purple welt covers the left side of her face, tracking across a swollen eye and cheek. Further down, large bruises dot her chest and side.

Lana puts the phone down.

She runs the shower and stands under it. Blood circulates in the water by the drain. It's still in her hair. Memories from last night tumble through her interior: the beating from the stranger and the early morning debrief, the ad hoc bandages plastered to her as she furiously typed up a report. Pushing through it, she tries to conjure her return to the motel, but it won't come. She gets out of the shower, swallows painkillers and gets back under the water until it runs cool.

Then she goes back to bed.

Drained and furious.

He got away with it.

•

The wake-up call was from New South Wales Superintendent Dwain Gorst, the man who got her into this mess. Lana calls him back, apologising profusely for the earlier conversation and explaining herself.

'Oh well then,' Gorst says, still miffed.

'The investigation is progressing. The shooter may be the man I ran into last night. We're following up all the necessary leads.'

'Tell me about Strike Force Diablo.'

'It's running pretty hot, as expected. Lots of churn. They're trying to cook with the kitchen on fire. That's how it feels. Their murder room is a complete mess. Paperwork piled up for days. And the senior men are at their wits' end. The rank and file under them, are . . .'

'Yes, detective?'

'There are irregularities, for sure.'

'I didn't send you up there to be coy.'

'The men are behaving as anyone might, sir. There's a lot of pessimism in the air. Lots of booze, worse than you'd think. Some of them are barely functioning. Dead on their feet. The rest are run ragged. Management's approach to righting the ship seems to be berating them regularly, threatening demotions and transfers. Our lot would have quit, but these blokes seem to think it's just another day at the office.'

'Any direct improprieties?'

'A bit of dirty money floating around. A couple of free meals and shouted beers. A few odd things I'm looking into.'

'Are you taking notes?'

'That wasn't the deal, if I recall.'

'Let's give it another week and then we'll talk about bringing you back.'

Lana moves the phone from one hand to the other, studying her bruises. 'I'd like to see the Amstell case out, if I might? He had a family, sir.'

'Oh, okay. Of course, of course. If you want to try your luck, have at it. If you could do both things, that would be a real bonus, detective. Two birds.'

Lana puts the phone down. Gorst is clear enough. It isn't *really* about Amstell, and very little of it seems to be about stopping the Diablo killer either. No, everyone seems to be working an angle.

Meanwhile . . .

Lana puts her face to the mirror.

Her breath fogs the glass.

'This,' she says. 'Meanwhile, *this.*'

CHAPTER 38

THE SUN BEATS DOWN on the roof of the car, baking the interior. Lana has a day of enforced leave. Unsure if it's punishment or reward, she keeps working, opting for impromptu surveillance on Maddy Santos. Maddy's place is wide open. She stalks around inside with a manic intensity, chain-smoking and talking on a phone with a long lead. She's rattled.

Just after eleven, Maddy comes down the front stair in a haphazard outfit (grey marl tank top, black bra, no shoes) and makes her way on foot to the main drag. Lana follows along, tailing her to a cafe, then to a service station for cigarettes, and then back to the house where Maddy changes clothes, has a brunch cocktail and hops a cab to Surfers Paradise.

Downtown, Lana watches her visit hotels and apartments. She can't see all the occupants, but the glimpses reveal Maddy calling on bleary-eyed women, upset at having been woken at midday. The pattern holds through to lunchtime—a bite and another cocktail—then continues into the afternoon, wherein Maddy changes gear. She visits nicer places, more upmarket motels, a fancy bar and an outdoor bowling club. Along the way, she makes calls from phone boxes. She's looking for someone.

Half an hour later, Lana loses her in an apartment building. Maddy goes in but doesn't come out. At a loose end, Lana drops by the station house, subjecting herself to a series of whistles and winces from the day crew. They gather round to survey the damage. Mark Evans takes a particular interest. 'Jesus,' he says, touching her jaw. 'That's pretty nasty.' He ducks and weaves, trying to catch sight of her injuries in the light.

'You should see the other guy.'

'I wish. I read the report. It's good work, Cohen. Nearly got him, by the sound of it. I'm praying you knocked his teeth around.' Without asking, he takes her right hand, studying the torn and blackened skin of her knuckles. 'I've got uniforms out at every dentist on the coast. If he gets his teeth checked this week, we'll have him. I thought they gave you the day off?'

Lana takes her hand back. 'I came in to check on some calls. How did your leads from yesterday pan out?'

Evans sighs. 'We've got something. Well, I think it's something.'

'Can I take a look?'

He thinks about it. 'Sure.' He leads her to the murder room and closes the door, sealing them inside the arctic cool. Evans points to a series of dark photos posted in one corner of the room. 'That's Lenny Gibbs,' he says. 'The socialite. That's what everyone around here calls him. Victim number five. Lenny was the second one he used the gun on.'

'Same gun as Amstell?'

'Same type. We've spent the week re-canvassing Lenny's neighbourhood. They found him a few blocks from where he lived, close to here, actually. It's getting really built-up around here, so my theory is, if we've missed something, it's probably here. And I was right. On the second go-round, we found an elderly couple who lived down the street from Lenny, and they reported seeing a bloke on a motorcycle parked in front of his place. Lenny had quite the pad down on the river. This motorcycle was just idling out on the street for a few minutes.'

'Sounds like our guy.'

'It certainly does after your team found the tyre prints the other day. We've been out there interviewing motorcycle owners left, right and centre. There are only sixty-eight men on the coast who own a van *and* hold a motorcycle licence.'

'Any crims?'

'Five.'

'That could be it,' Lana says. 'Hopefully one of them needs a dentist.'

'Here's hoping.'

A phone rings on a nearby desk. 'I better get this,' Evans says. 'I'm collating the field reports as they come in.'

He sounds meticulous on the phone, almost pedantic. As Lana listens in, she wanders the room, running her fingertips across the piles of paperwork. She idly opens files, turns pages, scans crime scene photos and maps. She picks up a stray coroner's report—Eddie Edgar, victim number two. No blood or saliva or semen at the scene, only traces of red wine on Eddie's face. In the background, Evans wraps up the call, and Lana takes it as her cue. She puts down the report and slips out.

The street outside is balmy. It's a Saturday and the footpath is bustling with tourists. Lana lights a cigarette and heads north on Orchid Avenue. Distracted, she turns a corner and nearly runs straight into Maddy Santos stepping out of a shopfront.

Lana spins.

Waits by a parked car.

Takes a look.

Santos crosses the street, makes her way down the opposing kerb, oblivious. She takes a corner and Lana follows her into a familiar street. A squat building sits in the middle distance and Santos makes a beeline for it. It's a dirty white brick place with shuttered windows: the building Ron Bingham and the Diablo men went into two nights ago. And now, this woman on the periphery of a murder case is walking up to the same unmarked door, ringing the same buzzer, and disappearing through the same dark doorway.

CHAPTER 39

HENRY LOCH SITS AT an outdoor picnic table beside the Yatala Pie Shop and watches the Pacific Highway. Last night's excesses churn in his guts like lava and the steak and kidney pie in front of him isn't helping. He switches it out for a second can of Coke and gets to work.

Henry spreads Sarah Utton's stuff out on the table.

The church flyer pre-dating her disappearance.

The uncashed cheque.

The case of pills.

What would Emmett say about all this? He'd go piece by piece, detail by detail. Henry reaches for the church flyer first. *Saint Andrews Catholic Church.* The street directory puts it across the border in Tweed Heads, only half a mile as the crow flies from the Brian Amstell scene.

Interesting.

The uncashed cheque is from Paradise Gaming Pty Ltd. Henry takes it to a nearby phone box and searches the Yellow Pages stowed under the receiver. No listing. He calls Anne-Marie at the station, and she puts one of the girls on it. 'Call me back,' he says, reading the booth number off the plate.

Back at the table, Henry studies the pill box. The blue pills are homemade. DIY Serepax, at a guess. Downers. But the orange ones are more professional. Dexedrine, stamped '15 mg'.

Strong.

He pops one to be sure.

Thirty minutes later, the phone rings in the booth and Henry picks it up. It's Anne-Marie.

'You took your time,' he says.

'Don't be a dickhead. You know how to work a pencil?'

'Hang on.' Henry yanks his notebook free from his pocket.

'You write with the sharp end,' she says.

'Yeah, yeah.'

Paradise Gaming Pty Ltd is a shell company, thus the delays. 'It took three calls to pin it down, but the tax office eventually pulled the right record. The company is owned by Christopher Donald Cole, a chartered accountant from Sydney.'

'Thanks.'

Henry stands in the phone booth, clenching and unclenching his hands. Overhead, the sun rolls back out from behind a bank of cloud, lighting the landscape. The air buzzes with possibility.

'Are we done?' says Anne-Marie, still on the line.

'I'm okay,' he says, hanging up.

New leads.

New day.

Feeling good. Feeling fast.

'Definitely Dexedrine,' he says.

CHAPTER 40

THE FIRST PILL GETS Henry home at lightning speed, his mind racing like the white lines under the car bonnet. The second pushes his home office hustle into overdrive. He works the Utton thing, driving connections out to their limits and finding a direct hit in the mess.

Christopher Donald Cole—the accountant who owns the shell company paying Utton—he's the key. The cheque is made out to cash, almost definitely for services rendered. Henry knows who to ask in the records room and one call puts Cole right in the thick of it. Cole's on the books: charged with solicitation of a minor on the Gold Coast in '78. But Cole never goes to court. He's repped by Matty Gordon, a high-priced piece of shit with lots of pull, so the charges get dropped.

Cole's arresting officers in '78?

Jesus Christ.

Ron Bingham and Mark Evans.

Diablo.

•

Henry hits the public library three blocks from his house. Newspaper archives are in the back, decades of black ink bullshit piled politely in wide metal drawers. The librarian smells the sweat and crazy on him, but Henry badges her and she pulls the editions.

There's the story from September '78—the solicitation scandal—and with it, a photo of Christopher Cole.

Bug-eyed.

All girth and menace.

According to reports, Cole's up on the coast for a taxation convention when it all goes wrong. In the piece, there's a quick summation of his business interests, but nothing else. No mention of Paradise Gaming. No comment from friends and family. No comment from Cole's Queensland business partner, Joel Delaney. It's a tight ship.

Then—

Henry knows that name.

Joel Delaney.

Knows it, but can't place it.

Henry walks, leaves the library, papers everywhere.

Back into the car.

Through the front door of his place.

The kitchen table where it's all laid out.

He sucks water and coffee and paces.

'Fuck it.'

Joel.

Delaney.

Henry goes at his notes, scanning, listing, checking, then re-scanning, re-listing and double-checking. It's insane, but it takes fifteen minutes to find the nugget. Joel Delaney is *everywhere* when he hits the right notebook, because Joel Delaney is one of the Diablo victims.

He's number six, with a bullet.

In between:

Lenny Gibbs and—

Brian Amstell.

The world around Henry flashes.

Nuclear hot afternoon fallout.

White walls. Clouds of ash.

It's all connected.

Amstell.

Utton.

Diablo.

Henry fishes out the church flyer and holds it up, praying on it, begging.

'Why keep this?' he says. 'What is it?'

Henry carefully spreads the flyer out on the coffee table, smoothing it flat. He stares into it. He smooths it again and—

There.

His fingers brush against indentations.

The ghost of handwritten text.

He fetches a pencil, rubs the side of the lead over the flyer.

An address appears.

CHAPTER 41

LANA WAITS UNTIL DARK before entering the white building. Maddy Santos is long gone. She erupted out the front door an hour ago, visibly upset, almost running as she made her way up the street. In the time since, no one has approached the entryway and the street is empty, as if the building emits a silent warning.

Lana presses the buzzer by the door.

'Wrong address, luv,' says a female voice through the intercom.

Lana peers around for a camera. Can't see it.

'Gold Coast CIB, let me in.'

There is a long pause.

The door clicks open.

Lana steps into a sparse square room. No furniture. Peeling paint. Dust and dirt on the floor. In the far corner, a narrow timber stair spirals up.

The building is four storeys high, and the first two floors are abandoned. On the third, Lana stops and studies the gloom of an empty office space, then draws a fast breath as she sees a man lurking in the darkness. As her eyes adjust, she can see that he is well back from the windows, just standing there in the dark with a cigarette. Lana backs out and continues up.

The staircase terminates at a white locked door.

Lana knocks. 'It's me.'

A bolt slides across and the door opens. Orange light washes out, followed by the muted throb of a Dean Martin track. An elderly woman sits by the entryway, her plump arms draped on either side of a small podium. Between her arms is a steel cashier's box. 'Five bucks, luv.' The woman takes Lana's money without comment, leaving her to wander through the reception area. It looks like a knock-shop of some sort. Thick shag-pile carpet, shabby artwork on the walls, a tiki bar. A hallway of doors branches off on one side. Down the far end of the main room, there's a billboard-sized image of an amber forest and underneath it, a sunken lounge.

A figure rises out of the lounge. It's a woman in a black leather dress, a mini with full sleeves. She has bright ginger hair and a matching ochre broach pinned to her breast. The woman yawns, rolls her neck, and says, 'Helen, who's this then?'

The woman at the podium says, 'She's a cop.'

'And you just let her in?'

'She paid her money.'

The redhead waves Lana over. 'Come 'ere. Watch the stairs, though. Carpet's wet. One of your dickhead brethren spilt a schooner of beer down there last night.'

Lana steps down into the lounge.

The woman flops back into the cushions and stares at the ceiling. 'Can I bum a smoke?'

Lana tosses her pack over. Up close, the woman looks a touch younger than Lana, but the thick make-up makes it difficult to tell. There's a strangeness to her. Something uncanny about the woman's eyes and how they sit in her face.

The woman says, 'Sit down. You're making me nervous. Christ, my hangover is killing me. Helen! Helen, get Tommy to fix me a bloody Mary. And get a drink for our guest here.' She looks at Lana.

'A beer's fine.'

'And a beer, Helen!' She takes a long drag off the smoke. 'What's your name, sweetheart?'

'Lana. Lana Cohen. What's yours?'

'Colleen,' she says.

The woman studies her. 'What happened to you, Lana? Someone tune you up? Is that why you're here?'

'No,' says Lana, resisting the urge to touch her face. 'Colleen Vinton?'

'That's right. You must be new in town.'

'On loan from Sydney.'

'Do Ron and Pete know you're up here?'

Lana adds Pete Reynolds to her list. He's a Diablo lead detective, and of course he's dirty. It's written all over him.

'I thought you were open to the public,' Lana says.

Colleen smiles, but it isn't pleasant. 'If only.'

They sit in silence while Colleen savours the cigarette. The drinks arrive, carried by a man—Tommy, it seems—who is shirtless and muscular for his age. Long greasy brown hair. Tommy's approaching sixty but he's very lean, in tight stonewash jeans over woven leather loafers. As he puts the drinks down on the coffee table, Lana spies a smudged Led Zeppelin tattoo on his shoulder, an angel in monochrome. With the drinks in place, Tommy stands around, looming over them.

Colleen says, 'What can I do for you, Lana Cohen?'

'I'm interested in Maddy Santos.'

Colleen takes a sip of her drink and winces. 'Christ, Tommy, go lighter on the tabasco next time, will ya? Fuck.' She coughs. 'What was that name again?'

'Maddy Santos. Late twenties, dark hair. Pretty.'

'Nope, never heard of her. You heard of her, Tommy?'

Tommy grunts.

'I just saw her come out of here,' says Lana.

'No, I don't think you did. I mean, *a friend* just came by, said the police were harassing her. I didn't like the sound of that. I've got to tell you, Lana, we get all sorts in here. I deal with *all sorts*. What's this Maddy woman supposed to have done?'

'I can't say at the moment.'

'But I need to blab my mouth off?'

'That's how it works.'

'Not round here it doesn't.'

'How long have you been running this place, Colleen?'

'You know, we had a lady copper who used to come by all the time not long ago. There was another bird before you. She was all right, wasn't she, Tommy? Can't remember her bloody name. Wasn't around for long, though, was she? Isn't that right, Tommy?'

Tommy grunts again.

Lana hasn't touched her beer. It's sweating on the side table.

Colleen says, 'Do you like girls, detective?'

Lana knows she hasn't mentioned her rank. Startled, she says, 'No.'

'Tommy has a really thick cock,' says Colleen. 'It looks like a beer can. I'd get him to show you, but even looking at the thing gives me a headache. I don't keep you around for your drink-making skills, do I, Tommy?'

Tommy just stands there this time.

Lana is unarmed but impulsively touches her side.

'Where are you staying?' says Colleen.

'I've got a place.'

'You know, we could probably find you easily enough. I'm sure someone at the station knows how to find you. I look after my friends, you see. I'm known for that. I mean, it'd be nice to send you something. A welcome gift, you know. Wouldn't that be nice, Tommy? Do you have a gift for Lana here?'

Lana glances at Tommy. 'I'm not sure how things are up here, but down south, we take threatening cops pretty seriously. Gets people into trouble.'

'Then perhaps you should fuck off back to Sydney,' Colleen says, and to punctuate her point, she flicks her cigarette into Lana's lap.

Lana brushes the butt onto the carpet and grounds it out.

Colleen tut-tuts. 'Never mind that, dear. Happens all the time. I tell you, the things spilt on that carpet over the years. Crikey.'

Lana stands up. 'Thanks for the beer, Colleen.'

'Tommy, show her out.'

'I think I might show myself out. You come anywhere near me, Tommy, I'm going to lock you up.'

'Yeah?' says Tommy.

'Look at my face.'

They let her go.

•

She's out on the street, two blocks away, when the fear spills over. Lana's hands shake so badly she can't light a smoke. Instead, she stands in the night air and weeps, finally letting out all the trouble of the last twenty-four hours.

CHAPTER 42

HENRY SITS IN HIS car, under a dark, swaying palm tree, and twitches. He hates surveillance work. Waiting around in cars reminds him of being a little kid: him and his brothers sitting out in the carpark of a suburban tavern, waiting on his deadshit parents. The longer the wait, the worse the damage when they got home. Those memories itch at him tonight, courtesy of his Dexedrine comedown.

Across the street, house lights begin to blink out. This is the address from Sarah Utton's church flyer. Some posh place on Mermaid Beach.

Henry pops the car door and makes his way over. He cuts down the side of the house towards the ocean. About halfway along he spots a soft glow emanating from a bedroom out back. He creeps down and watches.

A woman appears, naked bar for a pair of black cotton briefs. She takes a drink from the night table and sips it by the window, gazing out at the sea, oblivious to Henry crouched in the garden. The woman is beautiful. A cold, lean face set against beaming eyes. Her body is thin, but she looks strong. Henry zeroes in on the details—her breasts, the softness of her thighs, the pinch of her underwear around the white skin there. The woman polishes off the drink and moves away, disappearing back into the house.

Henry scurries back to his car where he sits in the quiet darkness. There have been very few women in his life. A couple of ex-girlfriends, a couple of one-night stands. He never has to work at staying single. Bringing people into *all this* feels like entrapment. A lot of women can sense it, can see the signs. He's prone to silent spells and staring into space. No friends or family, no childhood anecdotes. Only career goals and nightmares.

A loud knock at the window breaks the spell.

Hello?

Muffled.

He turns.

It's a face he knows.

He winds down the window.

A woman in denim shorts and a long-sleeved checked shirt. She has bruises on her face.

'How you doing in there?' she says. 'It's Henry, right?'

'Yeah.'

'I'm Lana. Lana Cohen. We met at the pub the other day. I'm working with Bruno Karras.'

'Oh, right.'

'Figure we should have a chat.'

'Now?'

'If you're not too busy.'

Henry feels sick at *busy.*

What has she seen?

'I know a place,' he says.

He watches her walk back to her car in the rear-view.

CHAPTER 43

LANA FOLLOWS HENRY LOCH to a quiet spot along the Burleigh coastline. He's keen on staying in the carpark, but Lana leads them down across the lawn to the dunes. It's late and cloudy. The place is deserted. The beach feels lonely and forbidden. She takes a flat bottle of scotch from the back hem of her shorts, has a belt and offers it to him.

He takes it.

'Are you okay?' she says.

'Long day.' He nods at her face. 'What happened to you?'

'I think I had a dust-up with our guy.'

'What?'

'Where have you been all day?'

'Out in it.'

'Well, I ran into someone at the Brian Amstell crime scene last night, and it didn't go so well.'

'Get a look at him?'

'No. He had a balaclava on. Late forties, early fifties. Caucasian. Fit.'

'Jesus. Why are you out here talking to me, then?'

'Beats me.'

It's a joke, but it doesn't land that way with Henry. 'I should go,' he says, handing back the bottle.

'Hold on. Aren't you curious about how I found you?'

'Not really. Why were you looking?'

'I wasn't, I was staking out the girl's place. Spotted you jumping the fence. Do you know Maddy Santos?'

'Is that her name? I never saw her before tonight. What's your angle?'

'You first.'

Henry takes a piece of paper from his pocket. It's a church flyer and on the back of it, he shows her the engravings of a handwritten address. 'There's a missing girl,' he says. 'I found this in her stuff. Figured she might be camping out back there.'

'Who's this girl?'

'Some Brisbane pro. Works down here from time to time.'

'I think the woman back at the house is Brian Amstell's mistress. Apparently, they used to work together. I've been tailing her most of the day. Bingham made me take a sickie because of this,' she waves a hand over her face. 'I thought I'd make the most of it.'

He takes a sip of the scotch. Doesn't say anything.

'I think Maddy knows a lot of prostitutes,' says Lana. 'She knows Colleen Vinton.'

'Do *you* know Colleen?'

'I do now. Had a bit of a run-in with her earlier. She's pretty interesting.'

Henry scratches his stubble. 'That's one word for it.'

'I was hoping she was all bark.'

'All bite, most of the time. If she's in the middle of this, it's already over. She's a protected species.'

'You're the second person to tell me that this week. Is that all you're working on, the connection between Maddy's house and this missing girl?'

'Give or take.'

'Yeah?'

He shakes his head, tight-lipped.

'How long have you been in this game, Henry?'

He takes another belt of her scotch. 'Long enough. What are you doing up here? I mean, what are you *really* doing?'

She takes the bottle back. 'Working my case.'

'Nah, I don't think so. They sent you up here to snout around. Everybody can see it.'

'Firstly, piss off. And second, even if I am a rat, I'm doing a better job working this case than your lot.'

'Maybe you're both things.'

'Maybe I am? Do you care, Henry? Sounds like you're on the way out, anyhow, and the Diablo crew isn't exactly circling the wagons.' Lana watches him chew this over. A dark current flickers and passes. He wasn't this wired yesterday.

'You going to report me for the B&E back there?' he says.

'No.' She gives him the bottle.

'Well then, what do you want?'

She's careful with the rest. 'Help me and I'll help you. I'm the new girl in town and you're getting the boot, but we both found Maddy Santos, didn't we? We could be onto something.'

'Nah.'

'Just no?'

'With people like you, you can never see the end of it.'

He walks.

Lana calls after him. 'Then why were you on Diablo in the first place, Henry? What's *your* angle? Why bother if you're just going to let them bench you? That can't be what you want. It . . .'

He stops.

Lana goes for it. 'What did Beggs say? You're here by *occulted political will*. What does that mean, Henry?'

He comes back fast, striding through the sand, pulling up close. He's furious and loose, radiating menace. 'It means I called in all my favours to get here. That's what it means, and it didn't pan out.'

'I've dealt with men like you my whole life,' she says, the pulse of her own upset punching through. It isn't just Henry. It's all of the men like him. And it's the tremor of the run-in with Vinton, and the assault, and years of other bullshit. Her face hurts. 'This whole thing up here is rotten, and that's where they put people like you, isn't it? With the rotten things, but . . .'

She can't finish the sentence.

He's too close.

Rabid eyes.

Covered in sweat and spit—

The beach drifts off its axis.

A wave of genuine pain.

Henry notices it immediately and helps her down to the sand. 'Take a breath. You're okay.'

'Oh wow,' she says. 'That was weird.'

'I'll drive you home.'

'Give me a sec. I'm all right.'

They sit there for a minute, both of them listening to the ocean.

'Look, Henry, I need some local know-how. I'm getting into trouble up here, and I don't want to be. Look at me. Christ . . . just tell me what you want in return. Name your price.'

He doesn't answer immediately. In fact, he seems to be ignoring her, looking at the sea and lost in thought.

Who is this guy? Lana thinks.

Henry stands up. 'I won't rat anyone out.'

'That's not what I'm after, despite the gossip. Help me and I promise you, I'll return the favour. I can help you with this girl. Whatever you need. Our side of the border might have something on her.'

Henry blows out a deep breath. 'I don't want to go back to Consorting. It's been years and years getting here and I don't want to go back.'

'Then don't fucking take it on the chin, Henry. Work with me. Take your shot. I nearly found the guy last night. We both found Maddy *tonight*. You never know your luck. Maybe everyone else is looking the wrong way, and for once you're not?'

He finishes the scotch. 'Yeah, yeah, okay. But you need to know something about me, just so we're square from the start.'

'Yeah, what's that?'

'I've killed for the people who pull my strings. That's how deep it goes. That's what you're messing around with.' He hurls the empty bottle into the ocean.

DAY FOUR

SUNDAY, 24 FEBRUARY 1980

JOURNAL OF EMMETT HADES

(SELECTED EXCERPTS)

I hit the Gold Coast in late '73. Sliding down the greasy pole, career ruin to outright oblivion. But it goes slow: a series of long days and bad stretches. Hot summers, warm winters. Mundane policing and clock-watching. I floated along on go-nowhere cases. Can't remember half of it now. Missing persons. A couple of armed hold-ups. Disco brawls. Cab line punch-ups. A series of break-ins and a hundred stolen cars. It's small-time, committed by teenagers and dickheads, and in the middle of it: me, totally lost.

Time marched on.

I deteriorated.

I started drinking more.

I raged.

Wallowed.

Whined.

Depression seeped in. Sullen nights turned manic. I hollered at the walls and a conspiratorial air settled over the house, and then my job. In the glow of every beaming coastal sunset, I experienced a soft kind of madness.

I know some of the dates by heart.

Late '74: suspended for drunkenness.

'75: skipped a week of work without explanation.

'76: my clearance rate plummeted, shitty work on repeat.

The gossip spread.

My debasement was clear to everyone. I could see it in people's faces.

'He used to be—'

'He was always so—'

In Brisbane, in the upper echelons, people wrote me off.

My one true blessing.

•

The slump was never going to last. I snapped out of it spring of '76. Went back to church, that was the main thing. With that in place, I had the advantage. No one expected anything from me, least of all recovery.

I got off the booze and got back to work. I put in solid time.

My cases turned around.

A year later, I slipped back into Homicide unopposed. They had a vacancy and I applied. The paperwork got rubber-stamped. No one important cared because no one remembered my greatness, only my downfall and ruin.

More good work ensued.

It was no flickering montage—I was still the shadow of my former self—but I solved cases.

By 1977, I was gathering steam, just in time . . .

If you know your Gold Coast history, '78 is when Ruben Davis and Teddy Adams got murdered. Two nasty homicides in the space of a year. And there I am in the thick of it. Not the cop genius, but not the flunky, either. If my life up till then was preparation, backstory, foreshadowing and premise, then that year was the main event.

1978.

The catalyst.

The driver.

And: my evolution.

The trigger.

1978.

That year is the spark creating everything as it is now, all that is surrendered unto me in this world. For when the devil truly reveals himself, there is no surer route to God. The killer forced my hand. He made me start this story. I mentioned him on the first page.

CHAPTER 44

AN ORGAN DRONE FILLS Saint Andrews, playing louder than needed and moving like slow-motion shrapnel through Henry's hungover mind. The congregation stands around wailing in their pews. Misshapen white people, for the most part. Intense suburban desperation, ominous and dank.

Henry slips into the back row. He's been loitering by the door, but an old woman in a wheelchair notices. He gives her a nod and sits. She turns back to the altar without comment. The priest up front is an old guy. Mid-sixties with silver wire-brush hair. Leather skin. Not the usual ponce. He looks coiled and strong, more like a Vietnam vet or a crim.

'Parishioners, do we ask for the Lord's punishment or is it granted to us as a lesson?' he bellows. 'That's what I want to talk about today. I want to start with a passage from the Book of Job, verse three. This verse has Job's song in it, the doom-laden number he sings after feeling the wrath of God, after having his children taken from him and his skin afflicted with disease, all without sin of his own. This is what Job sings in his book:

May the day of my birth perish,
and the night that says, 'A boy is conceived!'
That day—may it turn to darkness;
may God above not care about it;
may no light shine on it.
May gloom and utter darkness claim it once more;
may a cloud settle over it;
may blackness overwhelm it.
That night—may thick darkness seize it;
may it not be included among the days of the year
nor be entered in any of the months.

'This, parishioners, is the true mindset of Job. He is cast so low as to wish his own birthday removed from the calendar. Have *you* ever been that low? I hope not. This may *sound* extreme, almost melodramatic, but we've all wished for reversals though, haven't we? *I wish I hadn't taken that job. I wish I hadn't married my husband. I wish, I wish. I wish I had never been born at all. I wish . . .*'

Henry zones out. He hates religion, especially this sort. To pass the time, he scans the room, hoping for a glimpse of anyone resembling Sarah Utton. It's odd to think that this might be her parish, but Henry has met many religious sex workers in his time, found plenty of crucifixes and prayer books in brothel back rooms. He gets it. Everyone gets this stuff rammed into them as a kid and it can stick. He knows plenty of religious coppers, too. No, what Henry finds strange is that Utton chose this old-school fire-and-brimstone lot over the youth assembly down the road. *How did she wind up here? Why the flyer for this joint?*

When the service is over, Henry stays seated and side-eyes the congregation filing out. He doesn't recognise the first woman who catches his eye. She has long, straight black hair and a regal vibe. Dressed in black but done up to the nines, she moves slowly, with what looks like two daughters following close behind.

A minute later, he notices someone else coming past.

Cold recognition jolts him.

The woman from the house on Mermaid Beach.

Maddy.

That's the name Lana used.

Henry freezes and stares, unable to stop himself. Then heat erupts from his hands and neck, a churning dread and guilt, as if the woman could look across at any moment and recognise him. *Know him.* Henry woke this morning assuming the woman was a sick vision. Some drug-fuelled comedown fantasy. But this five-second glimpse of her here unravels all that. Today, she looks better than the fantasy. She looks real.

CHAPTER 45

OUTSIDE SAINT ANDREWS, THE congregation gathers on the bitumen under the Sunday morning glare. A row of brown gum trees lines one side of the courtyard. Underneath it, the old biddies are running a cake stall, serving lukewarm tea in styrofoam cups. Henry watches Maddy Santos gladhand her way around the parishioners, hugging and kissing people, smiling and swaying. She's a million miles from the stone statue Henry spied last night. Today she radiates warmth and respectability.

Henry keeps to the edge of the crowd, but to his horror, the woman walks his way. She comes within six feet of him and studies the gravel carpark in the next lot. Without warning, she turns and looks directly at him. 'Are you new?'

'I've ah . . . yes.' Nothing else comes.

'Did you know Brian? Is that why you're here?'

Henry senses a shift in her, still perfectly pleasant but watching him carefully. He slowly shakes his head. This is his answer. He knows it comes off awkward—maybe even slightly deranged—but it's the best he can muster.

'Well, it was nice to meet you . . .'

'Henry.'

She takes a step towards the carpark and stops. 'Did you see a woman come this way?'

Henry shakes his head again.

'Okay, then.'

Henry forces himself to wait fifteen seconds, then walks to the corner of the church so he can watch her. The other woman from inside, the one dressed in black that Henry noticed earlier, waits for Maddy in the carpark. The two of them start talking, but he can't hear it. They are standing at the bumper of a blue sedan, hissing at each other, Maddy gesturing around wildly, the shift Henry sensed in her erupting out. The woman in black seems unmoved by it. She stands back, arms crossed.

A voice behind him says, 'I thought that was you.'

Henry spins. It's Emmett Hades. His mentor. 'What the hell? What are you doing here?'

'This is my local,' Emmett says. 'What are *you* doing here?'

'I found God.'

'That'll be the day.'

'I'm following a hunch.'

'I can see that,' Emmett says, looking past Henry to the women in the carpark. 'Do you know who they are?'

'I know the younger one,' Henry says. 'That's Maddy Santos. Do *you* know her, Em?'

'Only to say hello to. She's not here often.'

Over in the carpark, Maddy storms over to her car and gets in. Her opponent does the same, backing out first, the gravel loose under the tyres.

'Who's the other one?' says Henry.

'That's Erin Amstell. Brian Amstell's widow.'

'No shit.'

Emmett watches the cars head down the road.

'I don't know if you've heard the news,' Henry says, 'but I'm off Diablo. They're sending me back to Consorting this afternoon. Lowell and I are both getting the boot. They're winding the whole thing up.'

'They're fools. What are you going to do?'

Henry's whole face drops. 'I don't know. That detective from down south, Lana, is offering to keep me in the loop if I help her out. She reckons Amstell was sleeping with Maddy. She's a rat, but it might be the only shot I have at keeping my foot in the door.'

'You know, I looked her up. She's a good detective. If you can keep her at arm's length, you might learn a thing or two riding alongside her. She's got some clout down south.'

'I want to keep up with the early cases for you. I said I would.'

'I know. Thanks, Henry,' Emmett says, but his gaze has shifted to something in the distance.

Henry follows Emmett's eyes over to the crowd of parishioners. They both silently watch the priest extricate himself and walk towards them. He's out of his robes now and looking even more like a tough nut.

Emmett says, 'This is Father Hanlon.'

Hanlon smiles at Henry, hand already reaching out. 'Who's this then?'

'Father, this is Henry Loch. He's a policeman.'

Hanlon says, 'Ah, blessed are the peacekeepers.'

'I'll take your word for it,' says Henry. 'I know your name. You're the bloke that keeps hopping into us in the papers.'

'Henry is on the strike force,' adds Emmett.

'Is he now? Have you come to seek the Lord's guidance, son?'

This prick, thinks Henry. 'A chat with the other bloke might be more my speed.'

'Satan?'

'Is he around?'

Hanlon pivots. 'I hope you catch him sooner rather than later. The murderer, that is.'

'Oh, same here, Father.' Henry takes his photograph of Sarah Utton from his pocket and says, 'Have you seen this girl?'

Hanlon studies it. 'I don't know if I recognise her. Emmett, do you know her?'

Emmett shakes his head.

'She's missing,' Henry says. 'I found a service flyer for this place in her things. I figured she came here. You sure you don't know her? Take another look.'

'I really don't. I'm not that sort of priest, detective. I don't remember everyone's name. Bad with faces too. Real bad.'

Henry nods. 'I thought that was your job?'

Hanlon takes out a fresh packet of smokes. Still eyeing off Henry, he unwraps the cellophane. 'You remember every dickhead you roust?'

'No, not by name. I remember the faces, though.'

'I don't remember hers,' Hanlon says, nodding at the photo.

After that, they stand there a while, sweating in their church clothes and saying little of consequence. One of the parishioners comes by. She gives Hanlon a cutting from the local paper and some movie tickets. When she moves on, Henry leaves too. He gives Emmett a goodbye nod but ignores the Father.

CHAPTER 46

LANA IS IN THE office when the call comes in. It's Henry, 9.30 am, off-duty and standing in some phone box beside a church on the edge of Tweed Heads.

'What we talked about last night,' he says. 'I'm in. Get a pen.' He tells her to look into Paradise Gaming. 'It's a shell company run in partnership with a Sydney accountant called Christopher Donald Cole. Show me you've got some juice across the border.'

'Why this Cole bloke?'

'His silent partner in the gaming company is Joel Delaney.'

Lana spots it immediately. 'Victim number six.'

'That's the one. His company wrote a cheque to my missing girl. Show me new information on this and we can talk about the rest.'

'The *rest*?'

'I've got more. But it's tit for tat.'

'Okay. Deal.'

Lana puts her hand over the cradle to clear the line, then dials outbound. She places a series of long-distance calls to Sydney, connecting up with the New South Wales Fraud Squad. She gets names in the bookkeeping industry and makes more calls, writing frantically on a yellow legal pad. It takes an hour, but the story starts to take shape. Top to bottom, things look pretty curious.

First, Christopher Cole is dead. He went out in a blaze of glory four months back: a cocaine-related heart attack in a CBD jacuzzi. The death was anonymously called in, almost definitely the handiwork of a working girl looking to *stay out of it*. His wallet was empty.

In life, Cole was dirty the whole way down. He crunched numbers for drug dealers, pimps, gangsters and dirty cops. He barely concealed it.

'Cole was a bloody good accountant,' says a guy in the New South Wales tax office. 'He kept all the shady stuff off the books. He was a fat stupid prick, and impossible to deal with on my end, but he knew a thing or two about tax law. I'll grant him that much.'

Lana digs further. She hits the family records and medical files. Turns out that Cole's relationship with Joel Delaney was personal, as well as professional. Delaney grew up in Newcastle, where Cole's wife grew up. The two families went way back. Robert Delaney—Joel's father—is the godfather of Cole's kids.

As Lana finds all this, Bruno compiles the local due diligence. He disappears for an hour and comes back unhappy. 'I dug up this Cole character, and it turns out Henry Loch made the same calls yesterday. Why am I following up on his leads?'

'Because I think he's got something and I'm trying to get it out of him.'

'What he's *got* is career cancer,' Bruno says. 'And that shit is contagious. He's off Diablo as of today, right?'

Lana shrugs.

Bruno doesn't buy the nonchalance. 'Have you been sharing information with him?'

'We've crossed paths.'

She tells him the lot.

Bruno slumps into his chair. 'Just to be clear, I'm not going anywhere near him. You do whatever you need to do, but I'm not working with him.'

'And Cole?'

Bruno reads out the accountant's run sheet. Cole has a 1978 charge for solicitation of a minor, nixed by procedural mishap. 'Got off scot-free because Ron and Mark dropped the ball.'

'Ron Bingham?'

'Yeah, and Mark Evans. But before you get too excited,' Bruno leans in, lowers his voice, 'I don't trust Ron as far as I can throw him, but Evans? He's too fucking boring to be corrupt. And he's all wrong for it. He's a Catholic, four daughters, the lot. For years he's had a hard-on for sex offenders. It's a crusade with him. There's no way Evans is letting someone like Cole walk unless . . .'

'There's upside. You think Cole turned confidential informant?'

'Something like that. He probably provided some other type of leverage. There had to be a bigger fish to let him walk this blatantly.'

'Interesting. I wouldn't mind going through all the Delaney stuff. How's the murder room looking?'

'Empty, I imagine. I don't know where everyone is. But we can't just set up shop in there.'

'Why not? We're assigned detectives. Come on.'

They walk the breadth of the station and into CIB. Lana puts her hand on the Diablo room door, offering up a silent prayer as she enters. Inside, Bruno sparks a cigarette. 'I can't do this without a smoke,' he says, grabbing a stray coffee cup to ash into. He stands there, squinting around at the oppressive paperwork. 'I fucking hate this place.'

LANA PLANTS HERSELF IN a broken chair and says, 'We've got a shonky accountant called Chris Cole, and there's this missing working girl Henry is looking for, Sarah Utton. Both of them connect to each other and to the Diablo murders. Let's hash this out.'

Bruno points his cigarette at a nook of the murder room and says, 'Chris Cole was in cahoots with one of our victims. We know that much. Mr Delaney.'

'And?'

'Cole and Delaney's shell company Paradise Gaming was writing cheques to the missing call girl that Henry's after.'

'Yep. And?'

'She has some connection to . . .' Bruno grits his teeth and makes a clicking sound with his mouth. 'She has a *possible* connection to our latest victim via his mistress? She had that Mermaid Beach address, right?'

Lana nods along. 'That's how Henry tells it. Utton had Maddy's street address written down. That's how he found her.'

'It's not much of a connection. It could be . . .'

'I'm listening.'

'It could be that Utton's dead. She's the eighth victim and we just haven't found her yet.'

'That thought has crossed my mind. Let's start from the top with Diablo, see if we can wind it all together. Go case by case.'

'Me?'

'You know it better.'

'Okay,' Bruno says.

Victim number one is Teddy Adams. Day manager at a massage parlour. Teddy was snatched up in December '78, strangled with a rope, then rolled into an old carpet and dumped on a residential street in Burleigh Heads.

Lana takes notes. Still writing, she says, 'Potential connections?'

'Sarah Utton was in the trade. Teddy was in the trade. Maybe they knew each other? Worked together or something. Small world down here.'

Victim number two is Eddie Edgar. 'Eddie was a bartender around town, but mostly at the Continental Hotel. He was a real piece of work, for sure, but not what I'd call violent.'

'What's the story?'

'A known associate of Teddy Adams. He died the same way. No convictions, but he was a perv, I reckon.'

Lana raises an eyebrow.

'He was almost forty and his girlfriend was sixteen. It's in the file.'

'Any links to Utton and Cole?'

'Nothing official but . . .'

Lana takes it up. 'But Cole's a perv too. And if Teddy knew Utton, then there's a chance Utton knew Eddie as well.'

'Could be. Could be.'

Diablo victim number three is Barton Westerby. Taken two months later, Barton is killed and dumped and it's all a match, except for one fact. 'He was mutilated before he died. The killer cut off his balls.'

'What?'

'You heard me.' Bruno makes a snipping motion with his fingers. 'No one talks about it round here. One of the science blokes says our guy used a pair of gardening secateurs, probably while Westerby was unconscious, but before he died. The secateurs were brand new. Our guy bought them especially.'

'At least they were clean,' says Lana.

'Don't,' says Bruno, no doubt recalling the crime scene photos. 'Anyway, that soaked up a few weeks of work around here. Apparently, the guys know every shop assistant in every plant nursery from Coomera to Coolangatta. I tell you, Westerby makes the least amount of sense, or did until the recent stuff. He didn't know Teddy or Eddie. He was just some suburban shithead, as I see it. A divorcee, living alone.'

'Connections to Utton or Cole?'

'None that I know of.'

Victim number four is, 'Fucking Violet Burke. She was a pain in the arse. Local prostie. Someone shot her out the back of Tugun, out in the sticks. They didn't treat her case as a part of Diablo until later, when he shot the next victims.'

'So this new MO with the gun is about him putting himself back under wraps after the secateurs thing? Back to basics. Cleaning up his act.'

'That's the thinking, yeah. If you could call it that.'

Lana draws a line across her notepad. 'Tell me about Lenny Gibbs, number five.'

Bruno shakes his head. 'He uses the handgun again. I actually met Lenny a few times, before all this. He was an ageing party boy. A real grey fox. You'd see him around town if you liked a drink. His case got noticed. Diablo was actually quietening down before him, but then everyone got in on the act after Lenny went. The media, tourism, local business, the pollies. They all woke up to the fact that there's bodies every which way. The taskforce rolled it all together and prayed, and then Joel Delaney came along with the same MO and it was a done deal at that point.'

'Bloody hell. It's pretty fucked up when you really look at it.'

'That's why I try not to look at it,' says Bruno. 'I need some fresh air.'

Lana sits there alone.

She can guess at the rest.

Christopher Cole and this Lenny Gibbs travel in the same rich guy circles, and rich guys like that always pay for it from time to time. Then Joel Delaney dies. Cole's buddy.

Then Brian Amstell dies.

Then this.

CHAPTER 48

FIRST DAY BACK IN Consorting and it's the same ol' same ol' for Henry Loch. Him and Lowell are back where they started, like a traumatic flashback. Back in the car. Henry cruising and fuming. Lowell riding shotgun, nursing a 3 pm beer.

'It's a bloody hot one,' Lowell says. 'Where are we going, anyway?'

'I want to check on a house,' says Henry.

'You're the boss.'

It's a busy afternoon on Carlisle Avenue, Mermaid Beach. The last of the summer tourists are on the street, trundling along, towels around their necks, crying toddlers in tow. Henry double-parks, waits, eyes fixed on Maddy's house, watching it shimmer in the heat.

Lowell necks his beer and burps. 'What's the job here?'

Henry ignores him.

Lowell reclines his seat and closes his eyes.

The car in front pulls out and Henry nudges into the park. He kills the ignition.

It takes an hour, but when she finally appears, it's worth it. Maddy Santos wears a white swimsuit and holds a long glass in her hand. For minutes, she stays at the window, scanning the street.

Lowell comes awake. He squints through the windshield, still half-dazed from the nap. 'Nice,' he says.

'I think she's involved in the Brian Amstell case.'

'Is that your excuse?'

'Piss off.'

'Maybe she's the killer,' says Lowell, putting his head back down.

Across the street, Maddy Santos pulls the blinds.

'She's done something,' says Henry.

CHAPTER 49

HENRY AND LOWELL CATCH a suicide call at four thirty. 'Known prostitute, Nicole Rose,' says the woman on dispatch. 'Right up your alley, gents. Location is Oak Avenue. Uniforms on scene.'

'Fuck me,' says Lowell. 'She could've pulled this shit yesterday. Who tops themselves on a Monday?'

'It's Sunday,' says Henry.

'And Nicole Rose? Jesus Christ. Of all fucking people.'

Henry pulls the car down a gear. 'Can you—'

'Hey, *you* love this Homicide shit, not me, mate.' They speed along in silence until Lowell quietly says, 'I hope it's a wrist job.'

'Lowell.'

'I'm just saying. I don't want to see her head sprayed all over the—'

'Shut the fuck up.'

'She always was a piece of work.'

It's true. They both know her, of course. They've rousted Nicole Rose a couple of times. She hated doing her stint in lock-up. Hated cops. Loved to run her mouth in the squad car. Unfortunately, she also had a habit of punching the other girls and pinching the occasional wallet. In all, a bad combo.

Her place on Oak Avenue is a six-pack block of flats occupied entirely by sex workers. They didn't work out of it. It's one of Colleen Vinton's properties and the set-up is Colleen to a tee: she pimps the girls and skims the rent off the top. A closed loop.

Up in the apartment, they find Nicole Rose slumped in the corner of her bath, a makeshift noose still attached to the shower rail. There's no note. The rest of the apartment looks untouched. Nicole cleaned up beforehand. The dishes are stacked. Goldfish fed. New liners in the bins. The whole thing rings sad as hell.

Lowell strikes up a conversation with the uniforms attending. He bums a smoke. Henry seizes the moment to wander the building, showing his picture of Sarah Utton around, hoping a death nearby might catch one of the girls in a reflective mood.

Only three of the tenants are home. The first two blow off his condolences—no love lost for salty Nicole—and they barely glance at the Utton pic. They recognise her, though. *She works sometimes. So what?* and, *Haven't seen her this summer.*

At the third flat, Henry almost has to beat down the door before a thin woman comes to the window. He knows her. They call her All Weather Heather. She's a lifer.

'What do you want?' she says, voice muted by the glass.

'Open up or you're going in for the night.'

Henry finds a small gathering in the apartment. Heather and two younger women he doesn't recognise. All of them are nodding off around a glass coffee table. He squats down and runs a finger across the tabletop. One girl looks on, blank faced, watching him like a late-night re-run. Henry wanders the flat. It doesn't take long to find what he's looking for. There's a heroin kit inside a saucepan in the kitchen sink. He bags it up—mainly for effect—and dumps it on the coffee table.

'Girls, one of you is going to talk. The other two are going to sweat it out in the station house.'

'We're diabetics,' says Heather.

'Come on.' Henry hands her the Sarah Utton photo. 'Where is she?'

Heather purses her lips. 'One of us might know. But if one of us talks, we all stay out of the clink, yeah?'

'That depends on how helpful *all* of you are. Wake her up.'

Heather nudges the girl beside her. She's slept through this so far. Heather passes her the photo.

'What do you know about her?' says Henry.

'Sarah,' says the woman.

'That's right. She's missing. You know where she is?'

'No.'

'When was the last time you saw her?'

'Couple of months back.'

'Where?'

'I . . . I wanna walk on this,' says the woman, pointing a loose hand at the drug kit.

'We've already done that bit,' says Henry. 'Where did you see her?'

'We did a job together. Off the books.'

'I won't tell Colleen,' he says.

'Jesus, Kimmy,' says the third woman. She's been silent up till now.

'I know, I know. But Sarah was paying large, and I needed the money.'

'You double-teamed with Sarah Utton?' says Henry.

'That's right.'

'Who's the john?'

'Some regular of hers. A rich guy. Rented out this swish ocean-front place down in Southport.'

'This guy have a name?'

'Nah,' she says.

'Come on.' Henry drops a small wad of cash on the table. 'You all walk *and* you get paid. Or you all go down and none of you get shit.'

'That's not the bloody deal,' says Heather.

'Okay, okay.'

'You're not normally this much of a cunt,' Heather snaps.

'I don't normally have to be,' says Henry. 'I think this Sarah girl is pregnant, and I think something bad has happened to her. I'd do the same for any of you.'

'Yeah right,' says Heather.

'Well, she certainly wasn't pregnant when I worked with her,' says the other one.

'You a doctor now?'

'No, Einstein, Robbie pays extra to fuck girls on the rag.'

'It's a thing,' says Heather, catching his look.

'That's why it was off the book,' says the third woman. 'Colleen doesn't let us do that sort of stuff. Says it attracts a nasty customer.'

Henry swallows. Takes a moment. 'You said Robbie. Is that the john? How do I find this Robbie?'

'Yeah, that's him. I don't know. It's not like I have his number or anything.'

'Tell me more about him. Come on.'

'He said he worked in real estate.'

'And?'

'Black hair. Fortyish, but nice looking.'

'Was it just him?'

'Yeah. He had a cleaner come in and strip the bed at one point, but yeah, just him.' She slumps back into the couch. 'Can you please leave us alone now?'

Henry takes down their names. When he's done, he points at the syringes on the table. 'Why are you three booting up this shit?'

Heather lights a smoke. 'There's a drought on benzos. Can't find them anywhere. You try working all night on bikie speed and coming down cold turkey. It's rough as guts. I'm not sitting around this shithole without a little something. Don't suppose *you* have anything?'

'You find me this Robbie's surname and his home address, and I'll see what I can do.'

He's halfway back to the door when Heather ashes her smoke and says, 'That's why Nicole topped herself, I reckon. She was clear of the hard stuff for years until last week.'

CHAPTER 50

IN THE DIABLO ROOM, Lana gets up to stretch her legs. She bends at the waist, pushes her palms flat against the dirty carpet. She's still there in downward dog when a lilting voice says, 'So that's how you got this gig?'

It's Anne-Marie, Ron Bingham's assistant. She stands in the doorway, jiggling a tea bag in a mug of hot water.

'You wish,' says Lana. 'What do you want?'

'Phone call. I'll punch it through.'

The call comes in.

'It's me,' says Henry.

•

They meet on a stretch of the boardwalk under the fading light. 'How was church?' she says.

Henry watches the waves. 'More interesting than usual. Maddy Santos and Erin Amstell know each other. They were both there this morning. If Maddy is Brian's piece on the side, he might have met her in church.'

'No shit. I didn't see that coming. Then again, in my experience, men like to keep it close to home. Fucking complete strangers is . . .'

'Risky?'

'I was going to say difficult.'

Henry closes his eyes and takes a deep breath, rubbing a hand over his mouth.

'You okay?'

'Long day, and it's only just getting started.'

'Calls?'

'Yeah. A suicide down the street. There's a bit of smack around, which is . . . not great. Here.' He takes a piece of paper from his shirt pocket.

'A girl I spoke to this arvo had a lead on one of Sarah Utton's johns. Name's Robbie. Works in real estate. See what you can dig up.'

'Sure.'

'What did you find on Chris Cole?'

Lana runs it down. He's listening, but she can tell he's not interested until the part where she says, 'Cole's dead. Had a heart attack a couple of months back.'

'I missed that.'

'Everyone misses something.'

'Yeah?'

'You know, down my way, there's a bit of an office myth that you meet your bloke in the first few days of a case. He's some deadshit at the scene or in the first run of door-to-doors. His name's usually in there somewhere. But with this, there's just too much to wade through. Too many moving parts.'

'Have you been in the murder room all day?'

She laughs. 'Can you tell?'

'It happens. Look, I've gotta go. I'm going to keep an eye on Maddy tonight when I knock off. I'll call you if anything happens.'

'Sure, I'll go look for this Robbie in the haystack.'

Lana watches him walk back across the esplanade, weaving between the traffic. Even as Henry recedes into the dinner-time throng, she notices that he stands out. He's bigger than everyone else, taller, but also slightly hunched. Even the back of him has a despondent air.

CHAPTER 51

BACK IN THE MURDER room, Bruno sits in a chair with a police file pressed to his face, a plastic container of stir-fry resting precariously on one knee. 'You know, I'm liking this Chris Cole and Joel Delaney thing. It's barely been picked over at all.'

'Who's the lead on Delaney?'

'Reynolds.'

'What's the story?'

'Delaney was shot on the water.'

'What?'

'Yep, out on his boat. Our guy motored up in his own boat and popped him twice, then pissed off. Happened only a few clicks from where they found Amstell.' He shakes the file in his hand and says, 'It looks as though Reynolds has been hell-bent on finding the boat. He's got some decent leads in here. A couple of eye-wits on blokes in tinnies, one in a speedboat. Even investigated the local kayakers. There's more over there.'

Lana follows Bruno's nod to a section of the murder room wall. As soon as she sees the pictures up close, Lana wonders how she could have missed them. The scene photos are of a man lying on his back in a tin boat. Joel Delaney died holding his fishing rod, dressed in blue speedos, with loose XXXX Bitter cans by his side. Closer in, she can see two black circles on his skin. One below his left eye. One on his chest.

Bruno says, 'I was there when they brought him in. Happened early in the morning. We had him in the coroner's office by lunchtime, even with all the fuss.'

'What was the trouble?'

'They think he was popped on your side of the border, just off Duranbah then the tide brought him up our way. We didn't care. It looked like our case, but, bloody hell, the New South Wales Water Police raised seven shades of shit with it. They're funny buggers, the water police. I guess they don't see a lot of action.'

'Yeah, I've heard . . .' Lana trails off as she zeroes in on a map adjoining the crime scene photos. Someone, Reynolds probably, has circled the site of the shooting. It's across the border.

Brian Amstell was also killed in New South Wales.

'Bruno?' she says. 'You got a minute?'

He trundles over, still holding the police file. Still absorbed, he turns a page as he comes towards her. 'Look at this.' Bruno's holding a newspaper clipping stapled to Joel Delaney's file. The clipping has a grainy photo of four men in black-tie outfits, all smiling for the camera. 'That's Delaney and Chris Cole,' he says. 'And next to them, that's Lenny Gibbs, number five. They took this for the *Bulletin* social pages about a month before Lenny died. I wonder if this got followed up?'

Lana turns back to the Delaney murder board. 'Who's the other guy?'

Bruno peers at the smudged fine print and reads, 'On the far left is Robert Emmery. Local real estate developer.'

Lana stares at the maps, the blood in the crime scene pics, the stray debris.

Both killed near the border.

The last two bodies.

The clock in the Diablo room ticks over, producing a loud mechanical thud.

'What name was that again?' Lana says absent-mindedly, still staring at the wall.

'Robert Emmery,' says Bruno.

Robbie.

CHAPTER 52

HENRY SITS IN A booth at the front of the Mermaid Beach McDonald's, watching the evening traffic. He sees sedans with sleeping children, single drivers unmoving in the shadows. Teenagers on the prowl. Bogans in utes. All of it silent against the rowdy backdrop of the restaurant.

'Are you going to eat that?' says Lowell, already lifting Henry's cheeseburger off his tray.

Henry grunts.

'Mind if I duck out early?'

'Sure. Have at it,' says Henry.

'Thank god. I'm going to try to get a ride in before I hit the hay. Syd's got a new place a couple of blocks from here, wants me to give it the once-over. You interested?'

Henry says, 'Nah, not tonight.'

'Jesus Christ, you're a stick in the mud today. You're acting like a right toss.'

'Yeah, well—'

'*Yeah well, yeah well.* Snap out of it, please. Go home. Have a fucking beer and a tug or run yourself a hot bath, whatever it is you need to do. I'm begging you.'

'Any other feelings you'd like to share, Lowell?'

Standing up, Lowell says, 'Just this,' and he puts his hand into his pocket and removes it with his middle finger raised. 'Okay, I'm off. I'll pay on the way out.'

'It's a bistro,' Henry says. 'I paid at the counter.'

Lowell has a few drinks in him tonight, thus the impromptu pep talk and general confusion. 'It's fucking weird this place,' he says, even though he insisted on coming here. 'I like it, though. It smells good in here.'

'Go on.'

Henry watches him make his way out onto the street. He staggers south and disappears.

Back inside the restaurant, a pimply kid in a uniform comes by to bus the table. 'You done here?'

Henry slides the tray over.

The kid works slowly. 'You a cop?'

'Apparently.'

'Cool. You ever shoot anyone?'

'What? Uh, yeah.'

'What's it like?'

'It's okay,' Henry says. 'Happens quick.'

'They give you a medal or something. Or do you get into trouble?'

'They sent me here, so the second one.'

'Here?'

'The coast. I used to work up in Brisbane.'

'Oh right, right. Cool.'

'It's not that cool.'

The kid stops what he's doing.

Henry looks at him. *Thoroughly stoned.* 'I have nightmares about it sometimes.'

'Oh wow. Have a good night, man.'

'Yeah, you too.'

•

Henry takes the unmarked to the Santos house on Carlisle Avenue, where he once again sits in the dark interior and watches her. The lights are on. Maddy moves around, sweeping back and forth by the windows, trailing a white silk nightgown.

By eleven, she's shown no sign of slowing down, and Henry has managed to psych himself up enough to knock on her door. *It's just an interrogation, just another—*

'Yes?' she says from inside.

'Police. Open up.'

'Go away.' There's a slur to it.

'Maddy Santos?'

The door flies open. 'How do you . . .' She peers into the darkness outside. 'Oh, it's you. I knew you were a cop, I should . . . show me your badge.'

'No.'

Henry walks in, slipping past her.

'You need a warrant for this.'

'I don't seem to,' he says.

'I'll call the police.'

She looks different up close. Without make-up, Maddy is toned down and less imperial. For the first time, he can see her eyes properly—a light grey-green—and in those eyes, he sees disquiet, uncertainty and fear.

'I'm not here to hurt you,' he says. 'I just want to ask you a few questions about your boyfriend, Brian Amstell.'

'I've seen you out there, you know.'

'Have you now?'

'Last night, this morning, tonight.' She stumbles a little. 'I must say, you're not much of a policeman.'

'So I've been told. Tell me who Brian Amstell really was.'

'Go fuck yourself.'

'No. I don't want to.'

'*I* want you to. You've gotta go.'

'No.'

Maddy staggers towards him, slowly bringing her arm around. She's so drunk that it takes Henry a moment to recognise it for what it is, a flailing punch. He grabs her by the wrist and shoulder and, in some strange waltz, moves her to the lounge and sits her down.

'You need a cup of tea,' he says.

She laughs at that. With exaggerated poise, Maddy retrieves a packet of cigarettes from the coffee table and puts one in her mouth. Struggling with the lighter, Henry steps in. 'Thanks,' she says, exhaling in his face.

Henry goes to the kitchen and boils the jug. She's out of milk, but he makes the tea anyway. 'You take sugar?'

'I don't want that shit,' she says.

Unsure what that means exactly, Henry brings the mugs out and sits in an adjoining chair, an uncomfortable wicker thing that creaks under his bulk. He takes out his notebook. 'Tell me about Brian Amstell.'

'I'm not doing that.'

'I saw you arguing with his wife at the church.'

'Jesus.' She closes her eyes, but the ember of her smoke glows. 'What's your name again?'

'Henry.'

'Of course. You even look like a Henry.'

'Do you know what you look like, Ms Santos?'

She opens a single eye, tries to focus. 'What?'

'A person in more trouble than she knows what to do with.'

'Some detective you are. The girl down at the servo could've told you that. Here's another hot tip for you,' and she lowers her voice to a conspiratorial whisper. 'The bottle shop guy knows too.'

'Tell me what's going on? Maybe I can help?'

She laughs again. 'Ahhh, you are a strange bird, Henry. Policeman, pervert, social worker.' She slides the mug of tea off the coffee table and takes a sip. 'Are we out of milk?'

Henry hands her a picture of Sarah Utton. 'You recognise this girl?'

Maddy says, 'No.' But she puts the photo on the table face down.

They sit there for a minute, sipping their drinks. Henry can hear the wash of the surf in the distance. He says, 'Tell me about—'

'Have you ever been in love, Henry?'

'I guess.'

'If you have to guess, the answer's no.'

He sits back, tries to look relaxed. 'Okay then, no. Have you?'

'No. Definitely not.'

'You weren't in love with Brian Amstell?'

She lies back on the couch, slips her shoes off. 'I wasn't fucking Brian. He did slip it to the assistants at the clinic every now and then, but not me. It wasn't like that with us. We worked together. And for the record, I don't give a shit about what he did or with whom. Erin is a stupid, selfish bitch. You can put that in your little notebook.'

'That's the wife, yeah?'

'Look it up.'

'What about this place?' Henry says. 'He owns half of it, right? If I let someone live in a place like this, I'd want *something* in return.'

'What? Like a blowjob?'

'At least a blowjob.'

'Ha! Well, there's this thing called *rent*, detective. I happen to pay Brian, *paid* Brian, oh I don't know . . . I paid for all this in cash. I work, detective, just like you.'

'Except I do my taxes.'

'Congratulations.'

Another pause.

'I'm sorry,' Henry says. 'I . . .'

'What are you sorry about?'

'The inference. I work with a lot of prostitutes.'

'And it makes you think all women are prostitutes?'

'No, it makes me comfortable with the idea that some women do it.'

'Hm. Do you fuck the girls, Henry?'

'No.'

'I don't know if I believe you. A lot of policemen do.'

'Some do. Does it matter?'

'It matters to you.'

'I don't need to pay for it.'

She smiles and closes her eyes again. 'I really thought we were getting somewhere there for a minute. I really did.' Maddy lays her head down on a cushion. 'Lies. Lies upon lies upon lies. Can you leave me alone now? Do you have enough? I have a lawyer . . . I can . . .' Her voice drops to a murmur.

Henry watches her fall asleep. He gets up, takes the tea mug from her chest—a light red ring on the skin there—then pulls her feet up onto the couch. He thinks about covering her with a bedsheet, but it's warm enough without.

'Maddy?' he says.

She doesn't stir.

He studies her body, the gently undulating breasts, the outline of a wide nipple. Henry scans her arms (a silver ring on her right index finger) and sees that her legs are toned—a runner, perhaps—and that her toenails are painted with clear enamel gloss. He squats down beside her. She smells of sea salt, sweat, sunscreen and vodka.

'Goodnight,' he says.

He locks the door on the way out.

CHAPTER 53

LANA COHEN LEAVES THE station house at eleven. She's tired. Her battered face aches. Dull pain in her bones, in her teeth and in the place behind her eyes. A half dozen Aspros since dinner haven't taken the edge off.

Out on the road, the late-night traffic is light. She keeps to the ocean boulevards, watching the dark expanse of the sea appear and disappear through the driver's window.

It's a void, coming and going.

I was thinking about Dad before the attack.

That strange fact returns to her now. She was walking through the moonlit crime scene by the river, and for whatever reason, it dredged up that history. Memories appearing out of the ether. That's all it is now, with him: memories appearing out of nowhere. Lana can go a whole month without thinking about him, but then spot a man in the crowd, or see a face in the paper, and feel the dark sting of longing. All these ghosts, all these apparitions of the younger man who disappeared, instead of the elderly, ailing father who might be out there somewhere, still alive. It made no sense.

But that's life.

There's no resolution, of course, no closure. She's given up trying to force it. The facts of life are like the Diablo murder room: an expanse of impossible magnitude, detail upon detail, day upon day, each part broken down and tamed, but the whole? The whole is chaos.

Unmanageable chaos.

Lana turns into her street. She parks by the motel, takes the steps up to her room, then undresses to escape the heat. The bed beckons, but a cold shower pushes it back. Instead of sleeping, she uses the mattress as a table, laying out her notes.

One missing girl.

One greasy real estate developer.

Two shonky accountants, both dead.

Six other dead people.

Two dozen broken coppers trying to put it all together.

Detail upon detail, day upon day, tomorrow begat tomorrow . . .

More of the same.

Lana turns on the TV for company and a priest appears on-screen, angrily denouncing the world.

'—and if this vile social pestilence continues unabated, there will be no remorse. None. At the wrath of the Lord, the land quakes, and the people are like fuel for a fire. It's in his book. It's in the hearts of—'

Lana leaves the Diablo stuff and goes to the closet. She pulls out her father's missing person's report. The field notes. The forgotten leads.

In the background, the priest keeps at it.

'—if only, if only. But it's clear to everyone that the Queensland Police Force cannot solve these murders. The will of the people is not being served by these men. These men are all bought and paid for by local gambling interests, local prostitution, and local vice. Drink and sex and dishonour are their currency. If the viewers tonight seek the answers to these murders, they'd be far better off with me and my congregation than putting their faith in this wretched lot, this—'

Lana holds up a picture from her father's file.

Where do people go when they disappear?

It's everything, isn't it?

All religion, all mysteries. The only game in town.

She lights a smoke.

She listens to the priest carry on.

'—and oh yes, rods are prepared for the arrogant, and blows for the backs of fools. I'm here now, calling on Superintendent Albert Beggs to do the bidding of the people and put these inept fools to work elsewhere. Replace them. Replace these hopeless, inept idiots.'

The reporter holding the mic seems completely unfazed by the priest's screed. She nods along without comment.

Lana stares at the screen. She studies the priest's face. It's all over him: he hates us, he hates the police. As the segment ends, they post his name in the corner. *Father Frank Hanlon. Saint Andrews Catholic Church.*

'Fuck you, buddy,' she says, out loud, to no one.

DAY FIVE

MONDAY, 25 FEBRUARY 1980

JOURNAL OF EMMETT HADES

(SELECTED EXCERPTS)

I want to document the beginning of Diablo, for prosperity.

It wasn't a clean start.

We had another unsolved case hanging over us.

Ruben Davis.

No one talks about Ruben Davis, because no one remembers him, because he's buried at the bottom of Diablo.

But for me, he's the point of origin.

The spark.

The eternal.

Ruben Davis was murdered mid-January, 1978. Someone—a man, by shoe size—came into his house in Broadbeach, through an unlocked rear entry, and attacked dear Ruben as he slept. The killer then dismembered his body with a hacksaw, bagged up the parts, and took them with him when he left. He did all of this in the master bedroom and, when it was done, the room looked like what it was: an abattoir.

'He liked the mess,' said one of the science people working the scene. 'Had to. Anyone else would have dragged the body to the en suite. There are tiles in there.' There was semen on the carpet.

When I came into the case, we knew nothing, not even Ruben's name. There was no body. Just a blood-stained, empty room. A friend of Ruben's with a spare key called it in. Ruben missed a date, and the friend checked the house. That's how we caught it.

They assigned me as lead, with Mark Evans backing me up. We worked the thing over and over.

Ruben Davis was twenty-six when he died. He was in construction, a labourer. On the weekends, he went fishing and played indoor cricket.

He had exactly two ex-girlfriends—both with air-tight alibis—and no history of criminal association or deviant behaviour.

We had zip, in other words.

No suspects close to hand.

No dangerous crims in the area at the time of the attack.

No motives.

Nothing out of the ordinary at all, except the crime itself. All of this mayhem seemed to happen to Ruben for no reason, by no known suspect, in a couple of hours on a weekday night in Broadbeach, before quickly slipping into history, repeated only in neighbourhood gossip.

This was the state of things before Diablo. When Teddy Adams turned up dead in December of '78, I still had Ruben's file on my desk. I was still receiving calls from his distraught parents and his older sister. I was still searching for clues. Couldn't stop myself. It was the blood that got to me. The concentration of it. The violence implied. I'd had a wild career—like all of us in Homicide—but I'd never seen anything like that before. I couldn't get my head around it. It was like I was drowning in the stuff, and I knew something new would emerge out of it.

•

The early days of Diablo passed with manic intensity. The killer put the first victim's body on a suburban street, so it caused a fuss. No one said 'serial killer' back then, of course, because Teddy Adams, that was the victim's name, was an isolated thing. The powers that be wrote Ruben's case off as an unmentionable failure. No connection made. And, to be fair, the MOs were markedly different. At the time, I didn't disagree.

And yet it was the Teddy Adams case—not Ruben—that drew together all the familiar characters of this story: Ron Bingham, Pete Reynolds, Mark Evans. They all gushed in, everyone wanting a piece of the Adams investigation because it represented everything the Gold Coast CIB laid claim to: easy work. They were so cocksure. The killer would be an aggrieved john from Teddy's brothel workplace or an errant crim circulating in Teddy's grotty underground. Someone close and easy. And solving this case would please the higher-ups and the underworld and the local media, and that's who Diablo served, right from the start. Superintendent Albert Beggs—the poisonous toad—and Colleen Vinton, and the dictates of newspapers and television anchors. They were the real masters. That was what all this was really about. It's why Teddy Adams got the whole team behind him and why Ruben Davis—difficult, bloody, absent Ruben—got swept under the carpet. I lost him to inconvenience and office politics.

But I never gave up on it.

I worked both cases.

From the outset, I assumed I would finish it.

Solve both.

I had nothing else.

Went at it every hour, every day, every fibre, to the bone. No one put in more work. I slept in the murder room. I ate in the murder room. I worshipped at its altars and took communion from the ghosts of Ruben Davis and Teddy Adams. I became the case, and the case went south.

'78 into '79 into ...

Two more bodies fall into the red pit with me.

Count them off:

22/2—Eddie Edgar

12/4—Barton Westerby

All of them living with me.

Dying with me.

Me, living and dying with their bodies and realising that I am not on the road to glory at all. I'm turned around. Slipping down. For my sins, I would stand in front of their blood-soaked visage every night, screaming, 'How did this happen? Tell me how it feels, God. Show me how a man can do this to his fellow man? Show me the grace and glory of this. Show me. Show me, show me, show me, show me, show me.'

But the answer never arrived.

I had to show myself.

CHAPTER 54

HENRY WAKES TO A seven o'clock call from a man named Wesley Bowman. 'Trina from Tropical Touch told me to give you a bell,' he says. 'Your photos are ready.' Bowman lives ten minutes down the road.

Henry walks the neatly trimmed concrete path onto the verandah of Bowman's white fibro bungalow. 'It's open,' calls a voice from inside. Henry pulls the screen door and steps in. The house is immaculate. Vintage furnishings, pristine order. The couch perfectly parallel to the coffee table. The table flush with the wall unit. In the adjoining kitchen, Wesley stands at the bench, dressed for work in dark pants and a grey short-sleeved shirt. He looks like what he is—a schoolteacher—but he's older than expected, a small bird-like creature with thinning silver hair.

'Fancy a cuppa, detective? How do you take it?'

'White with one, thanks.'

'A man after my own heart.'

Bowman plugs in the electric jug and switches it on. While they wait, he pulls a manila folder from a kitchen drawer and slides it over. 'There you go.'

Henry looks in the file. The top image is a photo of his partner Lowell Sennett, completely naked, flanked by two women. Lowell's face is manically contorted and odd, the camera lens catching him in the throes of orgasm.

'Quite the specimen, that one,' says Bowman.

'You could say that.'

'Did you take these? They're very good for an amateur.'

'Thanks, I guess.'

Bowman finishes making the tea and the two of them chat about teaching and cricket until Bowman suffers a coughing fit. At first,

Bowman takes a step back and, wide-eyed, motions that he's fine. But after a brief respite, the hacking continues and he disappears into the back of the house to cough in peace. To kill the time, Henry takes his cup of tea for a walk around the living room. There are no pictures on Bowman's walls. No family frames or artwork. Henry peers down the short hallway attached to the living room and the walls are blank there as well. With Bowman still absent, Henry walks along, ducks his head into the main bedroom. Like the rest of the house, it's neat as a pin.

'You okay, Wesley?' he says.

'Oh yes, just—'

The coughing continues.

Back up the hall, Henry comes across a closed door. There's a spare room and in there the walls are covered in black-and-white images. A bad vibe hits immediately. Henry feels a tremor. He puts his cup on a nearby filing cabinet and takes a closer look.

Every type of vice is represented in the photos, every possible contortion of biology and debasement, all of it contained in neat silver-rimmed frames and perfectly aligned. Henry spies celebrities, sporting stars, minor politicians and the odd Queensland police detective. In the centre of one wall, there are three larger images. One shows a famous American actor standing naked in some grimy hotel room. The second photo shows a line of seven women, some standing, some squatting, all of them pissing on a hooded man. The third shot, the centrepiece of the entire collection, presents a grim tableau: a twenty-something man on all fours. Behind the man is a woman dressed in a nun's habit welding a dark red dildo. Behind the tryst there's a crowd of other nuns gleefully watching on, all of them in various states of congress and undress.

'It's wonderful, isn't it?' says Bowman, startling Henry.

'It's . . . it's a lot, is what it is.'

'Oh yes, but the eye flow is nearly perfect. Like a renaissance painting.'

'Who took this?' He points to the image of the nuns.

'A friend. She has quite the eye.'

'Wesley, do you show people this stuff? And be honest because I'm a policeman. I can tell if you're lying.' Henry takes a step towards him, but Bowman doesn't seem to notice.

'God no. What do you take me for? This is a private collection. It's very private. The subject of that one, the one on all fours,' he points to the image of the man and the nuns, 'he's dead. It's all I have of him. I couldn't share that.'

'What happened?'

'Topped himself. It's an insane world where such a beautiful image could be the source of such sorrow, don't you think? It makes no sense.'

'He killed himself because of this and you have it on your wall?'

'His father's a priest, I've been told. Come on,' Bowman says, ushering Henry out.

'I don't love the idea of my photos ending up in there.'

'Does it matter?'

'Trina told me you were discreet.'

'I am.'

As they step back into the kitchen, Henry picks up his manila folder. 'Do you keep copies of all the work you develop, Wesley?'

'No. Well . . .' Bowman studies him. 'I'm not a fool. I keep copies of the things I think are important. The sort of stuff that could rub people up the wrong way, should I ever find myself in trouble. Or dead. When I die, things might slip out. It really depends on how violently I shuffle off.'

'Did you keep copies of these?' says Henry, his hand on the manila folder.

Bowman winks. 'Only time will tell.'

'It's quite dangerous what you do, isn't it?'

'Oh, I don't know, detective. Do you know what Susan Sontag said about photography? She said it's a violation. To photograph someone is to violate them. So, what you do is dangerous, too, I imagine. Now, Henry, you have yourself a good day now.'

CHAPTER 55

THE GOLD COAST CIB lunchroom adjoins the Diablo set-up and works overtime as workspace spill. This morning, Mark Evans has a microfiche reader mounted to a table in there, pushed into a corner. He sits hunched over it, headphones plugged into a portable radio, his face buried in the flicker and blur of the images. Henry watches from across the room, thinking the set-up has a strange cadence to it: Evans absorbed, reams of data flashing, a detective locked in with no distractions. But no output either. Just a man and his vortex.

Lana appears and starts fixing a cuppa.

Henry empties his dregs and says, 'How'd you go with Robbie?'

'You're not going to believe this.' She produces a photostat page from her pocket. 'That's Chris Cole, that's Joel Delaney, that's Lenny Gibbs, and that's Robert Emmery. Your Robbie. See this?'

Henry reads out the purple ink caption under the image, '*Local property developer.* Where'd you find this?'

'Someone attached it to the Delaney file. Been in there for months.' She flicks the page in his hands. 'Chris Cole, *two* Diablo victims, and your guy.'

Henry studies the image. 'Could be a coincidence? It's just a photo in the paper.'

'Nope. I thought of that. I looked it up. Chris Cole used to do Robert Emmery's books *and* Lenny Gibbs's books. He's listed on their tax returns from '69 to '76.'

'There you go. What's this?' Henry points to some handwritten scrawl underneath the photostat image.

'That's my handwriting.'

'Really? The Condom?'

'The Condor. Jesus. That's Robbie's home address. Can you read numbers?'

'In English I can.'

'What do you want to do with it?'

Henry casts his eye over to Mark Evans. The man remains transfixed. 'I've got someone who can confirm it from this.' He folds up the photostat. 'Then I guess I'll go and see this Robbie character and ask him about Utton. See if anything shakes out. You?'

'I've got Beggs in a minute. I've been told to stick around. Big news, apparently.'

'You reckon they're going to let you out today?' The bruising on the woman's face is still mottled and red, but she's pasted over it with make-up.

'Who knows? Do you have something else for me?'

'I'm working on it.'

They both hear Ron Bingham calling the Diablo squad together. It's loud enough that even Evans comes up for air.

Lana says, 'You coming to this, Mark?'

'What is it?'

'Beggs is here.'

Evans put his headphones back in. *No*, it seems.

'You better go,' says Henry.

CHAPTER 56

LANA FINDS BRUNO KARRAS slouched over a carpeted office divider at the back of the squad room. 'Is this another bollocking?' she whispers. 'How often does this happen?'

Bruno exhales slow. *Too often.*

Across the room, Superintendent Albert Beggs steps out of the darkness of Bingham's office and starts up without warning. 'I said three days, gentlemen, and I meant it. I thought I was pretty fucking clear last time I was in here. You dickheads had three days to dig this bloke up and it's been three days, so where are we?'

Bingham is planted in an office chair off to one side, almost out with the rank and file. He gives a disgusted wince and says, 'We do police work down here, Albert. Not miracles.'

'Police work? Police work!' screams Beggs. He snatches a folded newspaper from a nearby aide and tosses it at Bingham, collecting the man in the face. 'Have you read the fucking stories?'

'That priest is a kook,' spits Pete Reynolds.

Lana leans towards Bruno. 'What are they talking about?'

'Some priest over the border. He hopped into us on the late-night news and now it's on the front page of the *Courier*.'

Beggs turns to his entourage, 'Pick that up.' The whole room watches as a junior assistant kneels by Bingham's feet to reassemble the newspaper. Beggs says, 'You're all fucking finished. The good Father Hanlon, *he's* my miracle, not you. This holier than thou bullshit of his plays well up in Brisbane, and he's right for a change. That little rant of his has put the higher-ups *right* offside. They're finally letting me do what I should have done months ago, which is dump the bloody lot of you. You know what? Today's your last day. You've got till I wake up tomorrow to produce something, just one *goddamn shred* of evidence that moves this case forward or every last one of you . . . you're all done.' At which point, Beggs starts lazily pointing at random detectives up the front. 'Cairns, Bundaberg, Gatton, back in uniform. Emerald, Birdsville, Cunnamulla, all of you disappeared to fuck knows where. Goodbye. *Goodbye!* And you,' he says to Bingham, 'you can do your *police work* down at the local RSL, with all the other has-beens. You'll be getting the chop.'

'Fuck,' says Bruno after Beggs has stormed off.

'What do we do?' says Lana.

'Let's go and shake down some informants. May as well call in all my favours.'

'Can I meet you down at the car?'

'Sure. I'm going to need a smoke first.'

CHAPTER 57

LANA MOVES QUICKLY. SHE goes to a payphone down the street and calls Dwain Gorst in New South Wales. 'It's all going to hell up here, sir.'

Gorst seems delighted. 'Stay with it.'

'I don't think I'm going to close out the Amstell case. Time's up and it's still a bit of a whodunnit.'

'Collateral,' he says. 'It's unfortunate, but . . .'

'There's one other thing I've been meaning to follow up on. One of the Diablo victims has links back to Sydney, Christopher Cole. He's an accountant, recently deceased. Do you know the name, sir?'

Gorst pauses. 'No, I don't think I do.'

'Well, there are connections there somewhere and they tie into the local vice up here. I've got a much better read on this place now. Some of the coppers up here are really up to their necks in it. I'm more than certain that one of the Diablo leads, Ron Bingham, is dirty. He arrested Cole back in '78 for solicitation and the case looks shaky as all get out. They let Cole off, essentially. Then his business associate up here, Joel Delaney, winds up dead. He's their sixth victim. There's dodgy stuff all over. And a missing girl in the mix. It's a clusterfuck.'

Gorst hums to himself. 'Well, this *is* progressing. How did you unearth all this?'

'It's in the cases, sir. I'm still on the outs socially. No one's feeding me this stuff.'

'Okay, keep at it, Cohen. Be careful but stay with it.'

'Will do, sir.'

'I want to hear about the fallout, Cohen.'

'I'll do my best.'

Lana is still holding the phone when it disconnects.

CHAPTER 58

HENRY KNOCKS ON A motel room door on Oak Avenue, Surfers Paradise. Beside him, Lowell Sennett sweats through his shirtsleeves. 'Bit early for this lot,' he says.

Henry knocks again.

All Weather Heather opens up. 'Oh shit.'

'Relax, sweetheart,' says Lowell. 'This is a social visit.'

'Nah, no, not him,' she says, pointing at Lowell. 'I don't want that donkey-dick fuckwit anywhere near me.'

'Is your friend home?' says Henry, turning pages in his notebook, looking for the woman's name. 'I want to show her a picture. I think I've found her john. Just want to get her eyes on it.'

'She *might* be home,' says Heather, looking straight at Lowell.

Henry tells Lowell to take five, then enters the rank apartment, closing the door behind him. The blinds are drawn. A silent TV shimmers in the dark. 'I've got this for you,' he says, taking a bag of downers from his pocket. The pills from Sarah Utton's room. 'If you can help me, I can help you. Half now, half when I get what I need from your friend. It's Kimmy, right?'

Heather says, 'Yeah. She's coming back tonight.'

'What's your number here?'

Heather says it.

'I call and you answer, okay?' says Henry.

'I'm off tonight, so don't sweat it.'

'You girls still shooting up?'

'Fuck off.'

'Tell me.'

'You gotta turn the tap back on. It's only gonna get worse if someone doesn't get things moving. I can keep my head straight, you know, but these new girls, it'll only take 'em a few weeks to fuck it all up. Colleen won't let 'em work if she sees the signs. It'll be game over.'

'I'm on it.'

'Good.' Heather walks him back to the door. She slouches against the frame as he steps out. 'I'm glad you're back in Consorting, Henry.'

Lowell is lurking. 'What about me, Heather?'

'I miss you like a hole in the head.'

'Steady on,' says Lowell. 'You say that to the wrong copper down here, you'll wind up with one.'

Heather sighs. 'Yeah, no shit.' She looks at Henry. 'Was he always *this* much of a dickhead? I forget.'

'Pretty much,' says Henry.

'It's true,' says Lowell.

CHAPTER 59

HENRY PUSHES ON. THE man called Robert Emmery lives in the penthouse of the Condor, one of the tallest apartment buildings on the Strip. Twenty-eight floors up, by the Nerang River.

Lowell hits the intercom and gets the maid. She puts Mr Emmery on.

'Yes?'

'Police. Can we have a chat?'

Emmery buzzes them through without comment, a sure sign that he's in with the local boys.

In the lift, Lowell says, 'Why are we interested in this bloke?'

'He's a john. I just need to have a quiet chat with him.'

'Oh okay. Do you want me to put him down and then you do the rest?'

'No, I mean, I *actually* want to have a chat with him.'

Lowell turns his nose up at that. *Soft.*

The maid is waiting by the lift. She tells them Emmery is on a call and ushers them through to the living room, where she serves refreshments. With a cup of tea and a Monte Carlo in hand, Lowell and Henry stand in silhouette against the bright panorama of the coast.

'Bit fucking much,' says Lowell. 'I'd shit myself if I saw this every morning. Not a big fan of heights.'

To Henry, it looks like success. They are right up above the fray. The whole thing looks calm and neutered from up here. The Strip. The inner suburbs. The grid-like streets. All of it impossibly quiet and quaint.

'Gentlemen?'

It's Emmery. He's mid-fifties and well put together. Barrel-chested, square-jawed. He has slicked black hair, matched to a neat black house robe. He wears plastic glasses that somehow only exaggerate his swagger.

Lowell pipes up first. 'Quite the get-up you have here, Robert.'

'Thank you. Sit. Please.'

'Sorry to intrude,' says Henry. 'We won't be long.'

'No problem, gents. What can I do for you?' Emmery settles into his chair. He crosses his legs and brushes something off an exposed knee.

Henry hands over the picture of Sarah Utton. 'Do you know this girl? Recognise her?'

'No. Should I?' Nothing in his eyes.

'She's missing.'

Emmery adjusts his glasses, takes another look. 'I'm sorry to hear that. I hope you find her.'

'Why?' says Lowell.

It's a bad play. The aggro in Lowell's quip immediately puts Emmery into a rehearsed stance.

'A pretty girl like this, it's always someone's daughter or sister. I'd think any sane person would want her found.'

Henry looks out the windows. 'Mr Emmery, have you ever hired a prostitute? And before you answer, we work in Consorting so—'

'We've fucked a lot of prostitutes,' says Lowell.

In the background, the maid takes her leave.

Henry waits. He says, 'There's no shame in it. Do you hire women?'

'I'm a happily married man, gents, so I can't see what business that is of yours. And it's not outlawed last time I checked.'

'I'm pretty sure it *is* illegal,' says Lowell.

Henry leans forward, lowers his voice. 'The talk around town is that you take girls to a place in Southport and that you have particular tastes.'

'Oh, really? Look, you can't believe half of what you hear about someone like me.'

'Maybe this is the true half?' says Lowell.

'It's simply not the case. I don't cheat on my wife. Never have, never will.'

Henry says, 'If I go up and down the coast and show all the hotel clerks and cleaners your picture, and Sarah Utton's picture, and ask about your particular tastes, it's not going to turn anything up, is it?'

Emmery emits a subdued sigh. 'Well, I'd obviously prefer that you didn't do that, but no, it's not going to *turn anything up*. You know, gents, I have good friends on the Force. I wouldn't want something like this to jeopardise that. That would make more than a few people unhappy and I don't want a lot of . . . unhappiness around me.'

'Are you offering us a bribe?' says Lowell.

'No.'

Lowell huffs. 'Pity. Let's get out of here.'

They stand up.

Henry says, 'I'm not in the business of making people happy, Mr Emmery.'

'Detective Loch, I'm *well* aware of that. But the truth is, I don't know this girl you're looking for. I really don't know her.'

'Yes, you do.'

'No,' says Emmery. 'I don't.'

'Come on,' says Lowell to Henry, 'before you get us both into trouble.'

•

An hour later, Henry sits in his unmarked and watches the Condor foyer. He's alone, with Lowell out for a stroll. The wait is hot and irritating, and Henry is about to pack it in when he spots a familiar face crossing the street up ahead. It's Tommy Lomax, the dirty, ageing hippie. Henry knows Tommy well. He's arrested him twice. He's Colleen Vinton's henchman. The guy who tunes up the girls when they step out of line. The enforcer. A real piece of shit. That Tommy is now stepping into the Condor lifts, headed up to see Robbie Emmery, it's all the confirmation Henry needs.

CHAPTER 60

LANA AND BRUNO CRUISE informant to informant, from street corner to caravan park, motel to servo. By early afternoon, they arrive at the parking lot of an amusement park down on the Spit where Bruno leads the way to a rusted green kombivan with makeshift curtains strung along the windows. To initiate proceedings, he kicks a two-foot-wide dint in the van's side panel.

The curtains part. A head appears. The side door of the van rolls open and a man stumbles out onto the gravel. He's barefoot and naked except for a pair of dirty blue undies. Long, greasy hair surrounds his face.

Bruno says, 'Hi Brad. How's things?'

'I was asleep.'

Bruno makes a show of peering into the van's interior. 'Am I going to find narcotics in here, Brad?'

Brad comes straight out with it. 'I've got a few sticks of weed and some speed.'

On the books, thinks Lana. She turns to Bruno and says, 'Is this guy gonna give us something or are we banging him up?'

'Oh man,' says Brad.

'Not a lot of time to waste today, Brad. You better tell her whatever she needs to know, quick smart.'

'I don't even know who she is.'

'You don't need to know,' says Lana. 'Tell me about Teddy Adams.'

Victim number one.

'This stuff again? Look, I never knew him. Met him once, but I never knew him other than that.'

'Eddie Edgar?'

'He was a prick, if you must know. Used to sell me booze on the sly when I was a kid, which is half the reason I got into this mess. I sold him some gear two years back. That's it.'

'Not good enough, Brad. I'm trying to impress her,' says Bruno. He puts a hand on Brad's shoulder.

'Lenny Gibbs,' says Lana.

'Fuck. I don't know anything about this stuff, just . . .'

Bruno brings his cuffs out with the other hand.

'All right, all right. I might've heard something about the other one. Someone told me something at the pub the other night.'

'What other one?' says Lana.

'The doctor.'

'Brian Amstell?'

'I don't know his name. Some Tweed Heads guy. I don't even know if it's the right guy, okay? I just heard something that might be . . .'

Bruno says, 'Come on, Brad.'

'I heard he was a pill connect for some of the girls up here, okay? He had the good stuff, apparently, and now he's dead and no one can get their gear. I'm selling weed hand over fist off the back of it. People are fucking antsy.'

'Who told you about the doctor?' says Lana.

'A customer.'

Bruno keeps the cuffs out. 'Who might want to knock off someone like that, Brad? You just said you're doing pretty well off the back of it.'

'Hey, not me, man. Are you kidding? I don't even know what this guy looks like, let alone anything else about him. I just heard the story and, you know, put two and two together.'

'This bloke is a regular Sherlock Holmes,' says Lana. 'Ever considered a career change, Brad?'

'I have actually.'

They both look at him.

'Yeah, man, yeah. *Division 4* and that. I love it.'

Lana shrugs. 'I've worked with worse.'

'You must have some idea how these pills are getting up here,' says Bruno. 'I can't see a doctor selling direct. Not our bloke. Did you move a bit of this shit for him, Brad? Is that what you're trying to tell me?'

'Wasn't me. I wish.'

'Come on,' says Lana. 'Your future career with us depends on it, Brad.'

'Nah, nah. We all keep to our, you know, our own patches. Vovo was the street connect for that stuff on the coast. When she died, I just thought, oh well. But then I hear this other bloke died too, and it's pretty weird.'

Lana opens her notebook. 'This Vovo got a real name?'

'Yeah, Violet.'

'Violet what?'

'Violet Burke?' says Bruno.

Victim number four.

'Yeah, yeah, I think that's Vovo's last name,' says Brad. 'Could be.'

CHAPTER 61

AN HOUR LATER, LANA meets Henry across the street from a bakery on the edge of Southport. They walk through the broadwater parklands, leaving their respective partners to glare at each other and make muted conversation over meat pies. Bruno wasn't keen on the meet-up, but he was hungry, and Lana sprang it on him. 'Fifteen minutes.'

Standing off the shore, wind whipping, Lana tells Henry about Amstell and the drug rumours, and the possible connection to Violet Burke.

He seems surprised. 'That slippery prick. I talked to Brad a couple of nights back and he didn't say any of this to me.'

'How'd you go with Robert Emmery?'

'He's dirty as hell. But I can't get a read on how it all fits together. I need a day to myself, just to plot it all out.'

'That sounds nice,' says Lana. 'I guess you've heard the chatter about Beggs?'

'It was on the radio. Last day, huh?'

Lana pinches the end of her smoke as she inhales. She nods.

'You could be back in New South Wales tomorrow,' he says, 'with all this behind you.'

'Nah, I'm no good with open cases. They get to me. And we've got your thing yet. So what's the next move?'

'Cupboard's bare on my end.'

'You know, Brian Amstell had heaps of case files in his office. When Bruno and I did a walk-through, he had them in cabinets right there where he worked, where he could *see* them. If he's up to something, like selling drugs, that could be an interesting place to take a look.'

'No time for a warrant,' Henry says. 'You know, Lowell is the station's go-to for . . .'

Lana plays it nonchalant, waits him out.

'He does a bit of off-book search and seizure, if you catch my drift? Knows his way around a lock or two. How hot are you for this?'

'That's the thing about being a woman in this game, Henry, everyone expects you to be one hundred per cent on the level.'

'And you're not?'

'No one is. Can you set it up with Lowell? We can go tonight after the clinic closes. I'm at the El Dorado.'

'Okay then. Lowell loves this shit. But, one condition.'

'Shoot.'

'Have a look for a file on Utton.'

'I can handle that. What are you up to now?'

'I'm tracking down someone who can help with Emmery.'

'Anyone interesting?'

'Oh yeah,' he says. 'This lady's plenty interesting.'

CHAPTER 62

ANGELA OWENS IS A low-life reporter working the crime beat for the *Gold Coast Bulletin*. She isn't much fun to be around—mean, drunk and sober—but she's easy to work with. She has a cushy deal with the local coppers. They feed her inside skinny and cash-in-hand, and in return Angela pulls whatever punches she can. Lately, she's had to fall in line, putting her in a tender position with the Diablo men, but she won't be on the outs for long. Henry finds her in one of her regular haunts, tucked into the corner of Bogart's, a tavern off Cavill Avenue.

'Henry Loch,' she says, 'King of the Prostitutes. What have I done to deserve this?'

'Just a quick chat, Ange.'

'Pig's arse. I see your partner still maintains a completely unfounded disdain for me.'

Henry follows her gaze across the room to where Lowell sits at the other end of the bar with his middle finger raised.

'Yeah, he's not a big reader. Look, I need some background on a property developer down here. Robert Emmery.'

'Oh dear,' she says.

'Is it that bad?'

'Order a jug and we'll go somewhere quiet.'

It takes a few pots and some nudging, but Angela spills the beans. Robert Emmery is clean on the surface. A good upstanding family man. A married Catholic. Three beautiful children. All the trappings to go with it, too. He owns that place in the Condor and a weekender across the border. He made his money subdividing back-lots in Brisbane, then funnelled it into large, risky bets on commercial real estate down here on the coast. 'He's got his money in a lot of buildings you drive past every day, Henry. He's big time.'

'Is he a crook, though?'

'God no,' says Angela. 'He's an elite. That's why the crooks all want him around.'

Henry shows her a picture of Utton. 'I'm looking at him as a possible connection to this girl's disappearance. Any ideas?'

'That's Sarah, right?'

'You know her?'

'Of course. Who could forget that face? Worked out of Tropical Touch, if memory serves.'

'That's right. She involved in anything hinky?'

Angela glances around. 'Nothing specific.'

'I think she's pregnant,' Henry says.

'That's an interesting situation.' Angela takes out her notebook. 'Emmery's going to be the public face of the casino bid. You hear about this? That's the plan. Things are lucrative upstairs in the government at the moment. They're trying to take it legit.'

'A legal casino here in Queensland?'

'It's true. There's backing from all ends. The premier from on high and Vinton from below. It's going to be a gold mine, when it gets up.'

'And Emmery's the point man?'

'That's the plan. And if he's knocked up some local prostitute, that might put a dampener on things. There would be ripples all over.'

Ripples, Henry thinks.

It would be more than that.

CHAPTER 63

LANA COHEN PACES THE carpet of her room in the El Dorado, dressed head to toe in black.

Someone knocks at the door.

She checks the peephole.

It's Lowell.

He takes one look at her black get-up and says, 'Hey, Catwoman, go put on your detective get-up. You don't want to spook the neighbours when we break into this joint.'

'What if we get caught?'

'By who? The police?'

•

Brian Amstell's clinic is dark and closed up for the night. Lana and Lowell stand on the footpath across the street, casing it out. The place is deserted. Another dead-to-the-world Monday night.

Lowell pushes the balance of a Mars Bar into his gob and garbles, 'It's like a bloody bomb went off. I was hoping for a bit more excitement down here.'

'Welcome to the Tweed, buddy.'

He cocks his head. 'You hear that?'

'What?'

'I think I hear a crime being committed. We should investigate.' As they cross the bitumen, Lowell says, 'You married, Cohen?'

'Piss off.'

'It's an innocent question.'

'I'm married to the head of Internal Investigations.'

'Really?'

'No.'

Lana leads him down the side of the clinic through a narrow alleyway. Around the back, she points to a fire exit she remembers from the previous visit. 'You think you can handle that?'

'I'm not just a pretty face,' he says, kneeling down to study the lock. After a minute, he stands back up, puts his hand on the door and says, 'I hope there's no electronic alarm.'

'Lowell—'

He pushes it open.

Silence.

'No alarm then,' he says. 'It could be a silent alarm, I guess.'

'Are you joking?'

She follows him into the building. Lowell produces a flashlight and immediately checks the ceiling corners. 'No sensors. We're fine.'

The door to Brian Amstell's office is open. She points at the filing cabinets in the corner. 'I need these unlocked.'

Lowell pops the locks as quickly as if he had a key. Inside the first cabinet, he finds a spare set of keys and tosses them to Lana. 'Okay, what are we looking for here?'

'Anything related to Diablo? You check the victims' names. I'll do the rest.'

'Who was the first one again?'

'Lowell.'

He flicks through files. 'Yeah, yeah. Henry told me you were like this.'

Lana searches the name tags. 'Like what?'

'Like *this*. Boring.'

'That doesn't sound like Henry.'

'Henry likes boring.' He stops searching. 'Come to think of it, I don't think it was him. What have you heard about me?'

'Nothing much. That you're a fuckhead, mainly.'

'Steady on. Who said that?'

'Everyone.'

Lana comes to the U section and finds *Sarah Utton*. 'Bingo.' She has a black sports bag with her and slips the file in, then works her way up the cabinet from there. 'You got anything?'

'Violet Burke,' says Lowell, putting the file in the bag.

'Does Amstell have a file on himself?'

Lowell checks it. 'Nope.'

'I'm going to have a quick look around,' she says. 'Then we can get out of here.'

She checks the other offices. All the doors are unlocked except one, but the keys don't open it. Giving up, she concentrates on the front of the building where there is a filing system on rollers in a purpose-built room behind the front desk. Lana grabs a stepladder and flicks through, looking for relevant names and finding nothing of interest. The files are mainly for skin treatments, cancer recovery and various ailments of the elderly.

Back in Brian's office, Lowell is down behind the doctor's desk.

'Let's go,' she says.

'Okay,' he whispers.

He stands, but Lana can hear the shuffling of paper and clothing in the dark.

'You find anything?' she says.

'Nah.'

Lana grabs the sports bag and they hightail it back to the car.

'Hang on a sec,' says Lowell, going to the boot.

In the side mirror, Lana watches him put something inside.

She hits the ignition.

When Lowell slips into the passenger seat, he's cradling a six-pack of XXXX Bitter. 'Fancy a bevvie?'

Lana guns the engine without comment.

CHAPTER 64

FLYING SOLO, HENRY LOCH cruises the coastline, showing his grainy newsprint photo of Robert Emmery to anyone in hospitality. He gets a few hits—people know Emmery's face—but nothing lands. Nothing's right. Around 10 pm, he drives to the motel on Oak Avenue to check in on Heather and her friend Kimmy. At the door, Heather gets straight into it. 'She's here now.'

Kimmy is in the back room, asleep in a waterbed with black cotton sheets. Beside Kimmy lies a naked man, face down, a patchwork of scars and tattoos across his back.

Henry bends down and gently rubs Kimmy's shoulder. 'Wake up, darlin'.'

'What the?'

'You're not in trouble,' he says. He holds up his pictures of Robert Emmery and Sarah Utton. 'Is this the threesome you worked a couple of months back?'

Kimmy reaches over and clicks on a bedside lamp. Smarting from the light, she takes the photos, rolls onto her back, and brings the pictures in close. 'Yeah, that's him.'

'That's the first good news I've had all day.'

'Am I going to get into trouble for this?'

'No. But I don't think you should hang around the coast. You got somewhere you can go?'

'I'll think of something. Been meaning to leave, anyhow. Is Robbie in trouble too?'

'Maybe.'

'I hope not. He was nice to us, you know. I mean, he's a perv, but he never treated us bad or anything. I can't see him hurting Sarah.'

'Well, we'll see. Who's this?' Henry motions to the man in the bed. He remains passed out, despite the light.

'Some fucking guy,' Kimmy says.

'Those are Doomrider tatts. You better be careful.'

'Yeah, yeah.'

'And Kimmy?'

'Yeah?'

'I owe you one. You ever get locked up, you tell 'em to call me. Henry Loch.'

'You better pick up.' She snaps the light off.

'I will. Night.'

'Yeah, goodnight, Henry.'

Back out in the living room, he hands a bag of pills to Heather. She drops one immediately, pushing it down dry. 'You get what you need?' she asks.

'I did.'

'Fancy a drink?'

'Another time.'

•

Out on the street, Henry finds the night has cooled off. He makes his way back to the car, noticing a few drunks wandering through, and two women out for a jog. Further down the street, he spots a figure in the shadow of an apartment building, a man out for a smoke, obscured by the garden separating the building from the street. Henry watches the cherry of the man's cigarette glow, illuminating his face for an instant. A large furry beard and glasses. Something off about him, some detail out of place, but it's that sort of street.

As he draws level, Henry peers through the garden shrubs. The man is still there. A golden flicker shines out of his beard. 'That breeze has picked up,' Henry says.

The man silently steps back into the darkness.

Henry decides to leave it.

Just some fucking weirdo.

And yet, a little further down the street, Henry stops and finds he can't let it go.

The golden flicker.

Jewellery.

He met a guy—

Henry snaps, turns. No decision, all instinct. The bearded man is already off running. He's slipped through the garden of the complex and is halfway across the street. Henry ducks down, scurries across to a parked car and watches. The bearded man climbs into a green van. For a split second, Henry sees him clearly. The beard is a shabby costume piece, and under the costume, he recognises the face—or the shape of it, at least. But he can't drag the memory forward.

The van takes off.

Henry whispers to himself, 'Motherfuck.'

He races back to his car, hands shaking, fumbling the keys.

Driver's door opening.

Ignition, ignition, igni—

Clutch in, foot down.

He pushes himself to keep the car moving slowly. No sign of the van ahead.

As Henry creeps up the street, he calls it in, talking into the radio set as he checks the adjacent roadways. 'Dispatch, I'm tracking a vehicle moving in the vicinity of Oak Avenue. Green van. Possible Diablo suspect. Requesting all available units.'

'Roger that. Mobile units on their way.'

At Birt Avenue, Henry throws caution to the wind and hooks it left towards the esplanade.

The street ends.

Waiting at the red lights, Henry peers around frantically.

'Come on!'

The green van moves out onto the road further down. The driver must've parked out of sight for a minute before deciding the coast is clear.

Henry lets the van get moving before gently turning across the inter-section and following at a distance.

'Dispatch, I have eyes on the suspect. I'm on the Gold Coast highway heading south. Repeat, on the highway, heading south.'

In tandem, they drive down into Broadbeach, take a detour along the esplanade and then back out to the main drag where the van moves at a slightly faster clip, pushing towards the New South Wales border. In pursuit, Henry finds himself in a dream state, his hands tight around the wheel, eyes locked onto the van, his mind churning.

The costume beard.

Pudgy.

Familiar.

They hit Miami.

Then Burleigh.

The green van is the confirmation.

But the face? Henry struggles through the panic and fog. He pushes his mind.

They drive through Palm Beach.

Through Currumbin.

They're rounding the bend to Tugun when it clicks.

Daryl Millman.

The property valuer.

Owner of a green van.

Henry interviewed him the week previous, while running bullshit rego checks the day after Brian Amstell's death.

It's him.

Millman is the gruff bloke, wearing jewellery, wrist and neck.

The golden flicker.

At the movies on the night of the murders.

'Fucking *Star Wars*,' Henry says to himself. 'His favourite movie is *Star Wars*.'

He slaps the wheel.

Up ahead, the van moves a little quicker. Henry senses he's been made. He stays back but keeps on him. In the rear-view mirror, a squad car pulls out from a side street, joining the pursuit.

Henry lifts the radio mic and gives his car number and says, 'We're about to cross the border into New South Wales. Please alert the Tweed Heads Station.'

'Roger that.'

Millman takes them off the main road and into the back streets of Kirra. They snake through the suburbs, losing the squad car and then come back out onto Wharf Street and down to Terranora Creek. The roads are empty here. On Boyds Bridge they pass a single oncoming truck. Two squad cars in the rear-view now. No mistaking what's happening.

As they near the southern end of the bridge, the van slows to a crawl.

Henry matches it, keeping a hundred feet between them.

The van moves diagonally across both lanes, blocking the bridge. The park lights come on.

Henry grabs the radio. 'We've got a problem.'

Movement up ahead.

Henry's windscreen pops as gunshots boom and echo. He throws himself prone and the windscreen explodes, glass spraying. Glass on his hands, in his hair.

Tyres squealing.

Shouting.

More shots and flashes of light.

Terrified, Henry scrambles for his gun and dives through the passenger door, slipping out onto the bitumen.

The sound of running.

Glass crunching, sliding off him. Shards in him.

He peers over the bonnet. The van sits idling in the distance.

Fuck it.

Henry runs, gun trained on the driver's window and then down into the cabin as he comes round.

Empty.

A voice calls out, 'He went that way.' A patrolwoman. She points into the bushland beside the bridge.

Henry runs straight to it, jumping the guardrail, feet hitting the grass and gravel of the road shoulder. He can't see Millman but hurtles across the flat ground into dark scrubland, following shadows and movement, feet falling heavy.

Another shot rings out. A nearby tree sprays bark.

Henry ducks down and scans around. 'Daryl,' he yells. 'It's over.'

Another shot booms.

Henry waits, his breath impossibly loud in his chest. He looks out from the cover and fires at what looks like a man in the distance. When the retort fades, he can hear running and follows suit. Still without a visual, Henry pushes on.

The bushland gives way to a creekside road. House lights dot the distance. The roadway is empty and Henry figures Millman could be in the trees lining the creek. He heads that way. The sound of sirens in the distance now, and another sound underneath, a throttling industrial noise. Henry recognises it. It's a motorboat engine turning over.

He sees him then. Millman in a boat, moving away from the shore, a dark silhouette in the moonlight, white water parting around the bow.

Henry runs, aims his gun and fires.

Nothing.

He fires again, coming up on the mangroves.

The boat continues out.

Henry dives through the bush and wades out into the water, waist-deep, still firing his gun into the night, firing it until it's empty, but the boat keeps moving.

DAY SIX

TUESDAY, 26 FEBRUARY 1980

JOURNAL OF EMMETT HADES

(SELECTED EXCERPTS)

I'm writing this in my shed on a rough timber workbench beside a table lamp and a police scanner. That's how I heard the call last night. Oak Avenue. Green van. Possible Diablo suspect. Requesting all available units. Henry's voice. He sounded scared.

I left immediately, slipping into the Falcon without changing out of my house clothes. I know Oak Avenue. It's fifteen minutes from here and the streets were dead. As I drove over, I'll admit to being rammed full of emotion. I was thinking about Ruben and the blood and the other victims. I was mumbling their names again, feeling happy and sad and relieved and ready, all at the same time. That's nothing new. There's no correct way to feel in this line of work. There's just the stuff you let out and the stuff you keep in. Rupture and repair. A proper homicide investigation is all about that stuff. The everyday world gets put off kilter, and you try to put it back. In the doing, you ruffle every feather, turn every stone. You invite disruption in and break the case open. Fight fire with fire. Disorder versus disorder. It takes a madman or a villain to deal with the magnitude of it. The end is always difficult.

So last night, I let it all slip and slide around inside me. An old man out for a night drive, unsure of everything, but still trying to find an answer, anyhow. A glimpse. I don't know. Broken as I am, there seemed to be no purpose to my actions, beyond seeing the thing through.

CHAPTER 65

AFTER TWO HOURS SLEEP, Lana wakes to Bruno banging on the motel room door, barking, 'Get your stuff.'

They drive south into the dead of night.

Lana rolls her neck. 'What do we have exactly?'

'Your mate Henry has a bead on our guy. Suspect is Daryl Millman. He came across him last week doing rego checks. Then last night, Henry spotted him in Surfers Paradise and the guy bolted, got into a green van and legged it across the border. There was some sort of shoot-out on Boyds Bridge, but everyone's okay.'

'Boyds Bridge? How do I know that name?'

'You can see it from the Amstell scene.'

'No shit.'

'And get this, Millman absconded by boat. Henry chased him along Terranora Creek, almost through our scene, and out onto the river where, for reasons no one can really work out, Millman had a tinnie ready to go. The water guys are out there looking for him at the moment.'

'Did he go upriver or—'

'Don't know.'

'Do they need us for the search? What's the deal?'

'We're headed to Millman's house. He owns a place down in Coolangatta. Apparently, it's worth seeing.'

'So, this is our guy?'

'That's what they're saying.'

Lana winds down the window and fires up a smoke. 'Henry Loch, hey.'

'Yeah,' says Bruno, shaking his head. 'This bloody job.'

•

Daryl Millman's house is a low-set brown brick place in a wide street. It's on a new estate, inland from the coast. The estate is dark and barren, but not tonight. Tonight, the science team have the house lit up like a stage play. Lana counts more than a dozen officers standing in the front yard alone.

'Great night to knock over a bottle shop,' Bruno says as he shows his badge to the officer on scene. They pass through the cordon. 'What do you reckon?'

Lana says, 'Let's have a snout around.'

The house is heaving. Diablo detectives bustle through, shouting between rooms and squabbling with the science team, who seem to be fighting a losing battle to keep the scene intact. At the front of the house, there are two bedrooms. Both have single beds in them, but one acts as a library, the walls lined with books. The other is where Millman sleeps. All of it is pristinely neat and clean, and yet all the detectives wear disposable face masks because the entire house smells of rot and human waste.

Further in, the kitchen is so crowded with officers that Lana has to push her way through as if passing through a nightclub throng. As she sets foot in the rear lounge, she sees why the other men have stayed back. The lounge room is devoid of furniture. Down the far end, standing free of the walls, is a human-scale crucifix wrapped tightly in visqueen plastic. Under the plastic is a heavily decomposed body nailed to the cross.

'What the actual fuck?' says Lana.

A man in front turns around. It's Bingham. 'It's not good,' he says.

'Any idea who it is?' says Bruno.

Bingham looks past them, spotting a figure lurking in the corner. 'You tell 'em. It's your story.'

Emmett Hades steps into view. He puts his hand out to Lana.

'I was wondering when I'd run into you,' she says, but it comes out slow as she notices Emmett's get-up. He's in his bedclothes, as if he just stepped out for milk.

'Here I am,' he says.

'Glad you're here,' says Bruno, looking anything but.

Lana motions to the cross. 'What have we got?'

'An old friend,' says Emmett. 'Looking at the trauma around the joints, I'd bet money that's Ruben Davis. He was murdered in his home about a year before Teddy Adams, but we never found the body. I've been looking for him ever since.'

'That body's been . . .' Lana trails off.

'Yes, hanging up there for years, possibly. The science men tell me he's done some sort of amateur embalming, but it hasn't worked too well.'

Bruno's looking closer at the body now. Lana remembers that he worked the Davis case. 'He doesn't look right,' he says. 'He's kind of . . . wonky.'

Emmett swallows and says, 'Bruno, he cut him up, remember? The different parts are attached to the cross with zip ties and, as time has elapsed, the decomposition has—'

Bruno runs for it but doesn't make it. About three feet from the door, he trips and falls, chasing a plume of vomit as it erupts from his mouth.

The room goes quiet for a moment.

'Get him up,' says Bingham.

Lana and Emmett help Bruno out. They sit him down in a lawn chair. Lana gives him a cigarette, 'Here,' but Bruno brushes it away. She starts on it herself.

A minute later, Mark Evans sidles along. 'What's wrong with him?'

'He's sick,' says Lana.

'Fair enough.'

'Is there anything we need to be doing?' she says.

'No,' says Mark. 'Stay out here. We'll brief everyone in a few minutes. It's going to be a long day.'

'I'm okay,' says Bruno.

But he isn't.

CHAPTER 66

IT'S A BALMY SUMMER night, an hour before dawn, and the detectives out back of Daryl Millman's house roll up their sleeves and unbutton their shirts. To Lana, they look like a bunch of plumbers having a Friday night barbecue.

'Come on,' yells Bingham. 'Circle in.' He stands out on the grass with his secretary, Anne-Marie. 'We've got maybe four hours, at best, before the newspapers get a hold of this. From there, we've got a day, gentlemen. A day before they go to press with how we lost him. But if we can find him, we turn the whole caper around. You could all be going home tonight knowing you solved *eight* murders.'

Bingham passes the meeting over to Mark Evans and Mark says, 'The basic description of Millman is already out there. Every mobile patrol and uniform from Cairns to Sydney has it by now. There are roadblocks in place, up and down the coast. The airport staff are on alert. This prick is not going anywhere. Now, Anne-Marie has copies of all the personal information we have on him. Myself and Reynolds will be in the Diablo room all day, going through the paperwork and coordinating the search. Please stay in contact. Check in regularly. I'm going to hand you back to Ron, to coordinate further.'

As always, Bingham is far less eloquent. 'Time to fucking do this,' he says, and he puts the detectives in teams and divides up the work.

In their huddle, Lana and Bruno review the task list. It's New South Wales liaison, then helping out with the canvass of Millman's street.

'This guy has a wife, right?' says a nearby detective.

'Where'd you hear that?' says another.

Lana is head down in Anne-Marie's memo, barely paying attention.

'Apparently the wife is in some filing of Henry's.'

'Where is he?'

A familiar voice replies, 'Fuck knows.' It's Lowell Sennett. He's leaning against the side fence. 'At a guess, I'd say he's back at the station giving a statement.'

'I thought he'd be here by now.'

'So did I,' says Lowell. 'I guess he took his ejection from the taskforce personally. Seems to me he's been doing a pretty good job of it on his own.'

'And you?' says Bruno.

'Oh, you know me, mate. Team player.'

That gets a chuckle from the other men in the huddle.

Emmett says, 'I don't suppose you remember anything from the interview with Millman?'

Lowell takes a moment. 'I must've missed that one. That was all Henry. It's nice that you dressed up for this, Em.'

Bruno tightens his jaw. 'Lowell, do you have anything valuable to offer? Or are you just here to gloat?'

'Hard to say at this point.'

'Can it, you two,' says Lana. 'Bruno and I will deal with my side of the border and coordinate with the locals, then swing back when we're done. The rest of you can go straight out to the street canvass if you like.'

Bruno, eyes still on Lowell, says, 'Maybe you should go find your partner?'

'He'll be around somewhere.'

They break out.

Back out on the street, Lana finishes a smoke as Bruno waits in the car beside her. She notices Emmett and Bingham on the front lawn of Millman's house. Two old policemen in quiet conversation. Emmett looks bothered—confused almost—and he keeps talking, but as he talks, he's inching away from Bingham. Eventually they separate and Emmett walks to his car. Lana finds it an odd moment: the great Emmett Hades in his pyjamas, in his car, completely expressionless, staring out the windscreen at Bingham, who is staring back.

CHAPTER 67

BY 4.30 AM, HENRY is back out amongst it, creeping the suburban streets of the Tweed as a tangerine dawn tints the night sky. He's flying solo, searching the northern bank of Terranora Creek on foot. Millman could be out here somewhere, holed up and waiting. Henry explores the muddy creek beds and mangroves, jolting at every movement.

A lot has happened in the last six hours.

Breaking open the case.

The chase.

Getting shot at.

Giving statements.

Maybe solving the thing?

Maybe winning?

It's wearing on him. He's still damp from the river. His wallet is soaked. The junior detective who took his statement back at the station got a laugh out of that. 'Were you going to swim after him, mate?'

'I've had worse ideas.'

Now, as Henry wanders through the mud and ripe heat of the mangroves, a type of delirium takes hold.

It was hot that night too, he thinks. The night in the field outside Beaudesert.

Hot like this.

And lonely like this too.

Stumbling around, Henry feels all his bad energy beginning to boil, fatigue bringing it on. He cuts down a gravel path and into another thick grove of trees, disappearing into the darkness.

CHAPTER 68

LOWELL FINDS HENRY STAGGERING along some lone back street. He brings the car up alongside him and calls through the window, 'Hey, dickhead, are you hungry?'

Henry mops his brow.

'Get in,' Lowell says, popping the door.

Out on the main drag with the wind gushing through the windows, Henry sucks water from a steel thermos and tries to block out Lowell's banter. Lowell claims he found him through a dispatch call. Two constables spotted a bloke matching Henry's description wandering around the creek. 'It took another hour though, bloody hell.'

They stop at a bakery in Tugun where Henry wolfs down a sandwich and a cream bun. The food helps. It calms him down a notch. He says, 'How are we assigned today?'

'They've got everyone in Licensing and Consorting on the prowl for Millman up in town. They're scared stiff he's going to lash out on the Strip. Long odds if you ask me.'

'You been to the house?'

Lowell wipes flakes of pastry from his mouth. 'Yeah.'

'And?'

'Not good.' He forces himself to swallow. 'You hear about the bloke strung up in the living room?'

'There was chatter at the station,' Henry says. 'Was it Emmett's cold case?'

'Yeah, Ruben Davis. Emmett was there last night.'

'Really? How'd he seem?'

'Still mad as a shithouse rat. He was in his pyjamas.'

'He was right about Ruben Davis.'

'I guess. Your girlfriend was there too. She was asking after you.'

'How'd you go with her at the doctor's office?'

'Good, I think.'

Henry gets up from the table. 'Back in a minute.' He walks across the street to a payphone and slips a coin into the slot. Dispatch puts a call out to Lana's car with the box number and two minutes later, the phone rings.

She says, 'Jesus, Henry. That sounded close last night.'

'You'd know.'

'He didn't shoot at me.'

The phone clunks abruptly. Henry can hear her moving around in the phone box on her end, closing the door.

'Sorry. Bruno's lurking. I got medical files on Sarah Utton and Violet Burke last night. Haven't had a chance to really look at them yet with all this going on, but there's something else.'

'What?'

'I think Lowell pinched something from the office. He was real cagey when we were done. I think he slipped something into the boot of the car on the way out. Figured you should know. I just have a weird feeling about it. Why would he do that?'

'The sky's the limit with Lowell. I've seen him do all sorts of weird shit. Let's get together tomorrow when all this blows over and see where we stand on Utton.'

'Deal.'

'Anything else?'

'No. Congratulations, I guess. You kinda did it,' she says.

'It doesn't feel like it.'

'Give it time.'

Henry crosses back to the bakery. Lowell's inside getting the bathroom key. Henry watches him disappear down a side alley. With the coast clear, Henry moves to the car, leans in through the driver's window and pops the boot. A few feet from the traffic, under the morning glare, he takes a quick inventory of Lowell's stuff.

A half-empty bottle of Bundaberg Rum.

A cricket bat and sports bag.

An emergency firearm. Lowell's personal piece. A shotgun, sawn down.

A dog-eared James A. Michener novel.

A box of condoms.

A pile of skin mags.

Unopened mail.

And a medical file.

Henry grabs the file and walks. A few blocks over, he hails a cab and gets into the rear bench.

'You from Melbourne, mate?' says the cabbie.

'Fuck off, I'm a cop. Get moving.'

Henry examines the file. It's big. The name on the cover reads, Colleen Vinton. He opens it up and starts scanning text, forms, appointments, details. There are consultations and prescriptions. Names. Dates. Clinics. Henry's mind buzzes, harsh noise in his ears. On the last page, there's a photograph taped inside, a picture of Colleen that lights Henry up like a flamethrower.

It's a landscape image of Diablo victims and missing connections. Teddy Adams beside Lenny Gibbs beside Joel Delaney. All dead, but not in this picture. Here they're smiling, holding drinks. In the centre of the frame is Colleen Vinton and, holding Vinton's hand, is the young man from Wesley Bowman's lurid photo room centrepiece. This is a candid pic, from the same night. The man is naked bar for a leather thong. And Vinton, of course, is dressed like a nun, holding up a dark red dildo like a prized catch.

Henry flips the photo over and finds handwritten names.

The kid is *Peter Hanlon*.

Henry flashes back to Wesley Bowman and his sick photo wall:

Topped himself.

His father's a priest, I've been told.

Peter looks just like Father Frank Hanlon.

Brian Amstell's priest from across the border.

Henry forces himself to breathe.

CHAPTER 69

LANA AND BRUNO TALK to the Tweed Heads police and have a look through their nightly reporting, before switching gears and working the street canvass in Daryl Millman's neighbourhood. The canvass turns up stories of an otherwise ordinary man. Millman is a bit grumpy, by all reports, but mows his own lawn and waves to the neighbours. No parties. No strange comings and goings.

An early rego check with Millman mentions a wife, but no one living nearby saw him with a woman. Not one. A Diablo detective called Brian Siegler did the initial interview. Thing is, under mounting pressure, Siegler admits he probably didn't *actually talk* to the wife. He can't remember the details, either way. 'I was doing bloody rego checks, wasn't I? Maybe Millman mentioned a wife or said he'd been out with her? I don't know.' The whole thing is a shambles and, by early afternoon, Siegler is stood down *for being a boofhead*. Everyone at the crime scene is talking about it. Everyone's fuming.

Frustrated by the lack of progress, Lana and Bruno return to the station and work the case from their desks, helping with the frantic paper trail and endless calls. A team of detectives at Millman's work radio in, but there are no clues there: no one at the office gave two shits about him. He was a diligent property valuer. He played a mean hand of bridge on his lunch hour. He worked back, when needed. Millman wore a pungent cologne to the office every day, for reasons now clear—he lived with a corpse—but there was nothing else. He was a quiet, boring guy, apparently. The detectives on site describe religious knick-knacks in his desk drawer and three versions of the bible spread about. An interview with a secretary two partitions over mentioned a church group, and that he once complimented her on a crucifix necklace, but that's as kinky as he got. The extent of his outward madness.

The remaining items from Millman's house are also somewhat routine: clothing and personal effects, mail and papers, all above board. No drug paraphernalia. No porn stash. No sex dungeon or splatter film collection. He has *Rocky and Bullwinkle* coffee cups in the kitchen cabinet. Fridge magnets for the local mechanic. A wall calendar with dogs on it. Detective Reynolds—on speakerphone from the scene—puts it bluntly, 'Aside from killing people, ol' Daryl here might be the most boring bastard who ever lived.'

That's where it lands.

•

After a late lunch, Lana and Bruno take a break from it, just the two of them out in the station carpark. Bruno doesn't look so hot. He's getting flustered and tired. 'We could lose this guy,' he says. 'He's a fucking church mouse. Could be anywhere. No one will notice this bloke on the street.'

Lana agrees. They're at a bit of a loose end. 'Gotta keep moving, though.'

'I'm all ears.'

'What about the local churches?'

'I was on that for a minute. The girls inside have been running them down all morning. He's not a paid-up member of any outfit that they can find. But a bible basher like him, he's going to be a big wheel somewhere. It's literally all he did on the weekend.'

'Sounds fishy, like he's . . . I dunno.'

'Hiding out? Using an alias at church?'

'Could be. How'd you feel about a quick run around? Let's show people a photo of him and get it knocked over. Someone will recognise his face, surely, and then at least we'll have him squared away on that front.'

'It beats this,' Bruno says.

•

They split it up. A dozen churches, both sides of the border. Lana figures a New South Wales congregation is an either-way bet for a wolf trying to hide out with the flock. Going to mass across the river makes sense. There's less chance of running into a fellow parishioner on the street or at work.

Unfortunately, this line of enquiry doesn't pan out. At the first ten New South Wales churches, Lana meets priests of all dominations— rotund men with soft hands, tall ghoulish men in starched shirts, and young and bright-eyed zealots with neat hair—and none of them recognise Millman or show any sign of deceit. Lana walks the grounds and buildings of these places, showing Millman's image to anyone who'll look (committee members, florists, an organist, yard people) and, throughout, she comes up short. *He looks like one of ours,* is as close as she gets. But Millman doesn't belong anywhere.

By sundown, Lana finds herself at Saint Andrews Catholic, a place with a familiar name but not much else. Inside, walking gently up the carpeted centre aisle, she spots a man kneeling at the altar. Dressed in black, the priest is as still as the surrounding church. A soft flickering candlelight washes his face. He has his hands on the rail, eyes clenched shut.

Lana clears her throat, hoping to rouse him.

The man keeps praying.

'Excuse me?' she says.

Nothing.

Lana gently taps his shoulder.

The priest's eyes shoot open. 'Jesus wept,' he says.

'Sorry, Father. Sorry. I didn't mean to disturb you.'

'No, no. Oh, I, I think I was sleeping. Was I sleeping?'

'Praying or sleeping.'

'It gets to be all the same at some point.' He slowly gets up, his knees cracking audibly. As he turns towards her, Lana recognises him. It's the ranting priest from the television news. The police-hater.

'I'm Frank Hanlon.'

'Lana Cohen. I'm a Homicide detective working a local case.' She shows him her badge. 'Can I ask you a few questions?'

'You can ask.'

They study each other.

'It's all anyone can do,' he adds.

'Ask and ye shall receive, isn't it?'

'That only works with God.'

'I'm looking for a man called Daryl Millman, wanted in connection with an ongoing homicide investigation across the river. Do you recognise him? He's a churchgoer. We're doing the rounds.'

Hanlon takes the photograph and studies it in the low light. 'Hard to say,' he says, handing the picture back.

'Hard to say? So, a *maybe* then?'

'Give me a minute.'

Hanlon leads her out onto the parish steps and sparks up a cigarette from his pack, glancing over as Lana does the same. He says, 'Are you scared of dying, detective?'

'What?'

Hanlon holds up the cigarette.

'Oh,' she says. 'I reckon the stress is going to get me before these things.'

'Same here. It's not easy getting people to live by the rules, is it? I think I'd prefer a heart attack over lung cancer, all the same. Go out clean.'

'A copper can always go out clean,' she says, holding her hand against her temple like a gun.

'That doesn't work with my lot. So how did a copper like you get involved in this mess?'

'A few of the bodies fell this side of the border.'

'Oh, that's right.'

'I'm the only New South Wales officer on it at the moment.'

'That sorry lot needs all the help they can get,' he says.

'I'm familiar with your take on it, actually. Saw you on the local news the other night. Have to admit, I'm not sure you're any sort of authority on how a police investigation should be run. No offence.'

Hanlon chuckles. 'None taken. But in my defence, I know more than I want to about Gold Coast policing. You from around here?'

'Sydney.'

'Well then, I'm sure you've seen your share of it down there as well, but up here it's a nightmare. Corrupt to the bone. Diablo is just the last in a long line of it. Do you know Emmett Hades?'

'I met him last night.'

'He's part of my congregation. When they tossed him aside, that was the last straw for me. I preach to all types down here, you see. It's not just the good and the kind. I've got working girls, gamblers, drug dealers, a reformed pornographer, the lot. I get troubled souls from Sea World to Coolangatta. They all find their way south for some reason. I've got years and years of these stories and all of them are the same. Bad men with badges, running roughshod over everyone else, concealing their sins and corralling power. Men like the men you work with. Except Emmett, a rare example of a good one, who gets thrown away like street garbage.'

'Well, he was in his pyjamas when I met him. Is he getting help?'

Hanlon ignores it. 'He's a brilliant man.'

'I know. I've read the case reports. But . . .'

'What?'

'People change. Okay, I best get out of your hair. Can you have another look at this photo before I go?'

Hanlon gives it a longer look. 'I don't know this man.'

Lana flicks her cigarette onto the gravel drive, then steps down and grinds it out. 'You take care, Father. And go easy on Diablo next time someone shoves a microphone in your face. You're not helping.'

'I don't know about that,' he says.

'I do.'

'He who hates reproof will die.'

'Where's that from?'

Hanlon points to the sky.

CHAPTER 70

LANA ROARS OUT OF the church carpark and hits the streets. A few blocks away, she pulls over and radios Bruno. 'You'll never guess who I just ran into. Father Frank Hanlon.'

'Really?'

'Yep, and guess what church he's head of? Saint Andrews.'

'Sounds familiar.' He takes a second. 'That's Brian Amstell's spot.'

'Correct. I completely forgot. I just barrelled in there. Let me tell you, Hanlon gives me the creeps, and his church keeps popping up.'

'That's religion for you.'

'I'm going to have a harder look at him. There's something off. You turn up anything on your end?'

'Nothing. Dispatch is looking for people to head over to Millman's house. They found a stash of new evidence in the ceiling. Wanna go?'

'May as well,' she says.

Lana signs off and sits there in the car, waiting for a thought to arrive, an idea out on the edges of her thinking.

Nothing.

She's still sitting there when a car rolls by.

Dark green sedan.

Single figure inside.

Lana watches it go and knows it's Hanlon.

Just knows.

•

Ron Bingham sits in the gutter outside Millman's house, holding a hamburger in one hand and an empty beer in the other.

'Evening, sir,' says Bruno.

Bingham looks at them, glassy-eyed, his thinning hair every which way. The stench of sweat and second-hand smoke waft off him. 'Go on then,' he says without cheer.

Inside the house, Lana and Bruno locate a similar mood. The morning's excitement has collapsed into exhausted despair. There's no sign of Millman. The interior of his house is quiet. In the library, five Diablo detectives sit around on kitchen chairs, silently hunched over notebooks and loose-leaf pages. There's a lot of material. Boxes of it. Already grim, the scene is washed in soft yellow light courtesy of an overhead fitting filled with dead silverfish. 'Grab a pile,' says one of the detectives, a greeting of sorts, and he throws a box of paperwork at their feet.

'All this was in the roof?' says Bruno.

One of them points to the bedroom across the hall. 'In there.'

Lana takes a look. A two-metre square panel of plasterboard lies on the bed. In the room's corner, there's an equivalent hole in the ceiling.

'He had the ceiling cavity partitioned off,' calls one detective. 'The science blokes were up in the roof earlier in the day but went through the storage hatch in the laundry. The sneaky bastard had this other part sealed up so you couldn't see it.'

She hears Bruno ask, 'Who found it?'

They all laugh.

'Bingham,' says one of them. 'Our fearless leader decided to take a camp on the bed in there and noticed the ceiling joinery was out of whack.'

'Bloody hell,' says Bruno.

Lana goes back. 'What's it look like so far?'

'What you'd expect. Detailed. Boring. Scary.'

There are no chairs left in the house. Bruno brings in two milk crates from the backyard. The two of them sit on their crates in the hallway and get to work.

Lana flicks through a black cloth-bound notebook from a box. It's a logbook of some kind, containing short, abbreviated sentences.

E leaves the store, heads west.

E stops for fuel at the station on Pacific Avenue.

E turns in.

Bruno gives her a look at his. It's the same deal, but about someone called *T.*

Lana tries another book from the pile, then another. There are journals filled with routine daily life, tax and expense ledgers, shopping lists and tide times. There is a book of hand-drawn flowers. Five bible study manuals. Then there's the darker stuff that the detectives have already sorted into a separate box: notepads revealing illustrations drenched in gore, rambling pornographic prose dotted with profound and surreal violence, polaroid photos taped into one scrapbook that no one wants to look at a second time, and to-do lists for the various crimes they know Millman committed.

'None of it is recent,' Lana says to Bruno. There are no notes or mentions of the last couple of murders. It all seems to date back to '78 and early '79.

One of the other detectives nods. *We've noticed.*

Two hours later, Lana stretches her legs in the backyard. Another of the Diablo men is out there, a young Māori bloke named Bill Webber. Bill paces the yard reading one of Millman's notebooks, his face pressed up against it to see the text in the yard light.

Lana whistles to get his attention. 'Want a smoke, kid?'

'I'm all right,' he says, and keeps reading.

'Suit yourself.'

Lana watches him pace and read. She closes her eyes and works the tips of her fingers into the side of her neck. She's tense from the scalp down.

'Shit . . . holy shit.'

It's Bill.

She opens her eyes and sees that he's stopped pacing. 'What is it?'

'I better show the others,' he says, rushing past.

By the time Lana makes her way in, they're all standing around looking at Bill's book as he squats down, turning the pages for them.

'It's us,' Bill says. 'It's all of us.'

And there they are: every Diablo detective, listed.

Blurry street photos.

Newspaper clippings.

Names.

Addresses.

Phone numbers.

Photos of cars, photos of houses, photos of families, photos of pubs, lodges, churches and routines.

Bill turns a final page, and a sickly silence falls over the room.

It's a two-page spread dedicated to one particular cop.

'The man of the hour,' says Bruno.

CHAPTER 71

THE DIABLO SQUAD ROOM ran red hot all afternoon and drove Henry back out into the field. He caught a lift with a patrol back to his car, then circled back to Millman's neighbourhood where he checked stormwater drains and bushland and any other place the man might be holed up. He gave Terranora Creek another pass, stumbling across two uniformed guys standing by an abandoned tin boat, wondering what to do with it. They were five miles upriver from Boyds Bridge, but Henry couldn't confirm it as Millman's tinnie. It was too dark last night, and he was too adrenalised to remember much.

From there, the day turned. Fatigue crept in.

Henry thought about popping the leftover pills from Sarah Utton's stash but nixed it.

He ignored dispatch.

Avoided Lowell.

Refused to call in.

He drove, parked and walked.

Drove, parked and walked.

And he kept at it well into the night until hunger and silence pushed him homeward.

•

Henry comes in through the front door, drops his keys in a bowl, and slips his gun into a drawer. He doesn't bother with the lights. Instead, he eats two-day-old pizza and reads Lowell Sennett's stolen Colleen Vinton file under the glare of the range hood. It's big information, but he can't work out what to do with it. Doesn't have the bandwidth for anything else tonight.

As Henry stands there dazed, a thud echoes through the house. *The cat.* It's the neighbour's pet, but Henry leaves a bedroom window open for it. He walks down the hall and stands in the darkened doorway of his room.

'Where are you, buddy?'

Outside, a wild wind pushes the trees around, flapping the blinds. He slides the window shut, sealing himself in. The house came with a small, rusted shed on the edge of the property, a flimsy tin structure engulfed in lantana. Tonight, the shed door hangs open.

'Goddamnit.'

The thing will clang and scrape all night if he leaves it.

Henry unlocks the laundry, goes out.

The phone rings.

He goes back in and picks up the receiver.

'Henry?'

It's Lana.

'What's going on?' he says.

'I'm at Millman's house. They found a bunch of stuff in his roof. Paperwork, mainly. We're giving it a skim before batching it off for HQ. Look, he's got your street address in here. There are photos of your car, the house, the lot.'

'That's creepy.'

'Yeah, it's not good. Figured you'd want to know.'

'Thanks. I'll call you tomorrow.'

He puts the phone back.

CHAPTER 72

HENRY DECIDES ON ANOTHER slice of pizza and takes it back out through the laundry to the yard. The shed door rattles in the wind and the trees howl. In a few seconds, he has the shed door secured and the latch across. He gives the thing a kick, to be sure. Turning back, he spots something out of place. There's a column—a giant cylinder—propped up against the back of the house. It's beside the hot water unit. Must've missed it on the way out.

Henry squints.

It's a rug.

No, it's a *roll of carpet.*

He takes one more step in that direction before a shadow slams into him.

The world tilts.

Henry's throat burns.

Hands on autopilot, he tries to prise his attacker loose, his fingertips sliding in under the leather belt wrapped around his neck.

The shadow behind him grunts.

Sweat.

Fear.

Salt water.

Henry twists and, just as the vertigo of tunnel vision closes in, he gets a full hand under the belt. With something to hold on to, Henry snaps his head back. A sickening crunch rattles through the back of Henry's head and a spray of hot blood lands on his neck.

The man behind him stumbles, emits a low groaning sound.

He lets go.

Henry lurches forward, reaching for the grass as it rises up. He heaves, and the man comes in a second time, grabbing him around the legs.

Two hands crawl up Henry's body, blows landing on his chest and shoulders.

By dint of a hundred street fights, Henry knows how to survive this. He wipes the man's slowing punches away, then hits back: a blow to the side of his attacker's head—Henry's fist pounding into the wool of a balaclava—followed by a second strike to the man's throat. That almost does it.

The man freezes.

He's stunned, starts gagging.

He rips the face mask off, searching for air.

Henry pushes him off and stands up.

In control at last, Henry starts kicking the man, stomping down with the heel of his foot. In the chaos of it, he finally sees his face.

Daryl Millman.

Henry keeps kicking.

When Millman goes limp, Henry climbs onto him and places his hands around Millman's throat, squeezing his windpipe shut.

Millman writhes around. Feet and hands shuddering.

'Please,' he coughs. *'Please.'*

Henry keeps squeezing, hands tightening.

There are tears in Henry's eyes, but all the history and cop gossip is true. Past a certain point, his capacity for violence is endless. A thousand compounded versions of his father.

'Please,' says Millman one last time before going limp.

It's over.

Henry crawls away. Halfway back to the house, he vomits again, and his crying jag turns severe.

'No! No, you fuck. You fucking fuck,' he screams.

He races back to Millman's body and drops to his knees and weeps over the man.

'No, no, no.'

A black sky overhead.

The wind, alive again.

Night sounds.

Then Millman twitches.

The man coughs.

His eyes shoot open.

'Stay there,' Henry shouts. 'Don't you fucking move.'

He sprints back to the house, in through the laundry and down the hall to the bureau by the door where he collects a spare set of handcuffs. Henry grabs them and races back—slipping once in the hall—then flying back out the door to Millman, who is crawling away.

'No you don't,' says Henry.

He drags Millman to the Hills hoist and handcuffs him to the pole. As soon as the second bracelet snaps shut, Henry lets himself exhale. He sits beside Millman and gives a half-hearted laugh. 'Jesus. I almost had to dump *you* in that thing,' he says, looking over at the roll of carpet propped against the side of his house.

REST

WEDNESDAY, 27 FEBRUARY 1980

JOURNAL OF EMMETT HADES

(SELECTED EXCERPTS)

I was still awake when Henry was attacked by Daryl Millman. I was back at home, in my garage again with the police scanner on.

An officer out in Benowa required assistance.

Henry's address.

A man forcibly detained in the rear yard.

The Diablo suspect. Millman's name, finally out in the open.

'That's my boy,' I said. 'That's my boy.'

There were a lot of questions arising out of this, but by some miracle, Henry had finally done it. He had caught the killer.

And just like that, I knew my career was over.

Diablo defeated.

Case closed.

There wouldn't be another. Surely not. I was spent, my reputation in tatters, and not for the first time.

In the garage, I got up from the bench, my tired bones creaking, and made my way into the house.

I switched on the jug in the kitchen.

Put the milk out.

Waited and listened to the water churn inside the kettle.

But before the water had come to a boil, the strangest thing happened. I abandoned the tea and moved towards the master bedroom.

The rest is hard to remember.

Just strange vignettes.

My reflection in the mirror above the dresser.

My service revolver in my hand.

My eyes staring into my eyes, with the cold barrel of the gun pressed to the skin of my temple. It felt good. I figured the shot would be muted.

My revolver isn't a powerful gun. The snap of it wouldn't wake the neighbours, not in this street. Instead, the bullet would pop, and I'd slop down and that would be that.

A full stop, of sorts.

Quick.

Finished.

The end.

If only.

CHAPTER 73

THEY PUT MILLMAN IN the biggest interrogation room they had, with the lights on full. A doctor saw to him—'He'll live'—but he doesn't look good. There's dark, mottled bruising around his neck and mouth. A swollen eye and a swollen jaw. And he can't walk properly. They handcuff him to a chair, just to be safe, then leave him in the room alone for a long time. Millman doesn't seem to notice. Just stares into the bright white nothingness.

Lana stands in the back corner of the viewing room with Bruno. Henry Loch is front and centre, crowded by detectives. The mood isn't jovial. It's no celebration and most of the men are quiet. Only murmurs and insults. Coffee slurping. A sandwich being unwrapped. Audible yawns and BO like the plague. It's the slow, procedural end. Everyone wants it to be over.

There are two small speakers in the viewing room, each mounted to a corner above the window. Both speakers crackle and shudder in unison as Mark Evans and Pete Reynolds step into view. The two detectives take a seat across from Millman, both as upright and neat as job interviewees.

Evans speaks first. Gives the introductions.

Millman looks through them.

Evans turns on the tape recorder. He reads out the date and the details. He clears his throat. 'Mr Millman, would you like to take this opportunity to make a statement before we get started?'

No answer.

'A confession,' says Reynolds.

Millman remains still. After a beat, he says, 'I did it. I killed everyone.'

That causes a ripple behind the glass.

'Goddamn,' says Bruno, under his breath.

Ron Bingham dabs at his face with a hankie.

Millman says, 'I'm the guy you're all looking for. I did it. I had to.'

Reynolds turns and looks through the mirror at the squad. His skin has turned a sickly grey. He says nothing for a few seconds, just looks in at the detectives.

Evans, to his immense credit, stays calm. 'Mr Millman, what can you tell us about the body we found in your house yesterday?'

'His name is Ruben.'

'Ruben Davis?'

'I don't know. Ruben something.'

'Did you murder Ruben Davis?'

'I saved him.'

Reynolds says, 'Tell us about that.'

'I saved him. I saved all of them.'

Evans fiddles with his pen. 'Right. Right. Okay. How *exactly* did you do that? Can, can you walk us through it?'

'With Ruben, I choked him with a shoelace. He was dead for, well, the rest of it.'

And so it goes. Millman takes some coaching, but he talks. He tells them he targeted Ruben Davis because Ruben lived nearby and because he smoked weed in a local park at night. 'He looked like a sinful type, and I confirmed it quickly enough, after a brief investigation. He definitely needed saving.'

No one understands it.

But they push on.

Millman took Teddy Adams from the driveway of his home. Millman knew Teddy worked in the sex industry, had followed Teddy for a month. He *looked sinful* too, but Millman zeroed in on Teddy because he had a kid, deciding a 'pimp and an abuser for a father won't do'.

By day, Millman's job in property valuation put him on the street. *Fieldwork*, he called it. He had a lot of leeway. He wandered around. He peeped. He took field notes. Turns out that, years back, Millman had stumbled across the dead body of a child in a stormwater easement in a park—it was the same park where he later came across Ruben Davis. About the dead child, Millman said, 'That could have been me, that kid, if not for the grace of God. The people who raised me were not churchgoers, not by any stretch. They were of the sort who might do something like that.'

Reynolds keeps after it. 'What did you do with Teddy Adams after you snatched him up?'

'I rolled him in some old carpet and dumped his body on the street.'

Reynolds says, 'Like garbage?'

'He was garbage. They all were.'

He's completely insane.

Eddie Edgar is next. He 'sold booze and smokes to minors out the back of his filthy pub', and thus he had to go. Millman nabbed him on the way into his house, wrapped a plastic bag over his head and taped it shut. 'He was big. I needed to move quickly.' Edgar also went into a roll of carpet and onto the street.

Pete Reynolds asks, 'Why did Barton Westerby need punishing?' Reynolds is the lead detective on the Westerby case.

Millman clams up. 'I, I . . .'

He pauses.

The detectives give him a minute.

Evans fetches a round of tea and they wait it out.

Eventually, Millman comes clean. 'I knew Barton. I knew him from before all this.'

'How?' says Reynolds.

'The worst way possible. From when I was young. He was a family friend. Offered me a lift home one day and made a pass at me, the dirty pig. Tried to . . .' Millman breathes and shudders. 'I told my father what happened, and he gave Barton a hiding. He was a possessive man, my father.'

Evans says, 'Did you look him up?'

Millman smiles. 'Barton? Oh no. The idiot objected to his property taxes and his file came across my desk. Not a common name, is it? I had a look and, sure enough, it was the same old Barton. It all came back to me. I let myself go with him. It was a bit like that with Ruben, too, I guess. It wasn't what I wanted. Wasn't exactly what God wanted either.'

'Go on,' says Evans, quietly, sensing more.

'God doesn't like it when I lose control. It's not how He likes to do things. I moved too quickly on Barton and that . . . it stirred things up. I didn't plan it out properly. The secateurs and all that. I thought, *Oh gee, I've really blown it.* That's why I had to stop.'

'Stop what?' says Reynolds.

'My work. I was sure you'd catch me after Barton. You did, I guess.'

Evans says, 'Can we move on to Violet Burke?'

'Who's that?'

'Your next victim.'

'My what? I, I didn't . . . I don't think I know a Violet Burke.'

'Really?' says Reynolds.

'I don't know her. Is she dead?'

Evans rests his hands flat on the table. 'You can tell us, Daryl. It's probably not going to change things too much at this point.'

'Oh, I imagine so, but I didn't save anyone after Barton. He was the last one. And I don't hurt women.'

Evans says, 'She was a prostitute. That's against the rules, isn't it? You dumped her out the back of Tugun, right?'

'No. That wasn't me. I didn't shoot any prostitutes. Guns are *so loud.* I was shocked the other night during that, uh, the thing on the bridge.'

'Shocked by what?' Evans's voice is rising.

'The sound. I've never fired a gun before. Surprised I didn't shoot myself, to be honest. I dumped that thing in the river, quick smart.'

Reynolds says, 'What are you talking about?'

In the observation room, it's dead.

'What are you saying?' says Reynolds. He grabs Millman by the forearm.

Millman looks nervous. He stutters, 'I, I don't *know* what we're talking about.'

CHAPTER 74

THEY GO TO THE pub to celebrate. It's beer for breakfast. Diablo is done. After two rounds, the detectives let the mood lighten and they raise their glasses to Evans and Reynolds, their comrades back at the station, still knee-deep in the interrogation.

'Fuck it,' roars Bingham. 'He's a bloody nut.'

Lana tends to agree.

It was hard to spot the moment where Millman changed his tune, but it would be in there somewhere, on the tape. It would be in some small faux pas or strange word, some microscopic detail—the temperature of his tea, the look in someone's eye, the lighting—some trigger that pushed his delusions into high gear. Something that made him stop cooperating. It wasn't uncommon. Lana had listened to plenty of blokes cop to one crime and deny another, having done the lot. But it's weird that Millman refuted the gun crimes. It was usually the more violent, perverted stuff that crims swore off. Not the polite executions.

'Maybe guns are against God's plan?' says Bruno.

'Maybe,' says Lana. 'Have you seen Henry?'

'I don't know where he is.'

And now the sun is out, and the men are loosening their ties in the side awning of the Surfers Paradise Hotel. They're all laughing and eating grease-filled sausages with eggs. It's a good moment. All the better, because they know it won't last. Lana can already see the mayhem on the cusp of it, creeping in. It's in the seasick turn in Bingham's face. The rising tide of ego and adrenaline. The fast-moving comedown. She doesn't care. Lana hurls herself towards it, pouring herself another pot from the jug and knocking it back in three gulps. *Why not?* she thinks, because this is the strangest of sensations: a touch of belonging.

CHAPTER 75

HENRY DRIVES HOMEWARD, HAVING slipped away as the taskforce detectives decamped for breakfast. He takes familiar roads. It's early and the midweek traffic is sparse.

In the quiet interior of the car, the events of the day replay out of order. A visceral energy pumps through him, dredging up a lot of ill feeling. It seems to eclipse the rest: the backslapping and cheer—*the golden fucking win*—all subsiding into a rattling anguish. *It's unfair*, Henry thinks. His body hurts. His mind aches. There's no release in it, but there should be. They would all want him now. All his sins would be forgotten. A bright future opening up. But instead of joy, he feels the void-like emptiness of goals achieved.

It's nothing he wants to take to the pub.

No, thanks.

He wants to be alone.

And then he doesn't.

•

Henry parks in his usual spot under the palm tree on Carlisle Avenue. Across the street, Maddy Santos has her house opened up for the morning cool. Not a blind in sight. The sun is vivid in the glass.

It doesn't take long to catch sight of her.

She passes a window.

Comes back.

Stands there.

She isn't dolled up today. There's no sheer robe or swimwear. She wears a white t-shirt and dark cotton underwear. Has her hair out.

Maddy steps away from the window.

The front door opens and it stays open, like a gaping mouth.

Henry waits.

A minute later, Maddy comes down the front stair, still only half-dressed. She pads across the street to his car where she leans down to face him through the driver's window. 'You might be the dumbest fucking cop I've ever met,' she says, smirking.

'You wouldn't say that if you knew what I just did.'

'Oh, I don't know. Come inside.'

'I don't think that's a good idea.'

'It's not an idea,' she says. 'I'm asking you.'

He does it.

Hot bitumen.

Concrete stair.

The bright house, the living room.

Hallway.

Bedroom.

She puts her hands on his chest as soon as he's in there. 'Take this off.' Henry unbuttons his shirt. There are patches of maroon blood on his singlet. Welts and bruises. He watches her take in the stains and injuries.

'What happened?'

'Got into a fight.'

'You okay?'

When he doesn't answer, she kisses him and then she takes off her shirt and they fall into it. Her hands on his face. The smell of her hair. The strange inertia. She reaches between his legs.

'Fuck me,' she whispers.

'No.'

He slips her underwear down and stares at her body, her breasts, her stomach, her thighs. He gently spreads her legs and looks at the opening.

'Touch yourself.'

Maddy slides a hand down, draping a finger along the skin there before pressing lightly at the top.

'Like this?' she says.

He watches.

She moves her hand in circles. 'Like this?'

She lies back, eyes closed. Henry adjusts himself, moving his cock around in his boxers.

'Henry?'

He won't answer.

She opens her eyes and grabs him by the arm, pulling him onto her. Henry tries to get off, but she won't let go. 'No,' she says. 'No more watching.'

She struggles with his zipper.

He moves her hand away.

She tips him onto his back and makes her way up the bed, climbing over him, moving his eyes past her breasts and the swollen nipples, past her navel to the wet hair of her bush. Slowly, Maddy lowers herself over his mouth and he pushes his tongue in. As she thrusts against him, the warm skin of Maddy's midriff covers Henry's eyes, blocking the light and pushing everything else out.

CHAPTER 76

MADDY STANDS BY THE bedroom window, contoured in the streetlight as it cuts through the blinds. She pulls down a slat and blows a plume of cigarette smoke out into the night.

Henry sits up in bed, rubs at his injured neck. 'What time is it?'

'I don't know. You've been out all day. Must have needed it.'

'Can I buy you dinner?'

'Bit late for that.'

'I know a few places that'll be open.'

'That's not what I meant, but I could eat.'

They drive to a hotel in Surfers Paradise where Henry calls in a favour. He gets them room service takeaway and a table in the darkened bistro. They sit by the wall-sized windows, the ocean on the other side. They're alone.

'This is different,' Maddy says. 'You bring all the girls here?'

'We better talk about Sarah Utton. I know you know more than you're letting on. It's all over you.'

'Is it now?'

'I like you. I want to get it out of the way.'

'It doesn't work like that.'

'You can tell me anything.'

'No, not this. You could end up in trouble.'

'Trouble with who? I'm a policeman.'

She shakes her head. 'It doesn't matter to these people. You must know *that* by now. You've been around.'

'Do you trust me?'

'No.'

Henry sits back. He looks at the sky and the sea. 'Six years back, I killed a man in cold blood. Just popped him twice in the back of the head and—'

'Henry, don't. You don't need to—'

'His name was Peter Torney. You can look him up. There's bits and pieces about him in the *Courier*. He was a serial sex offender, children mostly. Operated out of Brisbane's inner north for years, but kept slipping through the cracks. Anyway, we got him, worked out who he was and where he lived, and, uh, he had to go. But the powers that be decided it was better if Torney just disappeared.'

'Why are you telling me this?'

'It's an exchange. I've never told anyone this. Do you want me to stop?'

'No.'

'They offered me the job of knocking him. I'd been trying to get into the detective squad for years, but the upper brass didn't think I was cut out for it. Too aggressive and too dumb. That's what they thought. And they were right, in a way. I'd been like that earlier on, raised like that too. It's who I was for a long time and I couldn't shake it. No one wanted someone like me in the CIB until . . . until they wanted someone *exactly* like me. And, against all my better judgement, I took it. I grabbed the guy from his house, put him in the boot of my car and drove him to a field outside Beaudesert . . . where I, I just shot him. Put him down like a wild dog.'

Maddy takes a drink, a slight tremor in her hand. 'Then what?'

'They sent me here and filed me in the Consorting Squad. I thought I was getting in on the act, but I wasn't. Not really. From that point forward, I was bought and paid for. They own me now, the higher-ups. It's been years. And all the while, I've had to live with what I did, on top of being under the thumb.'

'He deserved to die.'

'A hundred times over, but it doesn't make much difference. Sometimes it feels like . . .'

'Go on.'

'Nah, I'm getting melodramatic now.'

'That's an excuse. Say it.'

'Some nights it feels like he's buried in me, instead of the ground. Every happy moment, every big day, today even, even when I'm outrunning some of it, I'm still the guy who killed him that way. Just flat-out murdered him. Brings back a lot of bad memories. There's no exit from it.'

Maddy lights two smokes. She hands one across the table.

'I don't smoke,' he says, taking it.

'It'll help. I don't like hearing that it doesn't get better.'

'What can you tell me about Sarah Utton?'

'I think she's dead, Henry. I really do.'

'Who did it?'

'Powerful people.'

'Well, there's powerful people on my side of the fence, too. You know that now. They're looking for her.'

'Listen to yourself.' Maddy suddenly grinds out her smoke. She stands up. 'Do yourself a favour. For once, just leave well enough alone. Say no to them, like you should have with the other thing.'

'Are you leaving?'

'Thanks for dinner.'

'Can I see you again?'

'Maybe.'

'I'll come round.'

'If you do, leave *this* in here.'

CHAPTER 77

APPROACHING MIDNIGHT, LANA ROLLS out of bed and pukes twice in the motel room sink. On the way back, she finds a handwritten note under the door. It's from the motel receptionist. It says Dwain Gorst is waiting for an update. He's left three messages.

It's late, but she calls.

'I guess congratulations are in order,' Gorst says, sounding less than enthused. 'It's all over the *ABC News*.'

Lana leans over and turns on the TV. 'Yeah, big day up here, sir.'

'Is this Millman character a beat-up?'

'No. I like him for it. He's confessed to some of the murders without coercion. And the guy's house is really something. He had a dead body strung up in the living room of his house like a Christmas tree. There's nothing I can't see this guy doing.'

'Murder weapon?'

'Not yet, but they don't need it, sir. Not in my opinion. It's open and shut. They've got a legit confession and more supporting evidence than you can shake a stick at. He kept notes.'

'And the Amstell case?'

'He hasn't copped to it yet, but I think he will.'

'Well, that's that,' Gorst says. 'Clearing out a murder case absolves all sins, doesn't it? But clearing seven . . .'

'Grounds for canonisation, sir. And it's eight, actually.'

'Eight cases?'

'The body in Millman's house was a cold case.'

'Jesus.'

There would be no internal censure now, no politics to be had. Diablo was untouchable, for the time being.

Lana says, 'I can hang around for a few days to make sure our end is seen to, sir, if you think it's warranted?'

'Do that. I look forward to a full debrief on your return.'

'Yes, sir. So do I.'

'Good job, detective. This is a big win for you. I'll be sure to remind Assistant Commissioner Collins of your involvement, even though it's not quite everything we were after.'

'Don't suppose you can mention what that is now?'

'It's best we leave it there, I think,' says Gorst.

'And the other thing?' Her promotion. Her own team.

'I keep my promises.'

Dial tone.

Lana lies down on the bed and drifts in and out. Superintendent Beggs appears on the TV, smiling and waving at a crowd of reporters. A strobe of camera flashes flicker, followed by stock footage.

The Surfers Paradise station.

One of the crime scenes.

Millman's mugshot.

It cuts back to the studio.

A newsreader with a picture of Millman in the corner above the words *Gold Coast Strangler Caught!*

Lana lights a smoke. It seems like a daft name to her. 'Didn't strangle all of them, did he?' she says to the TV. She would have called him *The Valuer.*

The news bulletin continues. There's no mention of Diablo's fuck-ups or the last two years of rolling failure. No redemption angle on display. To hear it now, Diablo is a crack squad of honourable detectives. Winners, through and through. *At last, the residents of the Gold Coast can sleep soundly in their beds.*

Lana zones all the way out.

The news ends.

Ads play.

The broadcast cuts to a test pattern.

TEN DAYS LATER

JOURNAL OF EMMETT HADES

(SELECTED EXCERPTS)

I didn't end up killing myself. The timing wasn't right. That's as much of it as I can understand. I guess, I've lived my whole life with people, in squad rooms, on the Force, and I didn't want to die alone in my bedroom. I've also attended my fair share of suicide calls and didn't want to put some fresh beat cop through it or, God forbid, my house cleaner, Irene.

I decided to wait. To put it on hold.

That's how I'm thinking, if you can call it that.

And besides, I don't want to miss the rest of the story.

The closing chapters, the epilogue.

•

The end of Strike Force Diablo was a real spectacle. Henry Loch came over for dinner about a week after Millman was charged and he gave me the blow-by-blow. What I'm about to commit to paper is, to the best of my knowledge, as accurate as possible.

It started at the top. The commissioner—always a deft hand in these moments—got stuck into it with the premier and they pushed through a straight-up heroic police story for the press. Finding the right protagonist wasn't easy, mind you. Of all the Diablo leads, Ron Bingham wasn't fit for purpose (a fat, drunken cliché) and Pete Reynolds was far too ill-tempered and rotten. That left Mark Evans, the aloof pseudo-intellectual. He was barely functional as a lead investigator, but he became the hero. Not a popular choice, but it flew.

They relegated Henry to a bit player. His big moment was a three-minute interview with Mike Willesee, positioning him as the lucky street cop, the guy who found himself in the right place at the right time. When asked, Henry dutifully told the nation how indebted he was to *the leadership of Evans, and that he was 'just following up on Mark's leads' instead of mine. Henry chuckled and played dumb. There was no mention of the fight at Henry's house or Henry's own diligence breaking the thing open. No, Henry ducked out of frame as quickly as possible, and it was, at the heart of it, a deeply impressive political manoeuvre.*

A first look at the new Henry.

Behind the scenes, he had them by the balls. They offered to make him Sergeant Henry Loch, and he took it, but there was no big announcement. He didn't want that. He wanted something else. A smooth transition out of Consorting into Homicide. He wanted to move fast and erase history. They complied. From there, it was as if all the violence and mayhem of his career started to slowly play in reverse: blood seeping back into wounds, fists unclenching, street brawls coming apart, and the back-room deals falling into disrepair. Some of their power over him was relinquished, and his interior shifted alongside it. I could see it in him. Those bullets of Henry's—those two shining bullets—they both started moving back through Peter Torney's skull, back across the midnight grass field outside Beaudesert, and back towards Henry's revolver where they resealed and cooled.

It was a redemption story in the making. A brute force absolution.

What Henry wanted.

Blood for blood.

Inspiring stuff.

I've always found him inspiring.

And I know all this intimately because I know the dreams and damnation of compromised men. I understand them. I wouldn't dare tell his story without knowing it myself.

CHAPTER 78

HENRY LOCH FEELS GOOD. He pulls his car off the highway and makes his way back to the El Dorado motel on foot, cutting across the drive-through check-in, around the pool and up the iron terrace to a room at the far end. 'Open up. It's the police.'

Lana Cohen answers, looking like roadkill. She squints out at the morning glare and says, 'Bloody hell.'

'Another big night?'

'Big week.' She lets him in but leaves the door open. 'Where have you been?'

'Sick leave,' says Henry.

'Meaning?'

It means holing up with Maddy Santos during the golden days of a new romance. They've been sleeping late and staying in. Henry doing the cooking. Maddy lounging around drinking and watching, always an eye on the TV or the window or the clock. She didn't work—or didn't seem to—but she was always slightly on edge, perpetually unsettled until late in the afternoons when the booze piled up. Henry stayed sober and savoured the strange fever of it. The fucking and the long, slow conversations, a buoyant swell of optimism welling up. He had time to think. He had intuitions now. He had plans.

'I had to go see someone,' is all he says to Lana.

Lana slumps into a chair. 'It's nice to see you and all, but what do you want? I'm about to have a nap.'

'Come on, it's a work day.'

'Fuck off.'

'Do you want to know my secret?'

'Sure.'

He tosses her a brown glass pill bottle containing his remaining stash of dexies. 'Those belonged to Sarah Utton. Evidence in an ongoing investigation.'

Lana takes a look, tosses them back. 'I had a little problem with those a while back.'

'You learn something every day. Come on then, I'll buy you a cuppa.'

Lana tells him to go wait in the car.

•

They hit a cafe and grab takeaway tea, then walk to the beach where Lana removes her shoes and stands in the tide. Henry has to holler down from the foreshore. 'To be honest, I thought you'd be back in Sydney by now.'

'I'm stalling. It's nice to be around a big win. You've got to take it when you can get it in this racket.'

'Don't tell me you've taken a liking to the place?'

She smiles. 'You know, I have a little. Never lived near the ocean before, and we had a deal, if I recall?'

'I didn't think that would hold.'

'That's because you were thinking the wrong thing. Though I'm not sure you *should* push forward with the Utton thing now. Or is this little chat about something else?'

'No, it's Utton.'

'Might not be the best idea, Henry. All you have to do is sit there and be a good boy and they'll make you the new Mark Evans.'

Henry stays quiet. He brings a hand up to block the sun.

'You don't want it?' she says.

'Would you take it?'

'Sure. Do a couple of years down here in Homicide, wipe the slate, then go work somewhere else.'

'The slate's pretty dirty.'

'And you think finding the girl will seal the deal?'

'Maybe. In my experience, getting what you want from these people is different from keeping it. Finding Utton will give me another iron in the fire.'

'Insurance.'

'Yeah. I reckon it's bigger than it looks.'

Lana wanders up to the hard sand. 'Okay then, you better catch me up.'

Henry starts with his dirt on Robert Emmery, the property developer and Sarah Utton's pervert john. 'There's some weird casino bid on the cards,' he says. 'It's tied right in with all the locals. Emmery is bosom buddies with Colleen Vinton and a bunch of blokes at the station, all of it on the down low.'

'A legal casino in Queensland? Come off it.'

'That's what my source tells me.'

'And Utton's caught up in *that*?'

'I think so.'

'That is . . . not great to hear.'

'We'll tread carefully. What have you told your lot down in Sydney?'

'I've told them what I was *always* going to tell them. As little as possible. Do you know what my deal is, Henry? The deal that got me here?'

He shrugs.

Lana places an unlit smoke on her lips. 'My deal is a load of shit. That's what it is. You don't know what it's like down there. Our system's as dirty as yours. We just hide it better. We're not total yahoos like your lot, but it's the same thing. And they're all in it together, past a certain point. Your team, my team. It's all . . .' She stops, pats down her pockets for her lighter and lets the thought drift. 'Now and then, you get to solve a case, you know. And then every now and then you get a full stop like Millman. That's how it's supposed to be. But we both know what it *actually* is. It's more complicated. It's deals within deals within deals. A thousand shitty promises, up and down the line. So, *my* deal is . . .' She sparks up her smoke, takes a deep drag. 'My deal is, I give the boys down south something to gossip about at the police club, and in exchange, I get to come up here and do my *actual fucking* job as initially promised.' She laughs at the idea. 'What a mess. You probably don't see it, but we're the same animal, you and me. You're the bogan hard man, and I'm the skirt. We're the *yes, sir*; *no, sir*; *three bags full, sir* people. So yeah, I might hand off a piece or two about Bingham or Reynolds, if the occasion arises, but you, you're okay.' And with that, she exhales. 'Does that work?'

'It works.'

'So, what's the plan, Henry?'

'I've got a move I can make with Lowell. I want to know why he lifted Colleen Vinton's medical file from Brian Amstell's office.'

'Really? Your own partner? You really are keen to clean the slate, then.'

'Lowell knows something about Utton. I can feel it.'

Lana scans the horizon. 'You know what's so great about the ocean, Henry?'

'It's wet?'

'It doesn't give a shit about any of this. It's oblivious to everything.'

'I don't know,' he says. 'I think it's just a hole in the ground.'

CHAPTER 79

HENRY SQUIRMS IN THE passenger seat. They both sit there looking at Lowell's house. It's nicer than it should be. Gleaming white timber. Wide verandah. Flowering frangipani in the air.

Lana says, 'You don't have a place like this, do you?'

'It's his wife's doing. She's an academic.'

'And she married Lowell?'

It's Lowell's academic wife who lets them in. She's trim and tall. Much better looking than Lana imagined. The interior of the house is also a surprise too. It's alive and bustling. Four kids. Lots of loud conversation around the kitchen table. A radio blaring. And in the middle of the mayhem, Lowell Sennett, with two rounds of Vegemite on toast, on his day off.

'Here he is,' Lowell says. 'And you brought your girlfriend?'

'Is that true, Henry?' says the wife.

Henry makes the introductions.

The kids resume their shit-talking. The radio sprays: *In local news, the man known as the Gold Coast Strangler will appear tomorrow in a Brisbane magistrate court on charges relating to—*

Lowell says, 'I don't figure this for a social visit?' As he's saying it, his eyes drop to the manila folder in Henry's hand.

Immediate recognition.

'Can we talk outside?' says Henry.

•

Out in the backyard, they sit around a flaking wrought-iron table.

Lowell says to Henry, 'You never come round. What's going on? Are we okay?'

It's half-convincing.

Henry lays it out. 'The other night in Brian Amstell's office, you lifted this medical file and put it in the boot of our car. I want you to tell me why you did that, and I don't want you to lie to me.'

Lowell lowers his voice. 'Then you bloody well shouldn't ask.'

'I take it you're working for Vinton?'

Lowell looks straight at Lana. 'Not here, mate.'

'Never mind her. I don't care what you're into on the side. That's up to you. We've all got stuff we need to look after, but if you're on the inside with Vinton herself, I need to know about it, because it fits into this other thing I'm working.'

'Yeah, what would that be?'

'The missing girl I'm looking for. Sarah Utton. I've been showing her photo around, remember? She's one of Colleen's workers and Jack wants me to find her.'

'Jack the Bagman?' says Lowell. 'You never mentioned that.'

'That's how it is. The grown-ups are watching.' Henry places a hand over the file between them. 'Now, you didn't just stumble across this in the dark.'

'Maybe I was hoping to blackmail Colleen. Figured there might be some juice in it.'

'You're not that dumb.'

'I guess that's a compliment. Can I have one of those?' Lowell says.

Lana shakes a cigarette loose for him.

Lowell lights up, stalling. 'Okay. I don't want a bar of this. We can talk about my, ah, business arrangements some other time. But you're on your own with Utton, and I'm certainly not explaining myself in front of her.' He nods at Lana. 'We *broke into* that doctor's office, mate. The way I see it, I can take whatever I want, and I don't have to explain it to anyone. You've got no sway here.'

It's a strange move. Lowell is pushing back harder than he should be.

'Maybe you should take a look in there before you go shooting your mouth off,' Henry says.

Lowell takes his time, checking in with both of them as he turns the file around and opens it. Inside, there's a set of photographs. Lowell's eyes widen and the colour drains from his cheeks and neck. Then, without warning, he leaps up and grabs Henry by the throat, slamming him into the lawn.

'This is my fucking house,' Lowell hisses.

Lana tries to pull him off, lifting Lowell under the shoulders. This gives Henry his opening and he slams a punch into Lowell's side, knocking the wind out of him. The man crumples and Lana gently rolls him onto the grass.

From the house, a distant voice calls, 'Lowell? *Lowell?* Is everything okay out there?'

Lowell sucks air. 'Just tripped, luv.'

'He just tripped,' says Lana.

Heels approach on the hardwood above.

'Quick, get the photos,' Henry says.

They're spread across the lawn. Lana scurries around on her hands and knees. That's when she sees the images. Black-and-white blow-ups of Lowell, completely naked, accompanied by two women in what looks like a shady motel or brothel.

Lowell's wife appears at the window.

'We're fine. I just tripped over,' says Lowell a second time.

The wife waits a beat, then retreats into the house without comment.

'Fuck you both,' Lowell says, under his breath.

Henry dusts himself off. 'Mate, I had to do it. The big boys are onto you, and I'm not the one who's stepping out. That's on you.'

'Who has them?'

'At the moment, no one. But Jack put in the order.'

'So, this is what, then?'

'A shakedown,' says Henry.

'Fuck me.'

They all sit there on the ground. Lowell thinking it through.

Henry rubbing his neck. Lana straightening up the scattered images, pulling them into a neat pile.

'Jesus, Lowell,' she says.

'Can you stop looking at those?'

'I can see what she sees in you,' Lana says. 'No wonder you've got so many bloody kids.'

That breaks the tension.

Lowell and Henry laugh until they have tears in their eyes.

CHAPTER 80

LOWELL GIVES IT UP in one long burst. 'Colleen Vinton had her hooks in me the moment I got down here, and I didn't even know it. Couple of years back, I fell in love with the wrong prostie up in Cairns and she snapped a few photos of us together and traded them with the owner of the place where she worked, a place Colleen had a stake in. She's smart, Colleen. She sat on those photos for years, without a peep, and then when I got transferred down here, and after I got married, bam, it all rained down. She put the hard word on me the first day back after my honeymoon. I was bought and sold, just like that.'

'What does she have you doing?' says Henry.

'Nothing too reprehensible. To be fair, it's not a bad gig. Colleen's a hard person, but not if you toe the line. These days, I just do pretty much what I normally do. Visit with the girls and make sure they're happy. It's troubleshooting, mostly.'

'Meaning?'

'Collections.'

'For what exactly?'

'Whatever the girls need. It's mostly drug stuff and the occasional abortion. There's a pipeline. I ran it with that bird you're looking for, her and Vovo, until she got topped.'

'Who?' says Henry.

'Christ,' says Lana. 'Violet Burke. Victim number four.'

'There it is,' says Lowell. 'Violet and Sarah were the runners. I handled the money. Sarah set the whole thing up, apparently. That's what one of the girls told me. She went to the same church as Brian.'

Henry swallows. 'Jesus fucking Christ, Lowell. This is . . . you could've ended up in jail. Beggs would have thrown the book at you.'

Lowell doesn't seem fazed.

Henry says, 'Tell me how it worked.'

'Amstell was Vinton's connection for benzos up here. He's got a pill-press in the back room of that practice we cased the other night. It was across the hall the whole time. Amstell made good shit too. Vovo and Sarah took the orders and ran the packages. I collected the money and paid everyone off. Gnomes in the Drug Squad gives the rest of them a drink from this. So, before you get all high and mighty, you should know there's a chunk of this floating around the station. There's a bunch of blokes who knew something hinky was going on with the recent Diablo stuff. They all knew who Vovo was.'

'Did they know Amstell was hooked up with Vinton?'

'Of course. Everyone knew, mate. The last four murders all have direct ties to Vinton. Blind Freddy can see it. Vovo and Amstell worked with her. Joel Delaney did her books, and Lenny Gibbs was backing her on the casino bid. If you want to know why Diablo was running white hot but getting nowhere, that's your reason. It was like we were running a homicide investigation inside a minefield.'

'Do you know who killed any of those people?'

'Fuck no. There's no cover-up. It's just, it's a bloody mess, is all.'

No one speaks.

Birdsong from above.

The trees swaying.

'It doesn't mean it's not Millman,' says Lana. 'He's already copped to delusions of grandeur. If his whole thing is a moral crusade, bumping off people in Vinton's circle wouldn't be a bad place to start.'

Henry shakes his head. 'How does a property valuer from Southport know where to start with Colleen Vinton's inner circle?' He looks at Lowell.

'Don't ask me, mate. No one knows who bloody did it. Maybe Millman got lucky. There aren't many crooks on the coast who aren't connected to Vinton.'

'Let's ask him,' says Lana. 'I've got the pull.'

'Millman?' says Henry.

She rolls her neck. 'Yeah. We know where he is.'

CHAPTER 81

HENRY TAKES THE ANNERLEY exit and crests the hill of Dutton Park. They're on the outskirts of Brisbane, headed for Boggo Road Gaol where Daryl Millman is on remand.

'You ever been in here?' Henry says, as they make their way into the parking lot.

Lana shakes her head, no.

The jail is an ominous building, especially in this morning's grey weather. A squat collection of red-brick structures sitting behind a flat red-brick fence, rusted razor wire over the top.

'It stinks,' Henry says. 'You'll be washing it out of your hair for days.'

•

Millman is in Number 2 Division. A guard takes them over and shows them through to an airless concrete room containing a table and chair, both bolted to the ground. Daryl Millman is in there already, cuffed to the table. Lana's expecting the man to look like death warmed up, but he looks fine.

To start, Henry drags a steel folding chair across the floor, the sound of it scraping and echoing. He gives it to Lana then walks back to the corner and stands there with the spare chairs.

'You remember me?' says Lana.

Millman doesn't move.

'You remember him?'

Millman nods, keeping his eyes off Henry. The man's face is still pretty banged up. A week back, they formally upgraded Millman's murder charges to include Brian Amstell. Bruno—working follow-up—located Millman's dentist and found records pertaining to an appointment on

Saturday the 23rd of February, the day after Lana's altercation with Millman at the crime scene. She knocked one of his side teeth out in the scuffle.

'Want a smoke?' she says.

'It's a disgusting habit.'

'Beats killing people,' says Henry.

'That was work,' says Millman. 'Your dreadful work, which I had to take up for the glory of God!'

'Isn't there some rule about thou shalt not kill?' says Henry.

They've settled on this play. Henry will provoke and prod. Lana will console. It can't be otherwise. During the earlier interrogations, it came out that Millman hates Henry. Millman had been paying special attention to him—occasionally following him—since their first encounter, the day of the rego check. Millman can't really explain his fear and dislike of Henry. Whenever asked, he falls back on religious fervour. Evil dwells in Henry, apparently. He is *clothed in shame*, and so on.

Lana says, 'Daryl, I want to ask you a few questions about the gun murders, the later ones you're charged with.'

'I know nothing about those. I've already talked about this.'

'Maybe your memory isn't what it should be?' says Henry.

'My memory is excellent. I remember everything.'

'Maybe you're lying, then?' says Henry.

'Why would I lie?'

'I don't know. I don't know why you would string a dead bloke up in your living room, either. Seems pretty strange to me.'

'Through blood, the forgiveness of our trespasses.'

The room goes quiet.

The heaving of iron gates in the distance.

'Okay,' says Henry.

Millman stares hard at him. 'You of all people should read your bible.'

Lana senses a shift. 'Can I ask you a question, Daryl?'

'You may.'

'I want you to tell me everything you know about Colleen Vinton.'

'The adulteress?'

'I think so. She runs a network of brothels on the Gold Coast. She's a big wheel around town. What do you make of her?'

'A lot less than you, I imagine. I know what I've seen in the papers. That's it.'

Henry yawns theatrically. 'You know what I've seen in the papers lately? Pictures of your dumb arse. Looking at you now, I reckon I've seen you around before. You go to brothels, Daryl? Once or twice, maybe? Tropical Touch? The Pussy Cat? The White Light? Any of these ringing a bell?'

'That's a bold-faced lie.'

'I have a knack for faces. I don't have your memory problems, Daryl. Maybe it was the Night Cap?'

Millman rattles his cuffs. 'Stop this lying tongue. Stop it.'

'Tell us about Vinton,' says Lana.

'Is that what this is about?'

Lana produces a picture of Sarah Utton. '*This* is what it's about.' The idea is to keep him off kilter.

Millman studies the photo. His mouth makes an ugly wet sound as his tongue slides around inside. 'I've seen her.'

'Where?'

'Where the whores ply their trade.'

'Did you hurt her?'

'No. Never had the chance to help her.'

Henry says, 'I think you killed her.'

'No. Not me. I'd tell you.'

Lana leans over the table. 'Like you told us about the others? Come on. Violet Burke, dead, September '79. She was a prostitute, worked for Vinton. Two months later, Lenny Gibbs is dead in December, same year. He was a rich bloke, travelled in Colleen's circles. Then, in the new year, the accountant who did Colleen's taxes winds up dead. Joel Delaney. Then just two weeks ago, Brian Amstell dies, and we find out he has shady connections to Colleen too. Do you remember what happened two weeks ago, Daryl? Any of this sounding familiar?'

'I remember,' he says, slowly. 'I have a question for you now.'

Lana says, 'That's not how this—'

'Have you found the books in my ceiling?'

Lana doesn't answer.

'I take it that's a yes. Well, maybe you should try to find the details of these more recent murders in there. I was meticulous in my work, wasn't I? Always have been—at the office, at home—because it's all God's work. I took great care with it. Now, you won't find a word about these people you mentioned in my notes because I know nothing about them, and I didn't kill them.'

'Maybe you ditched some of your notes?' says Henry.

'You visited the Amstell crime scene,' says Lana. 'We know that for a fact.'

'I was curious. I went to all the crime scenes at one point. It's rare to find a companion on the path.'

'If you stop lying, we can help you,' Lana says.

'That's true actually,' says Henry.

Millman sneers. 'He who breathes out lies will perish. I don't lie, Lana. I never lie. My sins are absolved in the eyes of the Lord.' He raises his hands to the ceiling. 'I've done my part. What have you done? Either of you, with your threats and promises? Everyone is very keen on offering me redemption lately. *This* offer, *that* offer, *just say this, just say that*, but I am *already* redeemed. My conduit is happy. The one true God in Heaven is happy. I'm already . . . I'm already free. Oh, our Father, who art in heaven, hallowed be thy name—'

'Cut that shit out,' says Henry.

'Thy will be done on earth as it is in heaven. Give us this day our daily bread—'

They press him, but he won't stop.

'And forgive us our trespasses as we forgive—'

It works.

The prayer forces them out.

CHAPTER 82

BACK ON THE HIGHWAY, Lana talks it out. 'There's just no way. I don't buy it. I fucking do not buy it, Henry. Millman's crazy enough to have done it, but he's a hundred per cent right on the chain of evidence and, after what Lowell told us, my gut is screaming, *not our guy.*'

Henry agrees. Millman isn't right for the later killings, and if he's honest with himself, he never was. Right from the get-go, Henry considered the cases separate. He's always sensed some politic at work, a tide of conflation and dispersal. He remembers the photo from Colleen Vinton's medical file. That image pinned to the back flap. The men pictured. 'I don't care,' he says. 'I just want the girl. We get the girl first and then we can see how it all shakes out down the road.'

'Couldn't we take a run at Vinton herself?'

'She'll lawyer up. It's a waste of time, and it's dangerous.'

'Okay, what then?'

'I'm back in the office tomorrow. Let's keep working it on the down low.'

A grey bank of rain clouds sits in the sky ahead. Henry can see it all shifting around up there. A storm coming in from the ocean.

'You know what? Drop me at the station,' says Lana. 'I'm going to make some calls and then have another look through the files. I might get lucky. And I need to get my notes together. I need to call . . .' and she starts rattling off names.

Henry pushes the accelerator down.

•

It's after two when he gets to Maddy's house. The door's locked. Blinds drawn. She won't come to the door. The best he can get from inside is the sound of her occasional slurring and telling him to *fuck off* and *leave me alone.* There's no explanation for it. Henry spent the night at his place, but there was no argument or awkwardness last time he was here. Worried, he cuts down the side of the house and spots her through a back window. Someone has given her a beating. She has a black eye, a swollen mouth. A large purple bruise wraps around her thigh.

Henry loses it.

He runs back to the front of the house.

Kicks the door in.

Grabs Maddy as she scrambles up the hall and holds her as they slide down the wall together. 'What happened?' he says, tears in his eyes. 'Tell me.'

She shivers: drunk, frightened, something else. She doesn't speak. Only waits a beat, pushes away from him and crawls up the hallway to where a half-empty bottle of vodka spews its contents onto the carpet. She scoops up the bottle and takes a pull, then lies down on the floor and closes her eyes.

Henry crawls after her, kneels over her.

'If I talk, they'll kill us both,' she says. 'I tried to tell you that, and now look at me.'

'I'm going to stop them.'

'No you're not. They know who you are and they still did this. Think about it.'

'No. That's how scared they are. That's all it is.' Henry touches her leg, his fingertips on the bruised skin. 'This is what desperate people do.'

'They said they won't hurt you if I can get you to stay away from me. They promised.'

'It's too late for that.'

'No, it's not.'

'Yes, it is,' he says, reaching for her hand.

•

Maddy Santos stands by the bathroom sink and tells him everything. 'I was the chemist and Brian made the pills. That's what half a university degree gets you these days. I knew the Amstell family from church, which is a strange place to start a drug ring, but that's how it happened. We worked well together. It was clean. It was safe. I don't regret any of it, and I'd still be at it if Brian was alive.'

Henry studies her from his perch on the rim of the bath. 'You don't have to justify yourself to me. You supplied Colleen Vinton's girls, right?'

'That was part of it.'

'Who beat you up?'

'*Who* isn't the important part.'

'Sure it is. You know their names?'

'They wore masks.'

'What happened?'

'They saw me with you and thought I was having ideas.'

'About talking?'

'Yeah.'

'Talking about what?'

Maddy breathes out. 'The girl.'

He leans over and touches her. 'Sarah Utton?'

'Her and Vovo put the stuff around.' She pauses. 'Vovo did the upper part of the coast. Sarah looked after Miami to the border. One night, September last year, we had a meet. They set it for a bush road out the back of Tugun, right out in the sticks. It's pitch-black out there. Brian and I were counting out the money in the headlights of the car, with Vovo and Sarah watching on. While we're out there, these men come out of the scrub in balaclavas.'

'These the same guys who hit you?'

'Yeah.'

'Keep going. What happened?'

'I thought it was a stick-up at first, but they immediately grabbed Sarah and started dragging her off. Vovo started flipping out. She was high. She tried to fight them and one of these guys, he just pushed her back and shot her in the head. Then he turned the gun on me.

Brian started screaming at him to stop. *She's the chemist. She's the chemist.'* Maddy cries now. Through it, she mumbles, 'They said if we told anyone about it, they'd kill us. So we ran. Just got in the car and hightailed it out of there. The next morning, Colleen Vinton called me here at the house and said she could protect me, if I kept my mouth shut.'

'And Brian talked?'

'I think so.'

'Who'd he tell?'

'The police, Henry. Who do you think?'

'Did he tell his wife?'

Maddy nods. 'They're threatening her too.'

Henry gets up, stands behind her. He looks into her eyes in the mirror above the sink. There's something else in there. He takes a punt. 'You sure you don't know who these blokes are? I can fix this, but we can't go halfway. There's no upside in going halfway.'

'I think one of them was Tommy Lomax. He works for Colleen. He was a regular patient of Brian's. This gross hippie guy. Used to come in for VD checks when I was Brian's receptionist.'

'You see his face?'

'His eyes, and the guy reeks of incense. He has these weird shoes.'

'You recognised his shoes?'

She nods. 'Leather loafers.'

It makes sense. Lomax is Vinton's standover man and it all seems to circulate around her. But Henry can't put it together on the spot. There's no way Sarah Utton was operating in Vinton's orbit without her go-ahead, not with that many of the girls involved, but why would she send Tommy out into the night to break up a drug deal she was a part of?

'What about the other man in the balaclava?' says Henry.

'A cop, at a guess. Just from how he was.'

'Do you know how to fire a gun?'

'They scare me,' she says.

'That's the point of them.'

Henry walks out to the car and takes his throwdown piece from under the spare tyre in the boot. The street around him is dead. Only the rumble of the highway and the roar of the ocean. Humid as hell, too. No breeze.

CHAPTER 83

LANA HITS THE BOOKS, page after page. Fieldwork, records, case files. She revises her work, mapping out data on a piece of foolscap paper. Elements of it look startlingly foreign now. She can barely remember the final stages of Diablo before the abrupt end. But in there—amongst the mess of detail—she has a lot of unrealised links between Colleen Vinton and Brian Amstell.

For an hour, she pores over her bounty of medical files stolen from Brian Amstell's office. For the most part, the files for Violet Burke and Sarah Utton resemble regular medical records. Burke had bouts of bronchitis. Utton had a bowel condition. Both suffered prolonged addiction issues. But pencilled into the rear flap of each folder are dates and dollar amounts. Rudimentary ledgers. It fits with Lowell Sennett's account, but it doesn't help with locating Utton.

Lana sits there in the station house and turns it over in her mind. After a time, she begins to feel lost in it and hits the streets of Surfers Paradise for fresh air. She loops around to the boardwalk, propping herself against a timber rail with her back to the overcast sea.

'Not much of an afternoon, is it?' says a voice.

She looks over, the recognition taking a few seconds. It's Emmett Hades, the old detective.

'We met at the house the other week,' he says. 'The Millman scene.'

'I remember. I was hoping we'd run into each other again.'

'And here I am.'

'How far off is that rain, you reckon?'

'Still a ways off. Early morning, I'd say.'

'This humidity is shocking. This is a weird, bloody place to work, Emmett. It really is its own thing, isn't it? I'm drowning in it today, let me tell you.'

'I suppose you're aware of how it all turned out for me.'

She nods. 'You're not the first bloke I know who's had a bit of a hiccup up here.' She taps her temple. 'Gets to all of us sooner or later. It's sure as shit coming for me.'

Emmett smiles at that. 'What do they have you working on?'

'Just mopping up loose ends. Bits and bobs work, but it's bloody impossible to keep hold of.'

'If you're sticking around for a few more days, you should come round for dinner. I'd love to hear about your time down south. You know, it's strange, but of all the things I miss, the gossip is the thing I miss most. I might be able to live without the job, but the stories . . .'

'Oh, I get it. I'll come round. I'd love that. I want to pick your brain too.'

'Henry has my number. Give me a bell.'

With that, Emmett starts off.

Lana calls after him. 'Hey, can I ask you something? What can you tell me about this Colleen Vinton character?'

'Why?'

'I think she's in business with my dead doctor. And one of her runners is the girl Henry's after. Colleen's up to her neck in the Diablo stuff, as it turns out, but no one seems to care. Henry talks about her like she's invincible, like a force of nature or something.'

'Have you had a run-in with her?'

'Yeah. She scared the absolute shit out of me.'

'She scares everyone. If she falls, all of this will go with her. It'll just topple into the sea.'

'So, she *is* the kingpin?'

'People down here treat her that way. But she's not really a criminal mastermind. More like the face of progress. She's the *destructive* face of progress.'

Lana can't really get a read on this. 'Okay, thanks,' she says. 'Have a good one.'

'One more thing, if Colleen has the girl, you should look across the border. Somewhere near Lismore. That's where she puts a lot of her ill-gotten gains, apparently. Never been able to track it down myself, but I've never had your resources either. Not a lot of buy-in for catching Colleen Vinton in New South Wales. Your lot were always tight-lipped with their info on her.'

'I wonder why.'

Emmett smiles. 'I don't. Okay, I better get going.'

'Take it easy,' she says.

Emmett walks away.

CHAPTER 84

HENRY HEADS ACROSS THE street to the Surfers Paradise police station just as the streetlights blink on. He travels the quiet corridors of the building, finding Lana Cohen out in the empty Diablo bullpen, working at another bloke's desk. She has a phone unit on her thigh.

'Didn't expect you back today,' she says, barely looking up.

'I know what happened to Sarah Utton.'

That gets her attention.

Henry looks around. 'Where is everyone?'

'They're having a bit of a get-together over in Robbery. I wasn't invited.'

He drags a chair over and, in a low voice, tells her Maddy's story: the abduction of Sarah Utton, the shooting of Violet Burke, the two men in ski masks. 'I think one of them was Tommy Lomax, a guy who works for Vinton.'

'I met him once. He's bad news. So, he shot Violet over some drug dispute and made it look like a Diablo thing?'

'Sounds that way. You find anything here?'

'I did, actually. I had a strange run-in with your mate Emmett this afternoon while I was out and about. He told me a very interesting factoid about Colleen. He reckons she has a place across the border near Lismore. I've been on the phone for the last hour running it down.' She hands over a list. 'Vinton is clean as a whistle, of course, no paperwork on her, so I started ringing in title searches for different people. Called in a *lot* of favours. Do you know who *is* a registered landowner for a few places around Lismore?'

Henry looks at the list. 'Tell me.'

'Christopher Cole.' The owner of Paradise Gaming—cutting cheques to Sarah Utton—as well as Joel Delaney's old business partner.

'You're shitting me?'

'Nope. Lots of aliases and horse trading, but it's right there. The Cole family has properties all over the region. His brother-in-law bought a few places around Lismore a couple of years back, all in the same two-month stretch.'

Henry winces. 'Cole's in the bloody photo with Emmery. The one I've been using to ID the bloke this whole time.'

'What do you think? Great place to stash a missing girl for a couple of months.'

'It's all we've got.'

Henry jolts as a loud cheer erupts from the other side of the building.

'That's the party,' says Lana.

'I think we should get out of here. I've got a weird feeling.'

'Really?'

'Yeah. Get your stuff.'

Before they go, they check the records room for *Lomax, Tommy*. They find his rap sheet. It's long. Henry separates the file, and they spend a few minutes going through each page, line by line. 'Here,' he says, pointing. Christopher Cole paid Tommy Lomax's bail on public nuisance charges back in '77. A year later, Lenny Gibbs, victim number five, bails Lomax out for another infraction. Assault and resisting arrest.

'How's that feeling of yours now?' says Lana. 'Watch this.'

There's a phone in the corner of the records room. Lana uses it to call in Tommy's name to the New South Wales police archive and hits the jackpot. Her hand over the mouthpiece, she says, 'Arrested '76 after a domestic assault call-out. Place of residence . . .' She puts the phone down. 'It's one of the addresses. Same street name and—'

'My, my, my, what do we have here?' says a voice from across the room.

They turn to find Ron Bingham swaying gently back and forth in the doorway, a brown tallie of XXXX Bitter in hand.

'Ron,' says Henry, gently sliding the cabinet shut. 'Big night, mate?'

'Big enough, yeah. Yeah, big enough. I was just . . .' The man is catatonic. He scratches his gut. 'You're all right, luv, you know that? Don't know if I ever said it, but, luv, yeah, you're all right. I mean—'

'I was just about to come over,' says Henry. 'You want to come with me, Ron?'

'Where?'

'Back to the party.'

'Those fucking Robbery cunts. I fucking hate those cunts.' Eyes open and blank. 'Yeah, I might as well head back. Come on. Come and have a fucking drink with me, Henry. Come on, Sherlock, come have a drink.'

Henry whispers to Lana, 'Meet me across the road in five,' and darts over to Ron.

It takes some doing, but eventually, Henry coaxes Ron to the western lunchroom where about two dozen drunk plainclothesmen stand around in a circle yelling at each other. In the centre of the room sits an overflowing garbage bin piled with empties and above it, a piñata of sorts: a grey pullover stuffed with toilet paper and tied off at the bottom with masking tape. For a head, the piñata has a green balloon and on the balloon is a photocopied mugshot of Daryl Millman.

'You must be jumping for joy, son,' says one of the Diablo men, emerging from the fray. 'All the glory and none of the bloody court appearances.'

'Jumping for bloody joy,' says another man.

'What?' Henry yells, pushing his voice above the chatter.

'Ha, he doesn't know. Look at him! He doesn't even know, look!'

Pete Reynolds tosses a half-full can of beer at Henry, hitting him in the chest, spraying his shirt. 'Someone topped the bastard two hours ago. He's fucking dead. Bled out in his cell.'

'Here's to Boggo Road,' shouts one of the detectives.

'Here's to fast justice!'

Then:

'Millman's dead!'

'Millman's dead!'

'Millman's dead!'

Emboldened by the chant, one of the younger detectives gets out his lighter and lights the Millman effigy on fire.

It takes quickly.

Smoke pours out.

The entire room cackles.

Henry's frozen, beer seeping through his clothes.

Ears ringing.

What's happening?

It's pure chaos right up to the moment Bruno Karras grabs the fire extinguisher and lets rip.

CHAPTER 85

HENRY COMES OUT OF the station house looking worried and won't say a word until the car is moving. 'I want to visit these houses tonight. You in?'

Lana's game. 'You want me to phone through for warrants?'

'No. If Tommy and Colleen have Utton stashed in one of these places and she's still down there, we have to go straight in. It's all going to hell. We're . . . I think we're in trouble here.' Henry tightens his grip on the steering wheel.

'Hey, slow down.'

'They killed Millman,' he says. 'He's dead.'

He tells her the details.

'It could be a coincidence,' she says.

'We asked him about Utton. Showed him a picture of her, kicked the hornet's nest.'

'What now?'

'We check the houses and pray,' says Henry.

'And if we find Sarah, what then?'

'Let's cross that bridge when we get to it.' He turns into a side street. 'I've got to do something before we cross the border.'

That something is Maddy Santos. Henry pulls up to her house and goes inside. A minute later, Maddy slips into the rear seat behind Lana. The woman's in bad shape. Someone has given her a hiding, and she's drunk off her arse.

'I remember you,' Maddy says.

'Yeah, sure,' says Lana. 'What happened to you, Maddy?'

'What do you think?'

Henry gets behind the wheel, takes one look at Lana and says, 'The men we're looking for did that.'

'Why?'

'Yeah, why Henry?' says Maddy, slurring.

He shakes his head. Instead of answering the question, he pulls the car out onto the road.

A minute later, Maddy says, 'Where are you taking me?'

Henry tells her, 'I know a place.'

Maddy winds down the window, blasting the interior with hot air. She lights a smoke. Lana watches her in the side mirror. Maddy delicately puts her hand out into the wind and brings it back. 'It's starting to rain,' she says.

•

Across the border, the roads turn wild and dark. They hurtle down corridors of grey trees strobed by headlights. They're inland now, not a living creature in sight. Henry finds a holiday inn and pays for a room. Lana stays in the car. She watches Henry and Maddy embrace in the doorway of the room. She watches Henry hold the woman's head in his hands as he kisses her. The dissonance of it—this angry man moving gently—loads the moment, and a wave of heat passes through Lana's face and neck, a strange mix of desire and despair, as well as something else, something strong enough to momentarily cut through the fear, but harder to name.

•

Back out on the road, Lana hears the rain coming before she sees it. Seconds later, a curtain of water hits the windscreen, coming down so hard it feels like the glass might come in. Henry doesn't seem to notice. He turns the wipers on. Checks his watch. Neither of them speak.

Lana senses the end arriving, and figures Henry does, too. There's a twitch to it, a pulse Lana always clocks at the end of a big case. The big unlock. It always comes with enough adrenaline to push her through the final stage, out of squad cars and divvy vans and into suburban street blockades, night raids, through kicked-in doors and brawls and violence. The end always seems to have its own momentum.

'I think we've found the girl,' Henry says, snapping her out of it. 'Something about this feels right.'

'We'll find something.'

That's always true too, at the end.

It's an unravelling.

A collapse.

Revelations.

CHAPTER 86

THEY HAVE THREE ADDRESSES around Lismore. Three houses all owned by Christopher Cole. First up is the place where Tommy Lomax was arrested in '76 on DV charges. He isn't there tonight, though. No one is. The house is abandoned: a burned-out fibro number, sans windows. Henry and Lana have a good look through the rubble, just to be sure. On the way out, Lana fixes the beam of her flashlight on a wall of graffiti, spotlighting a crucifix with two cross-bars, an infinity symbol at the bottom.

'You seen this before?' she says.

Henry says no.

'Me neither.'

'Let's get out of here.'

•

Second on the list is a house on the edge of the Lismore scrub. From the roadside, Henry can see it isn't their spot. The house is occupied. Lights on. Curtains spread. A family inside. Three children and two adults, all in pyjamas around a flickering TV set.

Lana knocks, and the father lets them in without hesitation. 'Come out of that rain,' he says. He takes them to the living room and sits them down in front of the bug-eyed children. The wife asks if they want tea.

'I'd love one, but we aren't staying long,' says Henry.

The father is the local bookkeeper. He's heard of Christopher Cole and Joel Delaney ('I did a stint in Sydney') and he knows Cole owns the house, but it's trivia to him. He rents the place through the local real estate agency. 'I just pay the guy down the street. Has Cole done something?'

Henry shows the man a picture of Sarah Utton, and the man shakes his head. He passes it to his wife, and she shakes her head too.

Henry follows up with, 'Do you know a man called Tommy Lomax?'

Neither of them knows him.

'Are we in trouble?' says the wife.

'No,' says Lana.

They leave them be.

•

The third place is dark, tall bushland. Henry spots a gravel track leading in, barely visible in the downpour. A locked gate across the front. 'This is more like it,' he says.

'Are we going to radio this in?'

'No.' Henry reaches over and pops the glove box. He takes out a cotton bag and, from the bag, two handguns. He turns the car's interior light on and checks the serial numbers on each gun. 'You don't want this one,' he says. 'Here.' He passes her the other one.

'I have my service weapon.'

'So do I. Take both.'

Lana lifts herself off the car seat and presses the gun into the waistline of her jeans.

'Are you still good with this?' he says.

'Good enough. Let's get it over with.'

They take umbrellas and flashlights.

CHAPTER 87

THE HIKE IN IS fifteen minutes through a winding forest, rain sluicing down the trail, filling Lana's shoes. Out beyond the trees, the trail evaporates into open pasture. The property is nestled into a long hill and, halfway up, Lana can see the lights of a house.

They keep to the shadows. The house is an old Queenslander on stumps. No gardens. No fencing or pathway. The tin roof of the dwelling roars in the downpour, covering the sound of their approach, but also giving the place a dark, pounding energy.

Henry points to the stairs. They ditch the umbrellas and walk up, crouch by the front window. Lana takes the first look.

Lace curtains.

A dank room lit by gas lamps.

Two women sit in adjacent chairs by the fire. Both are dressed in black smocks.

Lana shakes her head at Henry and spins her finger. *Let's look around.*

They split up and creep the outside verandah, checking other windows. Lana finds another woman round back. She stands in the kitchen, washing out a tea kettle at the sink. She's wearing the same garb as the others, a black smock. Her face is buried under long peroxide hair.

Same build as Sarah Utton.

Henry and Lana reconvene at the front door, voices low, faces close.

'Anything?' says Henry.

'Someone like her in the back. No sign of Tommy.'

'Let's have a chat with them.'

Lana stands front and centre. She opens the screen door and knocks.

Inside the house, a woman shrieks. Footfall vibrates through the timber as a shadow crosses the window.

The lights go out.

Lana knocks a second time.

'That you?' says a voice.

'Police. Can we come in?'

Hushed whispers sound from behind the door, then it opens a little. A woman's pale white face appears in the murk. It's one of the women Lana spotted by the fire.

'Why are you here?' says the woman.

'Routine enquiries,' says Lana. 'Can we come in? Won't be a minute.'

'Is it important?' says the woman, spotting Henry.

'It is.'

'I guess that's okay.'

The woman's face disappears.

With one hand on her sidearm, Lana pushes the door open further, revealing an empty hallway. The woman is gone. The smell of incense and burnt timber wafts out.

'What the fuck is that?' hisses Henry, a hand gripping Lana's shoulder. He points past her at the terminus of the hallway.

There's a creature of some sort sitting there.

Two eyes shining in the darkness.

'Hello?' calls Lana.

She switches on her flashlight and moves the beam over to where the eyes are.

It's a fat grey possum, hunched over a kitchen saucer of dry food.

Henry curses.

'In here,' calls a voice.

They move in. Halfway along the hall is a doorway spraying warm orange light against the opposing wall. Lana takes a quick look around the jamb. The woman from before now stands by the fireplace. The lights are still out.

Lana says, 'Can we come through?'

'Is that fella with you?'

'He's here.'

'Landlord won't like it. Landlord says no men in the house. Can he stay outside?'

'He's a policeman.'

No response.

Lana and Henry slowly move into the room. In the light from the fire, Lana can see that the woman is younger than expected. In her early twenties. Long auburn hair.

Lana says, 'Can we turn a light on?'

'Sure,' says the woman, but she doesn't move.

'Why don't we all sit down,' says Henry. He makes for a threadbare armchair.

Once seated, they both open up their badges. The woman comes forward and looks. 'I know you,' she says to Henry. 'I know your face. You have a familiar ... presence.' She goes back across the room and takes a seat at one end of a long antique lounge.

'Is there anyone else in the house?' says Lana.

'Aries is out back. Tower is making tea.'

'Anyone else?'

'No,' says the woman.

'Anyone expected home soon?'

The woman speaks, but the surging rain on the tin roof drowns her out.

'What was that?' says Lana.

'No one is expected,' says the woman.

'I need to take down the names of the people who live here.'

'I'm Temperance,' says the woman. 'And there's Tower and Aries, as I said.'

'Can I have your full names?'

'No,' says Temperance. 'No other names. Landlord doesn't allow it.' As she says this, another of the women steps into the room.

'Doesn't allow what?' says the new one, placing a tray of tea and biscuits on the ground.

'Our dirty names,' says Temperance. 'That's Tower.'

'Oh,' says the new woman. She delicately pours out the tea. 'You both look wet.'

Lana takes her cup and holds it in her hands, letting the warmth seep through.

'Who is this landlord?' says Henry.

'We have to call him Landlord,' says Temperance.

'Isn't that his name?' says Tower.

'I guess.'

Done with tea, Tower walks across the room and stands beside Temperance at the settee. At a guess, Lana pegs the girls for stoned. They have the slow, even drawl of stoners, and this stuff about their names isn't a game. They both seem more than a little confused by the questions.

Lana pushes on and the interview plods. Eventually, Henry just comes out with it. 'We're looking for a girl. She's about your age. Her name is Sarah. This is a picture of her.' He gets up and reaches his arm out with the photo.

Still seated, Temperance leans out and takes it.

Then Henry twitches. 'What, what is that?' he says, pointing at the space on the lounge beside Temperance. 'Is that another possum?'

Lana peers around, trying to see.

'What?' says Tower. 'Oh, that. That's probably an elf.'

Henry recoils. 'A what?'

Tower turns to Temperance and says, 'I told you it was strong.'

Lana slowly turns in horror and looks at Henry's chair.

His half-empty teacup sits on the arm.

Somewhere in the house, a sound announces itself, a bassy rhythm that Lana thinks is a piece of machinery or thunder, but quickly the sound morphs into—

A third woman runs into the room, her bare feet slapping against the floor.

She's holding an axe.

'Henry!'

The woman rushes him, but Henry manages to bring an arm up, catching the axe handle under the blade with his forearm.

A sickening, crunching sound sprays from the connection.

He grabs the woman with the axe and they go over.

Hands grapple for the weapon.

Tower starts moving, reaching down behind the settee.

Lana knows it before she sees it.

Gun.

Tower lifts the rifle from its hiding spot, and in a single swift movement, fires.

Lightning in the room.

Chair fabric exploding by Lana's head as she dives away, landing on the floor with her sidearm already drawn, already squeezing the trigger as a jet of blood sprays the wall behind Tower and the rifle tumbles. Beside Lana, Henry throws the woman off him and Lana lashes out with the butt of her gun, smashing it into the woman's head until she goes limp.

It only takes seconds, but these are seconds with their eyes off Temperance.

Lana looks up, terrified.

But Temperance remains on the lounge, emotionless.

There's gun smoke in the air.

They can all hear Tower dying, gasping her last breaths.

Lana goes to Temperance. The woman is still holding the photograph of Sarah Utton. Lana stands close, brushes the hair from the girl's face.

Temperance's eyes refocus. 'Yes?' she says.

'Do you know this girl?'

'She's in the tomb,' she says.

CHAPTER 88

HENRY RUBS HIS EYES and stares. His father stands across the room, in the doorway by the hall. For some reason, his father is holding a pair of binoculars. He brings them up to his face.

'Don't you fucking look at me!' Henry shouts.

'Hey, Henry,' says a voice, a watery quality to it. 'You've been drugged. It's okay.'

It's Lana, but she's not facing him. Instead, she's on the opposite side of the room, looking down at a police detective at her feet. 'We've got to go,' she says to the detective on the ground, and as she helps him up, Henry's world shimmers and lifts. He realises he's been looking at himself from across the room. The shock of it blasts him along some strange tunnel of light and movement, back into himself.

'Can you walk?' she says.

'Yeah, I think so.'

'Take your gun out.'

He does it.

The woman called Temperance leads them through the house, past a dining room and into a kitchen then through a sleep-out to the rear stairs and the pouring rain. At first, the rain punctures Henry's delirium, but only briefly. The night world quickly seeps in. He sees ghouls and serpents as they run across the backyard of the house. He feels tentacles wrapping around the cuffs of his pants, thin arms gripping on. He frantically scans the night, searching for other monsters. He sees a dragon with the head of a rooster. He sees men from the past, waiting in the shadows. He sees a green sphere of light. And he hears his mother's voice, humming to the radio as he stumbles, trips and—

A black vortex opens up, some deep cratered hole, the sides of which rush past, flapping his clothes against his arms and legs.

No light.

No hope.

Total endlessness and—

Lana's hands grab onto him, hoisting him up. 'You have to keep moving,' she shouts. 'You need to concentrate.'

Henry finds some deep reserve of focus and holds onto it as they cross a paddock. Temperance is in front of him, leading them towards thick scrubland. In the scrub, the canopy provides respite from the rain, but the low visibility sparks Henry's nightmare-vision again. It's worse this time. His skin pops and sizzles. Flying objects shriek, their fangs dripping with bile. Human faces float by, all of them smashed open, beaten and bloody. Corpse upon corpse around him. Ghost after ghost. Henry can hear himself quietly moaning, but he holds on.

They press through the trees and back into the gale.

'It's not far,' yells Temperance.

Henry sees figures in front of him, walking across the grey landscape in the distance.

They're not real.

They're familiar figures, from his memory.

Even in the dark and the rain he knows they are transformed visions of himself and Peter Torney—the man he killed outside Beaudesert—and he knows this is a flashback, but he can't stop himself replaying it. He can't make Torney stop begging and pleading and crying and blubbering and shouting and now Henry feels the same coldness blossoming inside himself, the same dark sliver sharpening.

He remembers what Torney said at the end.

He hears it again:

Every day was agony, every day was—

Then the muzzle flash of a gun.

CHAPTER 89

AT FIRST LANA THINKS it's lightning.

Hard rain. New moon. No visibility.

Then a second volley of shots flash and she knows it's gunfire coming from the tree line on her left. Henry returns fire, hollering loudly over the shots, sounding completely haunted and feral. Lana grabs him and screams, 'Get the girl,' pushing him after Temperance.

She starts for the trees.

Another shot flashes in the night.

Wide.

They're guessing.

Another flash.

In the distance, Henry makes a jolting sound, but keeps moving. She hears him running in the grassy mud and water, the rain still slamming down.

Another flash.

Lana gets a read on the shooter, a general vicinity. She puts the area in the sights of her pistol and slowly walks towards it, keeping aim, staying low to the ground.

One chance.

The ground by her feet explodes, followed by the reverberated roar of the shot.

Lana keeps moving.

A human shape in the distance now.

Another shot.

Wide this time, but close.

One chance.

Only one—

Lightning arcs overhead, blasting an illuminated instant—white sky, white landscape—and there in it, a man, half-naked with a rifle, standing out in the open.

Lana fires twice.

The lightning fades back to night.

She runs, keeps firing.

Forty metres.

Thirty.

Another flash of lightning: the man prone.

Twenty metres.

Ten.

She comes up on the body, circles it and sees burnt holes in the man's chest.

Lana feels for a pulse. He's dead.

She looks at him. It's Tommy Lomax, eyes open.

'Hey,' calls a familiar voice.

Not Lomax, it's from the nearby tree line.

'It's okay,' says the voice.

She walks over, gun raised.

Mark Evans sits slumped against a tree trunk on the edge of the scrub. He's pale and sweating. Dying, at a guess. Lana can't see the injury, but he's breathing heavy, only a minute or two to go.

'I think, I think Henry shot me,' Mark says. 'How about that?' and he coughs.

'Why are you here?' she says.

'Ha, it's not called the Joke for nothing, Lana, it's not because you know . . .' and he gasps for air. 'You never know the punchline, not really . . .'

She puts a hand on his hand, gives it a squeeze.

'I hate the rain,' he says.

'I'll be back.'

Lana runs.

Back in the field, she finds three figures huddled around a circular hole in the ground, a camp light below and an earth floor. A bunker.

The tomb.

Lana collapses to her knees and looks at their faces. Temperance is drenched, muddy, wide-eyed, but calm. Beside her, under her arm, sits Sarah Utton, dirt-smeared and vacant. She's alive though, a grimy version of her photo. Then there is Henry. He's as pale as a ghost and crying openly, distraught and deranged by the drug. Underneath his wailing, Lana can hear another sound, some soft gurgling. She sees movement in his jacket and gently peels back the cloth. Henry's bleeding from the side, blood leeching out of his belt line, and there, above the stain, nestled in the crook of his arm, is a tiny baby.

REVELATIONS

JOURNAL OF EMMETT HADES

(SELECTED EXCERPTS)

Nothing on the Gold Coast is ever completely true. They used to call it the South Coast, back in the day, because it was the only thing south of Brisbane worth caring about. Such was the provincialism of Queensland, so wrapped up in its dreams of independence and legitimacy. They called it the South Coast right through the 1950s—not that long ago, really—and they only changed the name to besmirch the place once it got too big for its britches. They called it the Gold Coast to run it down, for its inflated land prices and its rising status.

That's the etymology.

The Gold Coast is a joke scrawled in history's ledger.

Early and predictive.

•

The Lismore shootings never got properly reported or investigated. The Gold Coast Bulletin *ran a page four story—HERO COP KILLED IN DRUG RAID—but it was too depressing for the front of the paper. They reserved the front for a higher-profile death: Daryl Millman, the monster, stabbed in prison. They put him in the big type and the Lismore incident slipped from view almost as fast as it appeared. It became trivia. A thing crime buffs and cab drivers knew. 'Yeah nah, you know, the bloke who caught Millman? Can't remember his name, but he died on the same day. Some drug bust gone wrong. Poor bugger.'*

That hero cop?

Mark Evans.

Henry was fine.

Well . . .

Almost fine.

•

Henry spent a night in hospital, then recovered at home. A week later, he and Lana brought Colleen Vinton in for questioning. Henry figured he'd soon have the testimony of an ex-Vinton employee (Sarah Utton), and the surviving girl from the house (Temperance) and it might be enough. That and the beginnings of a paper trail between Vinton and Lomax, and the Lismore house and the dreadful bunker, all catalogued by the New South Wales police force. It seemed like a good start.

Vinton lawyered up, as expected. A property developer by the name of Robert Emmery paid the bills, put his best solicitors on it. He even sat out in the station house reception and waited for her while she visited.

He didn't have to wait long.

Colleen said:

No comment.

No comment.

No comment.

From that point onward, the system worked like clockwork. The cancerous parts of the Queensland Police Force started throwing money around. The Internal Investigations Section gave Henry a visit; they showed a remarkable dedication to policy all of a sudden, grilling him on the Lismore raid and the lack of warrants and process. They told him they'd keep an eye on him. The inference: you can still turn this around. Even Jack the Bagman got in on the act. Despite being the instigator of Henry's involvement in the Sarah Utton case, Jack had the gall to set up a meeting. 'Now's a great time to look the other way, son,' he said. 'It'd be a shame for us to start digging up what we don't want to be digging up.'

'I've got the girl, and everything she knows,' said Henry. 'So, tell your friends I'm out. Fuck the consequences. I'm happy to roll the dice on this one.'

In truth, he was bluffing and praying. Sarah Utton was in a mental ward—practically mute—and the rest of the case was awash with messy, unresolved detail that no one wanted glued back together. On top of which, Henry still had Sarah Utton's baby. He refused to hand the child over—knew the kid's life was at stake—and he had, in that moment, the pull to buy some time. So, he bought a crib for the spare room of Maddy's house and slept in the next room with a loaded shotgun by the bed. Like I said, bluffing and praying.

Around him, the cancer kept spreading. Lana Cohen flew to Sydney and gave her debriefing on Diablo and Lismore. It was a closed meeting. No Dwain Gorst or union rep. It felt off, so she told them nothing. And from the moment she uttered her first refusal, Lana knew she was stone-cold fucked. Gorst's whole fact-finding mission was unsanctioned. The shooting was wayward. And everything else was way, way off-book. The meeting attendees thanked her for coming, then they fired her for insubordination.

But even that wasn't enough.

It kept spreading.

Colleen Vinton's house outside of Lismore burned to the ground. Someone dug up the bunker. It looked like an excavated swimming pool by the time they were through. Then every speck of New South Wales paperwork went into a closed archive. The finale chimed when the Queensland prosecutors declined to lay charges against Vinton. Whatever occulted force Henry and Lana stirred up, it spoke back and it was louder than the truth. Secrets can be like that.

CHAPTER 90

ONE AFTERNOON, SOMEONE KNOCKS on the front door of Maddy's house. Henry checks the window. It's Colleen Vinton. She's spruced up in black business attire, black sunglasses. The grim reaper in broad daylight.

'What do you want?' Henry says through the door.

'A chat.'

'Stay out there. You're not coming in.'

'Suit yourself, Henry. But I'm not a vampire, you know.'

Henry turns to Maddy. She's right there. She knows who it is, recognises the voice. He gives her the look and Maddy disappears down the hall to the master bedroom walk-in where they keep the overnight bag and the spare gun.

Henry steps out, leans against the patio railing. It still hurts to sit. Colleen eases herself into a canvas deckchair and digs around in her handbag for a slimline case of cigarettes. 'I suppose a cup of tea's out of the question?'

'I don't want to fuck around,' he says.

'Suit yourself.'

'What is this? A final warning?'

'Oh no, it's better than that. A final offer.'

'Yeah?'

'Half a million.'

'For what? The baby? I should slit your throat.'

Colleen laughs. 'That's very dramatic, Henry. No, you can keep Robbie's bastard. The money is for you, to leave the coast, give the kid a better life. It's a boy, right? You can start again somewhere. Go straight, for a change. Leave all this behind you.'

It stuns him. She's serious. 'Just go?' he says.

'That's the deal.'

'What's the catch?'

'No catch. Or none you need to worry about.'

'Are we talking openly, Colleen, or are you full of shit?'

'I'm a lot of things, but I don't lie to people.'

Henry tries to think it through but there's too much going on. 'Okay then, tell me how all this happened. I don't want to leave town without knowing.'

Colleen huffs out a long, exasperated breath. 'One day, everything I do here on the coast will be legal. The fucking, the gambling, abortions, drugs. The lot. But a legal casino is the first cab off the rank. That's the progress people can handle, Henry. The baby steps. There's *going* to be a legal casino here before the end of the decade. It's already happening. But for that to happen, I need a man like Robert Emmery in my pocket. A good *family* man, a church guy with political connections, but I also need him to have . . . weaknesses, I guess. I suspect you know all about Robbie's little appetites?'

'The period blood?'

'That's the one. Parting the Red Sea. All that. He's a strange one. But poor Robbie doesn't know the first thing about women or how they work. For all his bizarre tastes, you'd think he'd be interested, but, no, not in the slightest. You can get pregnant when it's that time of the month, Henry. Don't let anyone tell you otherwise.'

'It's nothing I need to worry about,' he says. 'I take it he got Sarah pregnant, and you snatched her up to make sure she had the baby?'

'Keeping a bad man on a leash is easy. But tying a good man down, that takes something bigger. Dirty photos and the usual don't work when you want to keep someone clean. You've got to think long term. I've learned that the hard way.'

Henry looks right at her. 'Is there anything you won't do for this plan of yours?'

'People don't like the answer to that question when they hear it. Look, in business, you're always dealing with contingencies. Sarah's pregnancy was a mistake. *Her* mistake. But it landed in *my* lap. Looking back, I could have bought her off with half of what I'm offering you, but . . .'

'You got angry.'

She looks away. 'Well, the woman did rip me off, and she was making plans of her own. I couldn't let that slide. The one thing I'll say in my defence is that I didn't know what Tommy was up to, god rest his soul. I didn't think he'd keep her in a bloody hole in the ground, or any of that nonsense. That weird cult he'd made for himself, out at Chris's place, I had no clue. I'm sure the late Mark Evans didn't know what he was dealing with, either. I really thought Tommy was smarter than that, but that's men for you. Now, is there anything else? Because I'd rather talk shop, if you don't mind.'

'What happens to Sarah Utton?'

'I'll take care of her, in the good way. And for the record, leaving the baby with you is fine with her. She wouldn't know what to do with it anyway. She can't look after a child in her state.'

'How will you get me the money?'

Colleen smiles. 'Drop by the place on Hannan Street. I'll have my girl put you on the payroll. I'll need to dole it out over the next couple of years, but I'm good for it. As long as you take care of the kid and disappear.'

He thinks on it. 'I've got terms.'

'I'm not sure I'm in the mood today.'

'I have your medical file, the one from Brian Amstell's office. It makes for pretty interesting reading. He kept a picture in the back of it.' Henry opens his wallet and removes the photo, holds it out for her to see.

It's all there on display:

Colleen and the dildo.

Diablo victims alongside her, smiling away.

The priest's son in the centre.

Topped himself.

Colleen tries to shrug it off, but her eyes say otherwise. 'What do you want?'

Henry ignores it. He points to the man in the centre. 'That's Father Frank Hanlon's kid. I've seen the other photo of him from that night. It's not like this one, is it? I think this might be the heart of the entire thing, actually. Was Father Frank another one of these good men who needed tying down, Colleen? Is this whole thing arriving off the back of a grudge between you and that priest?'

Colleen stubs out her smoke. 'I'm not sure I follow.'

'I don't think I know all of it either, but *this* asks a lot of questions.'

'It doesn't have to. What do you want?'

'I want you to keep your promises,' says Henry.

'Is that it?'

'And Maddy's out. You need to find yourself another pill-maker. That's over. Also, I want you to leave Lowell Sennett alone. He's out too.'

'No, I need Lowell, unfortunately. You can have Maddy. The baby will need a mother.'

'Well, no repercussions for Lowell, then.'

'I'll have to give him a mild touch-up. Is that okay?'

'I can live with it.'

Colleen gets up and shakes Henry's hand, but she keeps hold of it afterward, gently touching the lines of his palm. 'Henry, I just want to remind you that you're just one man. One man in a long line of them. So don't get any strange ideas. I don't like gossip. If I ever hear a whisper about that photo . . . it's personal. It's more personal than you'll ever know. So if you use it against me again, I'll come find you and I'll kill you, and I'll kill everyone who's ever been kind to you.'

'I believe it.'

'Good. Mark Evans always said you were smarter than you let on.'

Colleen makes her way down the stairs. At the bottom, she turns. 'Henry? One more thing. Your friend, Emmett Hades, can you try to convince him to stay out of my affairs? I know the man's in poor health, but I fear for his safety if he keeps going the way he's going. He can be very persistent.'

'Sounds like another threat, Colleen.'

She bounces her car keys in her palm. 'That's because it is.'

CHAPTER 91

LANA COHEN TOOK HER severance money and headed north. She had very little tying her to Sydney: a near-empty apartment in Glebe and a second-hand car she sold to a neighbour's kid. That's it. Most of her clothes went to the Salvation Army. There was no boyfriend or husband. No pets or close friends.

On her last day in town, she packed a week's laundry into a rucksack and caught a lift up the coast with a colleague, an old Homicide partner. At the border, she walked across Boyds Bridge to Queensland on foot.

•

Bruno Karras meets her at the Sands Hotel for a drink. 'Couldn't stay away, huh?' He has a schooner of beer in each hand. All smiles. He knows about her dismissal. They all do. Word travels fast.

'I've got something I want to show you,' she says.

It's a pile of photos of Gold Coast detectives stepping into a local brothel.

'What are you going to do with those?' he says.

'Finish the case.'

Bruno hates the sound of it.

•

A week later, one unseasonably cool evening in March, Lana comes by the house of Emmett Hades for dinner. She brings Henry with her. In his kitchen, they mill around. Henry mashing the potatoes. Lana at the table, sipping beer. Emmett tending to the T-bone steaks steaming up the room. The old man has the wireless on. The six o'clock bulletin plays.

Upset in the Labor Party continues tonight as—

Henry turns it off.

Emmett says, 'So that's it then?'

'Seems like it,' says Henry. His resignation letter is in. It's a done deal. He's already told them about his plans with Maddy and the baby. They're heading south, across the border and into the hills. When no one's watching, they'll jump ship to New Zealand and disappear completely. 'We're going to try a few places before we settle. I want some land.'

'How's the dad life?' says Lana.

'It's a wild ride.'

'Worse than night shift?'

'About the same. Harder on Maddy. She's had to wind back the booze a touch. What are *you* going to do now?'

Lana smirks. 'Got a meeting with Beggs on Monday.'

'You're joking,' Henry says. 'How'd that happen?'

'Ron Bingham put me forward for it.'

'Did he now?' says Henry.

'I think Ron missed me,' Lana says.

'That doesn't sound like the Ron I know,' says Emmett.

'I don't want to know,' says Henry.

Lana shrugs. 'What else am I going to do?'

Emmett passes around the boiled peas. 'I know *exactly* what you're doing. You're going where the case is. Diablo isn't completely done, is it?'

'It isn't?' says Henry.

Lana and Emmett exchange a look.

'I'm not one to argue with the master detective,' she says, with a laugh. No one wants the dinner to turn into work, so they drop it. But Lana feels seen. Emmett knows her, somehow, knows that she hates—more than anything else—the ache of not knowing. And he knows that's why she's back here. That's why she's on the coast. It's not just the job. It's the loose ends. To break the mood, she says, 'Come on, Emmett. Tell us about the Ruben Davis case? That's what I'm here for.'

He talks them through it, every detail.

He had the key piece of Diablo from the start.

•

Later that same evening, Lana steps outside for a smoke. Emmett puts the yard light on for her. It's painfully bright, casting long shadows off her as she wanders around the back garden. Pacing and smoking, she spends a minute staring at the detached garage, the flaking paint and crooked timber. She notices a green army tarp piled up beside the shed. There's a glimmering speck shining out from underneath it.

Lana squats down.

It's a two-mil cylinder of metal catching the light.

The spoke of a wheel.

Feeling a strange sensation, she pulls back the tarp.

A motorcycle.

Running purely on instinct, she gets all the way down on the ground and checks the tyres, seeing the familiar tread: a match for the Brian Amstell scene.

She walks straight to the garage and opens it, fumbles with the light switch, and sees the work room and the maps and all the planning and equipment. It's all in there. The prep work for the last three Diablo murders: Lenny Gibbs, Joel Delaney and Brian Amstell.

Lana understands it instantly.

Feels it.

No questions.

No hesitation.

She races back to the house, up to the kitchen, finding Henry and Emmett on opposite sides of the room. Henry's holding a dripping dinner plate by the sink and Emmett has his service revolver in hand with the barrel of the gun pressed against the side of his head.

Henry, his hands up, *easy now.*

There is an eerie pause.

Emmett pulls on the trigger.

Snap.

Pulls it again.

Snap.

A third time, everyone in motion.

JOURNAL OF EMMETT HADES

(SELECTED EXCERPTS)

PERSONAL EFFECTS, TAKEN FROM WOLSTON PARK HOSPITAL ROOM, COLLECTED BY DETECTIVE CONSTABLE LANA COHEN

EXHIBIT 33 B

I killed three people because I wanted to know how it felt. It was the best kind of investigating, but it came out of a strange time in my life, certainly. A period of unmooring and desperation. I've written a little about it here and there in my journals, but the texture of it—the grinding, relentless persistence of that chaos—is difficult to understand without having lived through it.

I wanted to solve the case.

If only I could get into the killer's mind, I thought.

If only I could find worthless people to dispatch, useless junk to repurpose, just to know.

If I could do that, I'd feel as the killer might.

I could re-enact his rage.

It could open something up.

Rupture and repair.

Every day back then, I could feel parts of that rage—living on the coast, in the cesspit of sin and depravation—but to act on it was the last piece, the full commitment.

I had to act.

My targets were made selectively. I sought advice. I made a list from sermons. Three organised crime figures, all central to Colleen Vinton, but all hidden away, delivered unto me by a conduit, like manna from above.

Then three acts in a dark progression.

Three displacements.

I killed them neatly, as a policeman might, then studied my emotions.

I felt the rush of new information, new sensations, new regrets and mistakes.

I shook things up.

I killed near the border, to bring in New South Wales expertise.

And it all worked.

I summoned Lana Cohen.

I activated Henry Loch.

I kept the Diablo energy up.

I solved the case.

I really did, you see.

I did my job.

And it could have been perfect had I succeeded in the fourth murder.

Had the gun worked. Irene unloaded it as a precaution, you see.

It's almost funny.

All my careful plans undone by the cleaning lady.

•

No past.

No future.

Just the endless present, rolling on, like the locked groove of a record, locked onto:

Today.

I had another visit in the hospital from Lana, now a member of the Gold Coast CIB. I don't hold a grudge. If anything, I feel closer to her than ever before.

'It's not bad,' she says, taking in the new gardens they've planted in the courtyard outside my room in the hospital.

'It could be a lot worse,' I admit. I miss my house. I miss everything. But it's better than what I deserve. It took a lot of work to keep me out of Boggo Road, but a trial would upset the apple cart, so Wolston it was.

To be honest, it's mainly the uncluttered nature of my days here that gets to me. Free time is the enemy. It's how the ghosts find their way in.

Names like curses, names like—

'Emmett?' *Lana says.*

'Yes?'

'Will you help me?'

'What do you need?'

'Advice. Mentorship. I have questions.'

'Fire away.'

'Will you lie to me?'

'No.'

'Do you promise?'

'I can promise you that much.'

She seems satisfied. 'I've checked the logbooks at reception. Henry calls you, doesn't he?'

'Now and then. He feels obligated. I keep telling him to stay away, but he won't listen. It costs a fortune to call from where he is. He sends me packages sometimes. He sent me a very interesting photo for safekeeping the other day, the most incredible artefact, this—'

'What about Father Hanlon?'

'Sure. The Father visits from time to time.'

'Do you know who else he visits? A man called Brian Wells up in Boggo Road Gaol.'

'I don't know a Brian Wells.'

'He's the man charged with the stabbing of Daryl Millman. I can't get anywhere near that case, but I thought it was interesting that the Father visits with him, and he visits with you and . . .'

I leave it a minute.

Silence is an asset for any decent detective.

'This is all news to me.'

Lana smiles, but there's no real warmth to it. 'I keep going back over my notes and there's an odd term that keeps jumping out. The conduit.

You've said it. I'm pretty sure Millman said it. Is Father Hanlon the conduit? Do you call him that?'

'Oh, we shouldn't talk about religion,' I tell her. 'I can't advise you on what the Father is, either. That's his job.'

'Okay then. What about this? I've often wondered how you knew so much about Colleen Vinton's operation for a straight copper. That's always seemed odd to me. And Hanlon, he must hear everything in that confessional of his. All the gossip.'

'It's a good church. It takes in all sorts. You should try it.'

Lana presses on. 'Do you know how Father Hanlon feels about Vinton? Can you tell me that much? I can't see how they're connected.'

I look up at the light beaming down and, for whatever reason, I let something slip. 'The son,' I say.

'The sun?'

'The forsaken. He . . .' I want to say more, but it's not my place. It's like one part of me wants to explain the gospel to her and one part of me wants to keep my promises. I guess, in my own way, I settled for some obscure halfway point. 'Give it time,' I tell her. 'Keep looking into it, but . . .'

'But what?'

'Be careful.'

'If I come back, maybe we can talk more?'

'I'd like that.'

We sit there.

Another minute passes.

I say to her, 'Do you know what I want to know? I want to know about your side of the case. Tell me all about it. Is that too much to ask?'

'No, no, that'd be fine, Emmett. You can tell me where I went wrong,' she says, nudging my shoulder.

We both laugh at that.

'Where do I start?' she says.

'In the beginning,' I tell her. 'It's where it all starts.'

ACKNOWLEDGEMENTS

I'D LIKE TO THANK Sian Baker, James Buckley, Brendan Fredericks, Chris Flynn, David Honeybone, Liam José, Jarett Kobek, Patrick McCabe, Kate Mildenhall, Angela Meyer, Andrew Nette, Shaun Prescott, David and Beryl Rogers, and David Whish-Wilson, as well as my agent Tara Wynne, and my team at Ultimo Press: Robert Watkins and Sophie Mayfield, alongside Deonie Fiford and Camha Pham. Special thanks to Clare, Ginger and Woody for their continued patience and support. This book would not exist without the inspiration provided by James Ellroy, David Peace, Don Winslow, Sara Gran, Derek Raymond, Jim Thompson, Megan Abbott, Joesph Wambaugh, and Peter Doyle. While historical accuracy is far from my primary focus, a significant amount of period detail was borrowed from the non-fiction work of Matthew Condon and Keith Banks, and many others. God bless Robert Pollard.

Iain Ryan grew up in the outer suburbs of Brisbane, Australia. He has been shortlisted twice for a Ned Kelly Award for his novels *Four Days* and *The Student*. He lives in Melbourne. Find out more about his work at iainryan.com.